PRAISE FOR IRIS MORLAND

PETAL PLUCKER

Funny, charming, and utterly captivating! I devoured this sparkling read.

— ANNIKA MARTIN, NEW YORK TIMES BESTSELLING AUTHOR

Petal Plucker was funny, entertaining, fresh and fan-yourself-worthy . . . Their enemies-to-lovers romance is both charming, tender and steamy, and you'll love both of these characters (and their families!) and their sigh-worthy happily ever after.

— MARY DUBÉ, CONTEMPORARILY EVER AFTER

Morland has created a masterpiece of a romance . . . one of my favorite [books] of the year.

— CRISTIINA READS

Humorous, raunchy, and refreshing, Petal Plucker has rightfully earned its way, in my opinion, as one of the best romantic comedy [books] this year.

— CAROL, TIL THE LAST PAGE

My One and Only

This book was gripping, well written & the chemistry between the characters sizzled throughout this wonderful read.

— AMAZON REVIEW

All I Want Is You

Another heartfelt, steamy, terrific story. This is an author who really knows how to create a story that catches a reader's attention and characters that capture her heart.

— BOOKADDICT

Taking a Chance on Love

Thea and Anthony are in for a surprise when it comes to the language of the heart . . . I am in awe.

— HOPELESS ROMANTIC BLOG

Then Came You

This story really pulled all my heartstrings. This was truly a beautiful story and makes you believe there really is true love out there.

— MEME CHANELL BOOK CORNER

Someone to Watch Over Me

Till There Was You

I'll Be Home for Christmas

HERON'S LANDING

Seduce Me Sweetly

Tempt Me Tenderly

Desire Me Dearly

Adore Me Ardently

TILL THERE WAS YOU

THE THORNTONS

IRIS MORLAND

BLUE VIOLET PRESS LLC

CONTENTS

For everyone who had a dream and wanted to break free.

TILL THERE WAS YOU

Jubilee Thornton swore when her coffeepot—the one thing she could rely on in a world full of chaos—spluttered, popped, and then seemed to breathe its last. Two tablespoons of coffee splashed into the pot below, and she was almost tempted to drink it anyway.

When had her life gotten this pathetic?

At the age of twenty-five, she'd never dated, never gone to college, never even left her hometown. She lived in a tiny apartment in Fair Haven, Washington, and worked at her sister-in-law Megan's bakery, The Rise and Shine. And to top it all off, today her coffeepot just had to die, because apparently getting her caffeine fix was too much to ask.

"Come on. Don't do this to me today," she muttered to the appliance in question as she began to fiddle with the controls. Despite trying everything she could think of to get it to start again, she had to accept that her coffeepot had finally kicked the bucket.

She could wait for coffee, she told herself. She worked at a bakery that served all kinds of coffee, although it was so busy in the morning that she didn't have time to drink any that she made for herself.

Taking a deep breath, Jubilee poured herself a bowl of cereal, only to choke when she tasted very sour milk. And because this morning could not go right, that had been the last of her cereal, as she'd yet to get more groceries for that week. *I guess I'll have to eat at work, too.*

She dumped the cereal and sour milk, her stomach roiling, her head hurting, and her feet aching, although her sore feet came from wearing stilettos the night before at what should have been the best party of her life—until it had crashed and burned like a train wreck on steroids.

Why am I always stuck on the sidelines of my own life?

It was a realization that hit her squarely in the chest. When everyone else around her was experiencing what life had to offer, here she was, doing a grand total of nothing.

Then again, what did it mean to really *live*? If she did it like people did in the movies, she'd go skydiving, or mountain climbing. Maybe she should go on a safari and hunt for lions.

She grimaced. Shooting large game sounded depressing, not liberating.

Jubilee had two hours until she had to go into work at The Rise and Shine. This job had been Jubilee's first ever: two years ago, she'd finally moved out of her parents' house after being coddled and placed in a protective bubble for the entirety of her life.

Having leukemia—twice—as a child tended to create overly concerned parents. Jubilee understood this. But that didn't mean she liked it.

Now she lived on her own and earned her own money to pay her bills, but it seemed so pointless in that moment. What had Jubilee really done with her life? Nothing. She hadn't gone to college because of her mother's fears that Jubilee would relapse. She hadn't moved away from her hometown. She hadn't even traveled out of the state of Washington. What would it be like to go someplace far away? Like Florida, or Iceland, or even Mongolia?

At least a certain stupid man won't be in any of those places, Jubilee groused.

She needed to make a change. What better way than to make a list of all the things she wanted to accomplish?

Picking up a pen, she nibbled on the end of it as she thought about what, exactly, she wanted to do with her life.

Finally, she wrote at the top: JUBILEE'S LIST OF THINGS SHE WILL DO WITHIN THE NEXT YEAR

Well, she would work on the title later.

Skydiving didn't appeal to her. Nor did mountain climbing. She wanted to experience things most women her age had already done. Things she'd always wanted to do but couldn't because of being sick.

When Jubilee completed her list fifteen minutes later, she laughed. Her heart lightened for the first time since last night.

Last night, when she'd kissed her long-time crush Heath DiMarco, and he'd kissed her back. Before pushing her away and telling her it could never, ever happen again.

"Screw Heath," she muttered as she pulled her hair into a ponytail. She stuffed the list into her back pocket before heading out.

Heath had been her oldest brother Harrison's best friend since Heath had arrived in Fair Haven seven years ago. Compared to Harrison—and Jubilee's three other brothers— Heath was unassuming. With his auburn hair and average height, with glasses perched on his nose, he seemed like the type of man who enjoyed a cup of tea and a nice chess game in the evenings. Add to that the fact that he was a fifth-grade teacher, and he should've seemed staid.

Safe. Normal.

Except no staid man kissed like Heath had last night.

Jubilee shivered as she walked to The Rise and Shine. She told herself it was because it was a chilly morning. Autumn leaves crunched under her boots, the wind whistling through the branches that became barer with each passing day.

The bell on the front door of the bakery rang as Jubilee entered. It was already busy, and Megan Thornton (formerly Flannigan) came around the counter in a rush. With her red hair in a messy bun and flour streaking her cheek, she looked more harried than usual.

"Thank God! Can you take over the register for a bit? I need to get finish this batch of cinnamon rolls," Megan said.

"Of course. I'll be fine."

Megan didn't wait to hear a reply before she hurried into the kitchen. When Jubilee had first started working in the bakery, it had taken a bit to learn how everything worked. How to make a latte, how to use the cash register. Jubilee was grateful that Megan hadn't kicked her out within the first month of her working there.

By the time Jubilee got a break, it was after her usual lunch break. *Megan really needs to hire someone else*, she thought tiredly. Her stomach growled, and she snagged two sandwiches from the glass case (one of the perks of working in a bakery) before heading into the kitchen. They had a bell at the counter that people could ring for service.

"You should eat something," Jubilee said as she handed Megan one of the sandwiches.

"Oh, thank you. I'm almost done with these cinnamon rolls." Megan let out a breath. "I think I might need to hire a third person."

Jubilee took a bite of her sandwich and just raised her eyebrows.

That made Megan laugh. "Fine, fine. You were right. I'll put up a job posting tonight." She unwrapped her own sandwich and moaned as she bit into it. "I didn't realize how hungry I was."

Just last night, Megan and her husband, Caleb—Jubilee's second oldest brother—had announced that they were expecting. Megan didn't look pregnant yet, but sometimes Jubilee caught her touching her abdomen, lost in thought.

Her oldest brother, Harrison, and his wife, Sara, were also pregnant. Jubilee sometimes found it strange to see her ne'er-do-well brothers settled down with wives and, in the next months, babies. If her own heart twisted with jealousy, she ignored it.

Jubilee felt the list in her back pocket, burning a hole in her jeans. As one of her best friends, Megan would be the ideal person to ask if Jubilee should add anything—or anyone—to her list. After she'd written down what she wanted to accomplish, she'd started a list of men she could date. Given how small Fair Haven was, it wasn't an extensive list.

"Hey, Megan," Jubilee said, "can I ask your advice?"

"What? Of course you can. What's up?" Megan finished up her sandwich and leaned back in her chair, her eyes gleaming.

"Well, I've decided that I'm tired of living in a bubble."

Jubilee pulled out the list and handed it to Megan. "So, erm, I made a list. Of things I want to do."

Megan's eyebrows rose. Unfolding the piece of paper, she scanned the list, saying nothing for a long moment. When Megan didn't say anything at all, Jubilee barely stopped herself from fidgeting in her chair like a little kid.

Megan hopped up and disappeared, the list still in her hand. Was she going to shred it? Burn it over the gas stove?

But then she returned with a pen and clipboard in hand. "This is a good start," she said, "but let's add a few more things, and names."

When Megan grinned, Jubilee couldn't help but smile back.

HEATH DIMARCO STOOD at the front door of The Rise and Shine and wondered for the millionth time how he'd gotten saddled with the task of picking up cupcakes for the teachers' meeting that evening. The kids had already gone home for the day, although most of the teachers would stay until the meetings started a few hours later. Heath had planned to go home for a bit, but now he had to pick up cupcakes. And avoid making a bigger ass of himself.

When his principal, Mr. Anderson, had asked him to pick up the damn cupcakes, he hadn't been able to come up with a good excuse not to.

I'm sorry, I kissed one of the bakery workers and then told her it could never happen again?

I'm sorry, I've been banned from that bakery for all intents and purposes?

He hoped Jubilee wasn't working today. He also hoped she was working today because he wanted to see her. He wanted to make sure she was all right after last night.

Then again, how would he know if she was all right? She wouldn't tell him, even if he asked her. And he'd fucked up —badly.

This is never going to happen, he'd told her just last night, his heart twisting with guilt at Jubilee's expression. The hurt, the humiliation. He shouldn't have let her kiss him. It had been a stupid mistake with long-term consequences.

"Are you going inside?" a woman asked behind him.

He jumped a little, startled, before pushing the door open and holding it for the woman to enter. She gave him an odd look before entering the bakery.

The scents of bread and coffee filled Heath's nostrils, and he almost allowed himself to be comforted by the homey smell.

No one was at the counter. The woman rang the bell, and then rang it again when no one appeared within three seconds' time.

"I'm sorry, I'll be right there!" Jubilee's voice called from the kitchen.

Heath gritted his teeth. He considered paying the woman in front of him to pick up the cupcakes and then bring them to him outside. Like a drug deal, except with cupcakes.

He didn't get to put his illicit-cupcake plan into action before Jubilee came into the bakery, her cheeks flushed. When she spotted Heath, though, she stopped short but not before colliding with the corner of the counter.

Heath winced.

"Ow! Dammit!" Jubilee rubbed her hip. "Sorry, how can I help you?"

"I need a loaf of sourdough," the woman replied.

Heath could just imagine the disdain on the woman's face. How far did the stick up her ass go?

Right then, his and Jubilee's gazes met. He rolled his eyes at the woman. Jubilee bit her lip, ostensibly to keep from laughing.

After Jubilee had finished with the woman, Heath stepped up to the counter and found himself unable to find the right words. Did he apologize? But then again, he doubted Jubilee wanted to bring up last night. Maybe he should just act like it had never happened. It had been a lovely dream, kissing Jubilee Thornton, with her soft lips and the sound of her sweet moans filling his ears—

"Are you here for your latte?" Jubilee asked. She fidgeted, looking especially young to Heath.

That always-present guilt inside him nipped at him. There were multiple reasons why he and Jubilee could never happen. One of them was that she was too young for him. The other? She was his best friend's younger sister.

A best friend didn't poach on younger sisters.

He cleared his throat. "Cupcakes. I'm picking them up. They're probably under Anderson."

"Oh! Yes. Let me go get those. They're in the back."

Heath couldn't help but enjoy Jubilee's ass in those tight jeans she always wore. He rubbed his temples.

When he'd moved to Fair Haven seven years ago, Jubilee had just been a kid. Heath had thought of her as a younger sister as he'd become friends with her older brother Harrison. As the years had passed, Jubilee had grown into a beautiful young woman. And to Heath's dismay, she hadn't left Fair Haven. She'd stayed to torment him.

He laughed under his breath. Jubilee was the last person who would knowingly torment someone. It was his own problem if he now thought of her not as a younger sister, but as a desirable woman. A woman who'd kissed him last night and had blown his damn mind.

"Heath, how are you? Did you recover from last night?" Megan asked as she and Jubilee both came up to the counter. "When did you finally leave?"

"Um, around midnight, I think." He'd left right after the kiss had happened. He hadn't wanted to tempt fate, especially being around Jubilee in that flapper costume.

"Here you go. They're all paid for." Jubilee pushed the box of cupcakes toward him, making certain their fingers didn't brush.

"Thanks." He hesitated, although he didn't know why. What could he say? He was sorry? He wanted another kiss? He was an idiot?

Both to his annoyance and gratitude, another customer entered the bakery. He took that as an opening to head out.

He couldn't stop from looking at Jubilee one last time: her dark hair, recently cut into a short bob, framed her heart-shaped face, her eyes a striking green. She was smaller than her siblings, no taller than five-five or so. In the last few years, she'd grown curvier, and at the moment, her cotton t-shirt gave a hint of cleavage every time she bent down.

He needed to get the hell out of here before he did something really, really stupid.

Distracted, he didn't realize Megan was coming around the counter to clean a table when he collided with her. Megan let out a surprised "oh!" while Heath just barely hung on to the cupcakes. Megan stumbled, falling to the floor but catching herself just in time.

"Are you okay?" he and Jubilee both asked at the same time.

He helped Megan up after he'd set the cupcakes down on a nearby table. Megan laughed.

"I'm fine. Are the cupcakes okay? That's the most important thing." She wiped dust from her jeans. "Those took Jubilee all morning."

"Jesus, I'm so sorry. I guess I've been far away today," Heath admitted. He made a point to avoid looking at Jubilee right then.

"No harm, no foul. Just don't tell Caleb. He's already way too overprotective." Megan stuck out her tongue, crossing her eyes. He and Jubilee laughed, but then abruptly stopped.

"I'll see you later," he muttered.

She just nodded and went to help the rush of customers that always came in during the afternoons.

As Heath grabbed the cupcakes, he noticed a folded-up piece of paper on the floor. He picked it up. Had Megan dropped this? Or Jubilee? He was about to ask them when he read the word *virginity* in looped script. And then a name: *Jubilee*. His eyebrows rose to his hairline. Was she writing a romance novel? Now he was doubly intrigued. She didn't seem the type, but appearances were deceiving.

But it was none of his business. Turning, he was about to find Megan to give it to her for Jubilee, but she'd disappeared. Jubilee was busy with customers, and he wasn't about to give her some weird note right then.

He told himself he'd keep it and give it to one of the

women later. He had a feeling it wasn't the type of note Jubilee would want lying on the floor for any unsuspecting customer picking up.

He stuffed the note into his pocket. The note remained there throughout the meetings that evening, and he'd almost forgotten about it by the time he arrived home four hours later.

When he pulled out the note and stared at it, almost wishing he could read its contents without opening it, he considered. What if it wasn't Jubilee's? What if it was *about* her, and if he gave it to her, she'd get hurt in the process?

That was enough of an argument to convince him to open the note and read it.

JUBILEE'S LIST OF THINGS SHE WILL DO WITHIN THE NEXT YEAR

- Make out with a guy
- Go to a concert
- Smoke a cigarette
- Go skinny-dipping
- Lose my virginity (see list of eligible men)

Heath sat down on his couch, staring at the list until his vision blurred. He hadn't looked at the list of eligible men. He didn't want to.

Because he would be damned if Jubilee did any of these things—most especially *lose her virginity*—with any man but him.

Except he'd told her they could never happen. Groaning and swearing, he dropped his head into his hands and cursed himself for being a giant fool.

CHAPTER TWO

J ubilee dumped her purse onto her bed when she arrived
home, searching through all the various items for that
damn list. Swearing, she dug around in her pockets, her
coat pockets, even inside her shoes.

No list.

Hadn't Megan returned it to her before Heath had come
into The Rise and Shine? She couldn't remember. She'd
heard the bell while she and Megan had been adding things to
the list, and then she'd seen Heath, and her brain had essentially turned to mush.

She texted Megan, *Do you have my list?*

To which Megan replied a few minutes later, *No, don't you have it?*

That meant that that list was somewhere in The Rise and
Shine. Jubilee almost considered going back to look around,
but that seemed like overkill. If someone picked it up, she
hoped they threw it away, thinking it was trash.

Oh God, she thought suddenly, *what if Heath picked it up?*

That thought sent a chill straight through her, although it

was mostly embarrassment she felt overall. She'd never live it down if he saw that list. He'd think she was insane, or slutty. Or both. Who made a list of things like "lose your virginity"? Only sad weirdos did that.

Jubilee pushed away panic, telling herself that Heath would've returned anything belonging to her. He was a good guy. A good guy she wanted to kick in the shins, but decent nonetheless.

Jubilee had moved into her apartment two years ago when she'd started working at The Rise and Shine. She'd never lived away from home before, and it had been a battle for her mother to let her go live on her own. Lisa had been convinced that Jubilee wouldn't take care of herself, or she would get overwhelmed with the usual types of things you had to do when you were an adult. Pay the rent, pay the electric bill, etcetera.

Jubilee had persevered, however, and although working at a bakery wasn't exactly her dream job, it paid those pesky bills and allowed her to get out from underneath her mother's overly concerned thumb.

While eating dinner, Jubilee checked her email. Her heart raced when she saw the email from Avila College, a small community college in Seattle.

She set down her bowl of soup and opened the email, only to let out a deep sigh of relief when she saw the words, *Congratulations, you've been accepted!* Jubilee had gotten decent grades in high school, but her second bout of leukemia had lasted through her freshman year. She'd gotten behind, and it had been a struggle to graduate with her peers, but Jubilee had managed it.

A community college wasn't as competitive as a state

university, of course. There was no reason she wouldn't have been accepted, but that hadn't stopped her from feeling nervous. Now she just had to tell her family that she was moving to Seattle to go to college.

Lisa Thornton would *love* hearing that news.

But Jubilee allowed herself a celebration for her good news. Pouring herself a glass of wine, she was about to turn on the Food Network when someone knocked on her front door. She opened it to find none other than her mother standing there with two bags of groceries in her hands.

"Help me with these," Lisa said as she handed Jubilee a bag. "Those checkout boys can never bag properly. I had to take the bread out from the bottom of the bag before I left the store."

Jubilee sighed as Lisa started unloading the groceries and putting them away in Jubilee's cabinets. Lisa periodically bought Jubilee groceries for no other reason than she was convinced Jubilee couldn't buy her own. Jubilee knew her mother did it so she could check up on her. It also amused her greatly, considering Lisa hadn't bought groceries on her own for years until Jubilee had moved out. She'd always had help to do that for her.

"You didn't need to bring me groceries," Jubilee said as she placed a carton of eggs in the fridge along with bottled water and almond milk.

"You barely have anything to eat here." Lisa clucked her tongue as she placed three more boxes of cereal next to the lone one sitting in the pantry.

"I was going shopping tomorrow."

Lisa didn't hear her, too busy organizing Jubilee's pantry

to her specifications. Jubilee gritted her teeth to keep herself from saying something she'd regret.

Lisa had never left Jubilee's side during her chemo treatments as a child. She'd taken Jubilee to every appointment, every test, every treatment. She'd brushed Jubilee's hair when Jubilee had been too tired to do it herself. She'd bathed her, sat with her, told her she would beat this leukemia and live a long, long life.

Jubilee hadn't realized until years later how much Lisa had missed out on with her five older siblings to care for her. Thus, guilt kept her from telling Lisa to let her live her own life, no matter how frustrating it was.

Jubilee rubbed her chest, right over the scar where a port had been placed during her bone marrow transplants. Sometimes she could still feel the needle under her skin, even though she hadn't had any treatments in over a decade.

"Why didn't you answer my text?" Lisa asked. In her sixties now, Lisa remained an attractive woman. She kept her hair a light blond, her makeup light but elegant.

As the matriarch of a large family, Lisa remained a fixture in her children's lives, even after they'd reached adulthood. After she had almost broken up Harrison and Sara, however, she'd since "calmed down," as Harrison had termed it. Jubilee had a feeling she'd only calmed down regarding her older siblings. Jubilee would always be the baby who needed to be protected.

"Oh, sorry, I forgot." Jubilee started eating her soup again, but it had gotten cold. She sighed inwardly.

"Are you coming home this weekend?" Lisa sat down next to Jubilee, her back not touching the cushion behind her. "Your father would like to see you."

Jubilee bit back a smile. "He just saw me yesterday at the bakery."

"You know what I mean. You haven't been home in a while. Your brothers and sister will be there."

"Really? All of them?"

"Most of them. Caleb is worse at responding than you are." Lisa tapped Jubilee's knee. "I'm worried about you. You work all day, you have no food when you come home, you live in this tiny apartment—"

"Mom, we've been over this. My apartment is just fine. I have food, I'm paying my bills. I'm taking care of myself fine."

"And so this is it? You'll work at a bakery the rest of your life?"

Jubilee flushed in embarrassment. She considered telling Lisa about her acceptance to Avila, but she bit her tongue. She wasn't in the mood to hear Lisa tell her that moving to Seattle would be a terrible plan. Ironic, considering that Lisa wasn't a fan of Jubilee working at a bakery.

"What do you want me to be doing?" Jubilee countered. "Move home and live with you and Dad for the rest of my life?"

"No, I'm not saying that. Don't put words in my mouth. I'm simply saying that I'm concerned about your choices, that's all, and you have to be careful with your health. If you have another relapse…"

"Unlikely, now that I'm an adult."

Seeing the worry in Lisa's face, Jubilee couldn't help but squeeze her mother's hand.

"I'm fine. I'm happy. Don't worry about me, okay?"

Lisa squeezed her hand back. "You'll come home this weekend?"

"Yes, I'll come. I promise."

After Lisa left, with Jubilee promising to get the landlord to look at her leaky window, Jubilee tossed out the now ice-cold soup and poured herself a second glass of wine.

Would her mother ever let her grow up? She didn't know if Lisa could let go of the sickly child Jubilee had been.

Her mother's continued interference only hardened Jubilee's resolve further. No matter what anyone said, she was going to Seattle, and she was going to live the life she'd always wanted.

WHEN THE BELL rang at three o'clock, Heath knew that his students' minds were already looking toward home.

"Okay, everyone have a nice weekend. Be sure to work on your multiplication tables for the test next week."

Heath worked at Fair Haven Elementary, which was the only elementary school in town. There was talk of opening a second one, though, considering that the school had had to hire more teachers to teach fourth and fifth grade. Those teachers' classrooms were housed in portable trailers on school grounds, something which had been met with loud complaints from multiple staff members.

"Mr. DiMarco, can I talk to you?" Jessie, a new student to Fair Haven Elementary, was a petite ten-year-old with a mass of curly dark hair. She'd been shy and quiet at the beginning of the school year, but Heath had been pleased to see her coming out of her shell and making friends lately.

"Of course. What's up?"

Jessie hesitated, glancing over her shoulder at the other students packing up, laughing and making their way out of the classroom for the weekend.

"How about you get packed up and then come find me when everyone's gone? Do you have to catch the bus, though?"

Jessie shook her head. "No, I walk home."

Heath cleaned his desk, stuffing folders of tests and quizzes and homework into his bag while supervising the remaining stragglers. He ushered the last two out the door, knowing full well they would miss the bus without another thought.

He shut the door to give him and Jessie a little privacy. Fifth graders were one of the best classes, Heath thought, because they were still young enough to like (and sometimes hug) their teacher, while being old enough to think for themselves. Heath couldn't count the number of times one of his students had said or written something that had blown his adult mind.

"So, Jessie, how are you? Is everything at home going okay?"

Jessie shuffled her feet. She looked uncomfortable, and Heath's heart went out to her. This was the hardest part about teaching: the human aspect of it. His students came from all walks of life. Some had wealthy parents, some had middle-income parents. Some had one parent, some only had a grandparent. Some children only ate breakfast if they came to school for it.

Heath had met Jessie's mother, Lana, who seemed like a sweet woman who worked hard to provide for her daughter.

Jessie's father had died in a construction accident three years ago.

"I just…" Jessie bit her lip. "My mom's not happy."

"Why do you say that?"

"Well, she gets sad a lot. Daddy's been dead forever now, but I'll come home and she's crying. But she won't tell me why. I'll try to make dinner and do the laundry to help her. Last night she told me that she's lonely."

Heath had a feeling Lana wouldn't love that her daughter was talking to him about her issues. Before he could tell Jessie that, Jessie blurted, "I want you to date my mom."

Heath had to stifle an incredulous laugh. Putting on his best I'm-taking-you-serious face that he used so often with kids this age, he said, "That's very kind of you and I'm honored you thought of me. But that's for your mom to decide, not you."

"You won't even try? You'd like her. She's not fat like a lot of the moms here. She gets her hair done at the fancy salon!"

Heath's lips twitched. "I've met your mother, and she seems like a lovely person. But I'm not going to date her." Rising, he handed Jessie her backpack. "Now, how about we get you home before your mom worries about where you are?"

Heath shook his head as he gathered his own things. He'd have to have a chat with Lana tonight. He didn't want Jessie to misconstrue anything he'd said, considering the delicacy of the subject.

The thought of dating made him think of Jubilee—and her list. The list sat on his bedside table, mocking him, telling him he was an asshole for reading it.

And yet…

Heath cracked open a beer the moment he arrived home. His apartment had two bedrooms, one of which he used as an office. It had been built within the last two years, with brand-new appliances, carpet, and even a washer and dryer. Yet sometimes Heath felt like his place didn't feel like home. It seemed barren. Even after putting pictures on the walls and letting Rose decorate, it felt like someone else's place.

After two beers, Heath grabbed that damn list and sat staring at it as the TV buzzed in the background. He knew the list—two lists, technically—by heart at this point.

Jubilee and someone else had listed five names of men in Fair Haven "worth dating." Heath knew all the names, although he actually knew only one of the men: Ash Younger, Trent Younger's brother. Ash worked as Trent's accountant for his restaurants, and although he was charming and handsome, Heath was well aware of Ash's reputation as a playboy. There wasn't a single woman in Fair Haven he hadn't slept with or tried to sleep with, or so the rumors went.

Jubilee deserved better than a player like Ash Younger.

The other names were bachelors who often hung out The Fainting Goat, Trent's bar and a popular hangout in Fair Haven. They were the guys who liked pretty women and had no intention of settling down. Would Jubilee really go home with one of them and lose her virginity without a second thought? None of those guys would care enough to make sure her first time wasn't just good, but amazing. What if they hurt her, even accidentally?

The thought made Heath's stomach turn. And worst of all? The thought of Jubilee with any guy sent his mind into a total tailspin.

He folded up the list and put it into his wallet, promising

to return it tomorrow. Jubilee usually worked at The Rise and Shine on Saturdays. He could give it to her then.

As the evening waned into night and Heath depleted another beer, he took out the box that held items important to him. Rose's first tooth; a photo of his parents, dead these many years; Rose at her high school graduation; a letter from his fourth-grade teacher, Mrs. Dunby, who'd inspired him to become a teacher in the first place.

One thing was missing, however: a lock of Jubilee's hair.

He knew that Rose's ex Johnny had stolen it—for whatever twisted reason—when he'd broken into Heath's place earlier that summer. Heath hadn't mentioned it to Rose, because how could he without explaining why he'd kept it?

It had been Jubilee's twenty-first birthday the night she'd given it to him. She'd had her party at The Fainting Goat, along with a few friends from high school and her brothers keeping watch. Heath had arrived by himself, not realizing that it was Jubilee's birthday.

Jubilee was radiant that night. Normally a little shy, she became exuberant and affectionate as the drinks were poured into the night. Heath hadn't planned on staying late, but he was mesmerized by Jubilee that night.

He also knew very well that she was completely off-limits. Harrison had become a good friend after Heath had moved to Fair Haven. He wouldn't jeopardize that friendship—no matter how beautiful his younger sister was.

When it got close to midnight, Harrison and Caleb were helping Jubilee to her car, her friends too drunk to do anything but laugh at anything anyone said or did. Jubilee staggered, giggling, before telling her brothers she needed to pee.

Heath watched as Jubilee meandered down the hallway to

the restroom. When he heard a thump, though, he rose and went to make sure Jubilee hadn't fallen. Or gotten stuck somewhere.

He found her on the ground, digging through her purse. Her red lipstick was smeared, her dark hair a tangled mess. She grinned up at Heath when he approached her.

"I thought I saw you glaring at me," she joked. She giggled. "Are you drunk, too?"

"No, I'm not." He squatted down in front of her. "Can you get up?"

"Yeah, yeah, I'm looking for something…" She resumed digging around in her purse before pulling out a pair of…scissors? "There they are!"

"Jubilee, I'm not sure—"

"Oh, don't worry. I meant to do this earlier, but I forgot." She took a large piece of hair that had fallen from her up-do, opening the scissors around it and was about to start cutting.

"Wait, what are you doing?" Heath stopped her before the scissors closed over the hair. "Don't cut your hair now."

"No, no, you don't get it. You know I was never allowed to cut my hair? After chemo, I lost it all. Twice. It took five years to get it this long again. My mom wouldn't let me cut it." Determination lit her features. "But tonight I'm going to cut it all off."

Seeing how determined she was, Heath said, "How about you cut off a small piece? Just a little one. Then when you're sober in the morning, you can go somewhere and get it cut."

Jubilee narrowed her eyes at him, assessing. "You're probably right."

"Probably," he said with a grin.

Taking the scissors from her, he separated a smaller lock

from the piece Jubilee had been about to cut. It wasn't in an obvious spot, so hopefully Jubilee wouldn't be upset at its loss in the morning.

"You sure about this?" Heath asked.

"Do it. Or I'll do it myself."

Considering how uncoordinated she was, Heath didn't want her injuring herself accidentally. Before he could rethink this mad plan, he pulled the lock straight and snipped it about an inch from her scalp. It fell into his palm, silky and dark.

"Your prize, madam."

But as he tried to hand her the lock of hair, she shook her head. "Keep it. I don't need it."

Right then, Harrison came around the corner, and Heath put the lock of hair into his pocket. Harrison helped Jubilee up, thanking Heath, and then she was gone, the scissors left on the floor like some bizarre symbol.

Heath had kept that lock of hair ever since. When he'd next encountered Jubilee, she hadn't said a word about it. He had a feeling she'd forgotten it in her drunken haze.

He snorted, closing the box of mementos. It was better this way. He didn't need to keep thinking of a girl—no, a woman—who could never be his.

Jubilee had no idea about his past, and he planned to keep it that way. Even if it meant he could never act on his attraction to her.

CHAPTER THREE

"There he is." Megan tilted her head toward the bar. "And he's not with anyone, either."

Jubilee smoothed her hair, fighting the temptation to check her lipstick for the thousandth time. After losing her list, Jubilee had been so concerned about who might have seen it that she'd been tempted to abandon the scheme altogether.

Megan, however, refused to let her. "Who cares if someone found it?" she'd said. "You made a resolution and you're sticking with it, woman."

Jubilee, Megan and Mark Thornton's wife, Abby, were at a bar that had recently opened in Fair Haven. Normally they'd go to The Fainting Goat, but Jubilee hadn't wanted Trent, or worse, any of her brothers, to find out what she was doing.

Tonight would be the first time she'd ask a guy out. How had she managed to get to the age of twenty-five without doing something like this? How embarrassing.

Her first "target" (Megan's word) was Ash Younger. Ash was handsome and tall, his arms bulging through the cotton of his t-shirt. Jubilee heard him laugh at something the bartender said, the sound making her jittery.

Ash was way, way, *way* out of her league. Why had she agreed to this? She was insane.

"You don't have to do this," Abby said. When she'd learned of the plan, she'd been wary. Megan had countered that Jubilee needed to live her own life for once. Abby hadn't been able to argue with that.

"No, I want to do it. I do." Jubilee took a drink of her cocktail, the alcohol calming her nerves. "I'm ready."

"Get him." Megan winked.

Jubilee felt the beat of the music pump through her, and by the time she'd gotten to the bar and sat down next to Ash, she had almost convinced herself she wasn't at all nervous.

Ash didn't notice her at first. He looked lost in thought as he drank his beer. Jubilee wondered why he'd come here instead of his brother's bar. She had a feeling it might be the same reason she'd come here: anonymity.

"Do you come here often?" she asked.

He turned, his eyebrows rising when he finally saw her. "What?" he yelled. "I can't hear you!"

"Do you come here often?" she yelled, except right at that moment, the music changed to a quieter song, and her voice rang out through the bar.

Jubilee turned scarlet. Ash laughed.

"I know you. You're Lizzie's sister, right? Julie?"

She winced inwardly. "Jubilee."

"Oh, right."

He grinned, and it dazzled her for a moment. Her heart pounded. But then she thought of another man's smile, another man's laugh, another man's kiss—

She forced all thoughts of Heath aside. *He isn't here and he's not my problem.*

"It's a weird name, I know," she said.

"Oh, believe me, I know weird names. Me and all of my siblings have terrible names."

"Really? What's yours?"

He snorted. "I'm not nearly drunk enough to tell you that." His eyes sparkled as he took in her low-cut top, her skirt that barely came to mid-thigh. "But how about you keep me company and see what happens?"

Jubilee glanced over her shoulder to see Megan giving her a thumbs-up. She coughed to cover an embarrassed laugh.

Ash bought her another drink after she finished her first cocktail, and by the time she was near to finishing the second, the buzz of alcohol and the obvious interest in Ash's eyes were all that mattered. She might be a virgin, but she knew when a man was interested. And Ash was interested.

"Okay, but obviously pumpkin bread is better than cinnamon rolls," Ash was saying, thrusting his beer out as if to prove his point. "Cinnamon rolls are way too sweet."

"Pumpkin bread can only be eaten in the fall. Who eats pumpkin bread in March?"

"I do."

"Oh, I bet you do." Jubilee giggled. "Do you bake it yourself?"

He waggled his eyebrows. "Come over and taste for yourself."

She almost choked on her drink. Ash pounded her on the back, but then his hand wandered until it rested on her thigh. She felt it like a brand. Suddenly, the bar seemed too hot, and Ash was too close. Why had she wanted to do this again?

"Jubilee," a voice said over her shoulder. She stiffened as she turned to see Heath right behind her. His voice was level, but tense. "Megan's looking for you."

Jubilee blinked. "Where is she?"

"Outside. She asked me to come get you."

Ash hadn't moved his hand from her thigh, but at Heath's glare, he slowly removed it. He didn't apologize, however.

Jubilee groaned inwardly. The last thing she needed was two stupid men getting into a brawl over her.

"I should go, then. I'll see you later, Ash."

Ash shrugged. "Suit yourself."

Heath took her elbow and maneuvered her through the crowd. Instead of going outside into the cold, however, he led her to a semi-private alcove near the restrooms.

"Wait, where's Megan?" It took Jubilee's alcohol-soaked mind a second to put everything together. "Are you serious right now?" she blurted, her anger rising.

Heath didn't even have the decency to look abashed. "Do you even know Ash Younger's reputation? He's a playboy. He takes women home for one night, maybe two. But he doesn't date them."

She was so stunned that she struggled to find a reply. "What does it matter to you? And how do you know I don't *want* to be one of those women?"

Heath's face closed. He was agitated, pushing his fingers through his auburn hair, his jaw clenched. Jubilee had never seen him like this, like a wildcat barely leashed.

"I know you. You aren't like that. You'll go home with him and get your heart broken—"

"Like I said," she interrupted, raising her voice, "what the hell does it have to do with *you*?"

He looked surprised. Did he think she didn't have her own claws? She was about to leave this tête-à-tête when he growled, "I'm your brother's friend. I'm just looking out for you."

She blew out an exasperated breath. "You're my brother's *friend,* Heath. Not my brother. Now go away. I'm not having this conversation."

"Will you just listen to me for a second?"

His voice was so strained that Jubilee hesitated. If he wanted to talk, fine. He could talk to the wall behind her; she didn't have to listen.

"Look, you have a right to date whoever you want," he said, although he sounded pained as he said it. She was annoyed enough to be gratified by that. "But don't go after guys like Ash. It isn't worth the heartbreak."

"How do you know he'll break my heart?"

"Because guys say things around other guys they'd never say around women. Believe me on that."

Jubilee considered him. The alcohol was beginning to wear off, although everything still seemed to be moving in slow motion. And it didn't help that Heath looked as handsome as ever, with the dim light glinting off his auburn hair, his glasses falling down his nose. He pushed them up periodically, and Jubilee found that beyond endearing. Why did he have to be endearing? Or handsome? Or so nosy she wanted to strangle him?

"Fine, I believe you. Are we done?" She waited.

"If you're intent on whatever it is you're doing—"

"I am."

"Then let me vet the guys. I can tell you what they're really like."

Jubilee let out an incredulous laugh. "Where would you fall on that list?" she couldn't help but counter.

Heath narrowed his eyes. "I'm not on the list."

"Of course not. Fine, I agree." Before she could rethink her words, she added, "If you agree to my conditions."

"Fine."

"Really? Don't you want to hear them?"

"Whatever they are, I agree."

"If you get to vet the guys, I want you to teach me how to flirt with them. Make them want me. Teach me how to kiss. Everything."

She hadn't planned on saying that. She could've bitten her tongue in half, but seeing Heath's eyes widen, his breathing increase, almost made it worthwhile. Almost. She forced herself to steel her spine and not melt in the face of his censure.

But there was no censure. Only a croaked reply: "Okay, I agree. Shake on it?"

He put out his hand. After only a second's hesitation, Jubilee shook it.

He then closed his fingers around her hand and leaned toward her. "If you think this will make me back down, you're wrong."

"Ditto."

They stared at each other, the tension increasing until Jubilee trembled. She licked her lips, and Heath narrowed in on that small movement.

Please kiss me. Kiss me and make me forget everyone but you, she thought desperately.

He inhaled a deep breath, then pulled away. "Let me take you back to Megan," was all he said.

When Jubilee returned to Megan and Abby's table, she just shook her head when they asked her about Ash.

It's not Ash Younger I have to worry about.

WHEN HEATH ARRIVED HOME, he couldn't think straight. All he could see was Jubilee—and with Ash's hand on her thigh.

He growled under his breath. Raking his hands through his hair, disheveling it even further, he groaned. He was an *idiot*. How could he have made that bargain with Jubilee? "Flirting lessons"? Jesus Christ. As if he could teach her how to flirt, how to kiss, how to make him want her without making her his completely.

He got into the shower, the hot water clearing his thoughts a little. He could always tell Jubilee he'd been drunk and that he wouldn't agree to anything so insane. He could tell her that she didn't need lessons on making a man want her. Hell, he'd seen the way Ash had been looking at her. She didn't need any help from him.

Scrubbing himself down, he stayed in the shower until the water began to run cold. It was close to one in the morning, but Heath knew he wouldn't be able to sleep anytime soon.

He turned on the TV in the living room, mostly to have some kind of noise drown out the voices in his head. Except that every time he saw a dark-haired woman on the screen, he thought of Jubilee. He ended up watching some ridiculous infomercial about a knife set. Luckily, the presenter was male and older than Heath and had a booming voice that could shake walls.

The night waned on. Heath drank a beer, brooding. When

his phone began to ring, he thought at first that the sound was coming from the TV. It kept ringing, and he realized it was *his* phone.

Who would be calling him this late at night? Worry pierced him: Was it Rose? Or Jubilee? Yet when he looked at the number calling, it wasn't one he knew. He let it go to voicemail.

A minute later, his phone rang again. Same number. Annoyed, Heath picked up. "Hello?"

"Is this Heath DiMarco?" a voice Heath didn't recognize asked.

"Who's calling?"

"My name is Rich, but that's not important. You might have heard my name from your sister, though."

Heath's blood turned cold. "What the hell do you want?"

"Just that I know that you're going to testify against Johnny Porter. I wouldn't, if I were you."

"Is that a threat?"

Rich chuckled, but it wasn't a cheerful sound. "Johnny may be in jail, but that doesn't mean we're going to let him stay there. Either keep your nose out of this, or you'll get it cut off."

"You're crazy if you think I'm going to back down from putting that asshole in jail for the rest of his life." Just the thought of what Johnny had done to Rose made Heath so angry he could barely think straight.

"Except I doubt you'd want your secrets put out there for everyone to know."

Heath could feel the noose tightening around his neck. "I don't have any secrets to tell," he lied with surprising ease.

"Really? I doubt that. Let's just say that we know all about

Gregory Kirkland. Keep your mouth shut, and nobody will ever know. Oh, and if you don't care about your own secrets, I'm sure you care about your sister's."

The call disconnected. Heath struggled to breathe. His throat tightened, and he coughed and gasped for air. Panic clawed at him, but he forced it aside. He had to think. If he gave in to panic, he would lose everything.

No one knew about Gregory. Hell, Heath had only been an acquaintance of his. They'd lived in the same apartment building when Heath had been attending college. Gregory had been in his forties and had seen a lot of life's underbelly. He'd gotten his act together, though, and found steady employment as a janitor at an office building in downtown Seattle.

Heath had lived with his friend Troy. Troy hadn't been a great student, and when his grades had continued to plummet, his parents had threatened to stop paying his tuition. Desperate, Troy had gotten involved with none other than Johnny Porter.

Troy had assured Heath the drugs he was selling for Johnny weren't dangerous. They were illegal, but nobody would die from them. "I need the money," Troy had said. When Heath had pointed out that most people would get a job, Troy had countered that he needed more money than a part-time minimum-wage job could give him.

So, Heath had looked the other way. He'd justified it by saying that Troy was only doing it to stay in school.

Then Heath had come home to find an ambulance outside the apartment, and EMTs coming and going from Gregory's apartment. Gregory had overdosed that morning. His girlfriend had found him hours later.

And when Heath had confronted Troy about it, Troy had admitted he'd sold Gregory drugs.

Everything had gone to hell, and then Heath had gotten arrested for selling drugs along with Troy before Johnny had come to their rescue.

Heath laughed bitterly. Rescue! Johnny had made Rose promise to stay with him—and endure his abuse—to get Heath set free and the charges against him dropped and erased. And Heath hadn't known the depths of his sister's sacrifice until this summer, when Johnny had decided to threaten Rose once again.

The drugs, the arrest, Gregory's death—all three would destroy Heath's reputation and career. He couldn't teach children with something like that on his record. He would have to move, find a new job, lose everything he held near and dear. Worse, though, was the thought of Rose's pain being broadcast to the public. Heath couldn't bear the thought of his sister being hurt again. She was happy and in love with Seth Thornton now; Heath wouldn't let anyone jeopardize that.

He lay in bed for hours that night, staring at nothing, until exhaustion finally forced him to sleep.

Jubilee checked her phone for what felt like the thousandth time that day. Irritation filled her when she saw that Heath hadn't texted her. He hadn't texted her since their *encounter* at the bar last Saturday. Now it was Friday, and Jubilee was itching to finish work and march over to his house.

Or so she thought. She didn't know if she had the balls to do that. What had she been thinking, making that bargain with him? When she'd gotten home and slept off the alcohol, she'd woken up with almost more regret than pain in her head. But she'd been so frustrated at him interfering that she'd wanted to shock him. She hadn't expected him to say yes.

She hadn't told Megan or Abby what had happened with Heath. She'd only said that she'd decided that Ash Younger wasn't the guy for her and she'd "try out" a different one that weekend. If Megan had sounded skeptical when Jubilee had told her this on Monday, she hadn't tried to pry any further information from her, either.

"Jubi, hey? Did you hear me?" Megan poked her in the side. "You've been far away today."

"Sorry, just distracted. What did you need?"

Megan bit back a smile. "You know what? You can head home. I only need to close up, and I doubt too many customers are coming in now."

"Are you sure? I was supposed to stay until six o'clock like normal."

"I'm sure. Get out of here." Megan made a shooing motion.

Jubilee didn't hesitate. Grabbing her things from the back, she said goodbye to Megan and headed home.

Except that the thought of going to her apartment, to sit and be lonely and think too hard about everything, didn't appeal to Jubilee in the least. It was already way past sunset, and the wind whistled through the trees. Jubilee's breath fogged, and she shivered. Stuffing her hands into her coat pockets, she decided to walk home first and then decide.

After eating dinner and changing her clothes, Jubilee almost lost her nerve. What if Heath wasn't home? What if he was home, but he told her to go away? How humiliating. Her stomach churned as she imagined all sorts of scenarios.

"Did I make myself a promise?" she said to herself as she began to put on her shoes. "I'm not going to let Heath beat me."

She wasn't going to be that shy wallflower anymore. The girl everyone overlooked. The girl everyone assumed was too delicate, too naive, to take seriously. She wasn't going to be that girl any longer.

She only knew where Heath lived because she'd stopped

by with Rose one evening a few months ago. She just hoped he was home at all tonight.

When she saw Heath's car in his driveway and a light on inside the first-floor apartment, her heart started to pound. She almost lost her nerve right then. Taking a deep breath, she told herself to remain calm, cool, collected. She'd seen how Heath looked at her. She only had to use that desire to her advantage.

The moment Heath opened his door, Jubilee suddenly found all the words she'd imagined saying disappearing. His eyes widened in surprise, and he seemed just as speechless as she was.

"Jubilee? What is it? Has something happened?" he asked worriedly.

A nervous giggle burst from her. She clapped a hand over her mouth. "Why do you always think something terrible has happened?"

"Because you're at my house without telling me you were coming?"

"Good point." She shivered, her breath puffing white in the cold air.

"Jesus, it's freezing. Come inside at least."

Jubilee followed him into the living room, the apartment cozy and warm. A bottle of beer sat on the coffee table, jazz music on in the background. She hesitated, not sure if she should sit down. Clutching her purse, she couldn't help but notice that Heath wore a dark green sweater that made his eyes seem brighter. A five-o'clock shadow darkened his jaw, and his hair was long enough to curl against the neckline of his sweater.

Heath was lean, but rangy. He wasn't as big as Jubilee's

brothers, who were all too tall for their own overly inflated egos.

"So are you sure everything's okay?" Heath asked her. He looked tired, dark circles smudging the skin under his eyes.

Jubilee chewed on the inside of her cheek. *Just say it. Don't be a scaredy-cat!*

"I wanted to start our lessons tonight," she finally blurted.

Silence filled the room, except for the dulcet tones of a cello playing from the stereo. Heath didn't react, except Jubilee could make out how tense his shoulders suddenly were. How, if she squinted, she could see his jaw tightening.

"I shouldn't have agreed to anything like that. It was a mistake," he said, not looking at her.

Her heart fell, but despite wanting to run back home like a terrified bunny rabbit, she forced herself not to back down.

"Why not?" She moved closer to him, looking up at him from underneath her eyelashes. Megan had told her about that trick, and based on Heath's jaw tightening further, it worked. "We're both adults. We can do what we want."

"It's not that simple. And anyway, I'm not some playboy. I'm a fifth-grade teacher, for God's sake."

"You're saying I should go ask someone else?"

His fists clenched, but he finally shrugged. "If you'd like."

"All right. Well, I'll call Ash. He gave me his number, before you so rudely interrupted us. I'm sure he'd be more than happy to take me up on my offer." Taking out her phone, she dialed his number. They both heard it ringing—once, twice—then Ash's voice: "Hello?"

Heath took the phone from her hand and ended the call. "Not him, Anyone but him."

Jubilee rolled her eyes, taking her phone back. "Now

you're being an idiot. What do you want, Heath? That's the real question here."

"I know that if you get involved with Ash Younger, you'll regret it."

"Then fulfill your end of the bargain. You can vet the guys, but you have to give me lessons. Simple."

"It's not—" He blew out a breath before laughing softly. "How did I ever think you were sweeter than your brothers? You're worse than them."

She smiled at the somewhat backhanded compliment. "If you think they're stubborn, you have no idea."

Groaning, Heath collapsed onto the couch before patting the cushion next to him. "Sit down, then. I'm not doing this standing up. I'll get a crick in my neck."

"I'm not that short!" Jubilee sat down beside him, keeping a few inches between them despite what they were about to do. Her palms became sweaty, her breathing coming faster and faster.

"Don't be nervous. Here, take a deep breath for me. In, and then out." Heath's gaze searched hers. "We don't have to do anything, you know."

"It's not about having to do it; it's about wanting to do it. That doesn't mean I can't still be nervous."

His lips twitched. "Fair enough."

Jubilee suddenly became overly aware of her own body. Where did she put her hands? On her lap? She crossed her arms, but that seemed even more awkward. She finally put her hands down by her sides and tried not to fidget like a kid bored in school.

"Where should we start?" Heath asked.

"I want to know how to attract men. How to flirt. What do you find attractive in a woman?"

"You didn't seem like you needed help the other night."

"And yet I ended up going home alone." She pursed her lips. "So, answer the question."

"Okay, well…" He considered. "I guess any guy will say they like women who are confident. Who can take charge, who know who they are."

"And have big breasts?"

Heath coughed a laugh. "A nice rack is great, but not a requirement. And anyway, I prefer to call myself a breast connoisseur."

Jubilee felt her cheeks heating up. Rifling around in her purse, she pulled out a notepad and started taking notes.

"Are you really writing this down?" Heath asked, incredulous.

"Yes, because I'll forget everything. Now, keep going. I want to know everything." She pointed her pen at him. "Don't hold back. I'm not some delicate flower."

"Beauty is one thing in a woman, but it's that extra something that attracts me. Any man," he added hastily. "A woman who has her life together, who can have a conversation."

Jubilee clucked her tongue. "That's boring. Are you really telling me some eighty-year-old crone with a mustache and bad breath would be attractive to you if she were witty and had a decent retirement fund?"

Heath laughed, and the sound filled Jubilee with delight. "Okay, fine, I'm not sure I could do bad breath. The mustache could maybe be overlooked."

"You're such a liar. Go on. How should a woman flirt with you? Make you want her?" Jubilee realized she sounded breathless as she asked the question, and she stared down at her notepad so Heath wouldn't see her expression.

"I like when a woman teases. I also like when she touches me—nothing overt, but in small ways. And cleavage helps, too, although I prefer nice legs and long hair."

Jubilee wanted to ask if he hated short hair—considering she'd just cut hers into a bob—but she bit her lip. "And what should she talk about?"

"Anything but her exes." He smiled wryly. "That goes for the guy, too. Run away from guys who can't stop talking about their exes."

"Is that it? Just be pretty and touchy-feely, and you get a guy?" Jubilee was skeptical.

"Pretty much. Men are easy." He leaned toward her slightly, making her catch her breath. "I'll tell you a secret, though."

She licked her lips. "What?"

"I love a woman's neck. The pale curve of it. I love to kiss a woman right...here..." He pushed her hair to the side to expose the soft skin right below her ear. He blew a stream of air right there, making her shiver, but he didn't kiss her. When he moved away, disappointment filled her.

Do you really want to attract men? Or do you just want to attract Heath?

"Well, this is helpful. I'll use this when I go out this weekend."

Heath's heated expression turned cold within an instant. "Will you be trying to get Ash Younger again?"

"Maybe. He seemed interested, until you pulled me away from him."

"I was trying to protect you."

"I don't need someone to protect me. I've had people trying to keep me in a bubble my entire life. I don't need a fifth older brother, thank you very much." As she bent down to get her things, Heath stopped her with a touch on her arm.

"Just so you know, I've never thought of you as a sister." His voice was low and warm.

"Not even when you first met me?" She rolled her eyes. "I don't believe you."

"Okay, maybe then. How old were you? Sixteen?"

"Eighteen. But I'm not that kid anymore. I haven't been for a long time." She rose and slung her purse over her shoulder. "I should head out. I'll see you later."

Before she could leave, though, Heath stopped her again. "Wait. Before you go flirting with any guy in town, I should give you my list."

"Oh, that's right. Of suitable men." Her lips quirked. "How about you text me? I'm sure you'll want to be thorough."

His gaze scanned her face, his eyes inscrutable behind his glasses. Jubilee could smell his scent, a warm and spicy aroma that made her want to bury her nose in the crook of his neck. It didn't help that his sweater hugged his muscular arms and pecs, leaving little to the imagination.

Desire made her mouth water. Her heart pounded until she felt dizzy.

"I just want you to be careful, all right?" he said quietly. "You know what I mean?"

She was tempted to ask him if he really meant that he didn't want her with any man but *him*. But then why would he go to all of this trouble to set her up with someone else? It made no sense.

Without thinking, she pushed her hair away from her neck. Heath tracked the movement, and in that moment, she could feel his lips sliding down the pale curve of her neck to her collarbone, kissing a path toward her heart.

"Bye, Heath," she whispered.

He opened his mouth to reply when a knock sounded on the front door. His expression turned to a frown before hearing Rose's voice.

"Heath, it's freezing out here! Let me in!"

Heath moved to open the door when Rose came inside with a breathless laugh.

"I guess I could've checked to see if it was unlocked." Her eyes widened when she noticed Jubilee. With her dark hair tipped with blue and her blue eyes, Rose was a beautiful woman. She and Heath didn't look much alike, although Jubilee sometimes noticed a resemblance in their smiles. Their eyes both wrinkled when they smiled.

"Jubi, hey, what are you doing here?" Rose looked at Heath. "Am I interrupting?"

"No, I was just leaving. Bye, Heath, Rose."

Jubilee didn't wait for a response from either before hurrying to her car and driving away, trying to tell herself she wasn't making a huge mistake by getting mixed up in this absurd scheme.

HEATH WATCHED Jubilee practically sprint from his place before turning to his sister. Rose had her hands on her hips, a what-is-going-on expression on her face.

He sighed. "Come on in. Want a drink?"

"Sure. Then you can tell me what that was all about."

What *had* that been all about? He'd gotten so close to kissing Jubilee a second time. It hadn't helped imagining her flirting with him, smiling, touching him. Letting him touch her, too. He grabbed a beer from the fridge and handed it to Rose, who had sat down on the couch where Jubilee had just been.

"I didn't realize you two were having—what? Dinner? A date?"

"It wasn't either of those things."

"Huh." Rose opened her beer and took a drink. "Then tell me why Jubilee looked so flustered when I came in."

He growled. "Leave it alone, Rose. It's none of your business."

She sighed. "I'm not trying to be nosy"—he snorted at that—"but I know when you're being a dumbass. If you like her, why not ask her out? She's clearly interested."

"Who says I like her? Like that, anyway."

"Now you're being stupid." Rose rolled her eyes, setting her beer down on a coaster. "I know about the lock of hair. I know it was Jubilee's."

Heath froze. How would Rose know about that…? Then he put two and two together. "Johnny," he said with a groan.

"Johnny. He tricked me into going with him because I thought he had Jubilee. He had her hair, you see." Rose smiled sadly. "But I realized later he'd stolen it from *you*. Why did you have it at all?"

Heath considered telling his sister to go away, that this was none of her business, but she would never let it go. Besides, he was tired of secrets. He couldn't tell her every-thing—not about Rich's threats if Heath testified against

Johnny, or Heath's own darker secrets—but he could tell her this.

He told her the story of how Jubilee had cut her hair on her birthday and given him the lock. Since then, Jubilee seemingly had forgotten all about the incident, but he'd kept the memento anyway.

"I don't know why I kept it," he said with a shrug. "I should've given it back. Or thrown it away."

"I think you know exactly why you kept it. So the real question is: why not act on your own feelings?"

Because she's too young. Because she's my best friend's little sister. Because I've done things that she would hate. Because I'm not the man for her.

"She's interested in dating someone else," he said finally. "It's a moot point now."

"That's why she stopped by? To tell you she's dating someone else?" Rose shook her head. "Fine, keep your secrets. I'll get them out of you eventually."

They chatted for a little while longer, Rose updating him on her classes, about Seth's woodworking. Heath loved seeing his sister so happy. Seth Thornton had brought her out of her own shame and darkness and into a life that she'd always deserved.

Seeing his sister, though, always filled Heath with both joy and guilt. Joy, because he'd missed her when she'd essentially disappeared from his life years ago, and now they lived in the same town. Guilt, because she'd made a deal with the devil to save him, and now he feared it wouldn't be enough, if Johnny and his cronies had their way.

"Don't let Jubilee go," Rose said seriously as she was about to leave. Heath had offered to drive her, but she'd borrowed

Seth's car since she'd yet to get her own. "If you really care about her. You'll regret it if you do."

"How did you get so wise?" He kissed her forehead. "Don't worry about me."

"I'm serious. I know what it's like to be alone." Her eyes shimmered with tears, but she brushed them away. "Oh geez, it's late. I better get going. I'll see you later."

He told her goodbye and then returned to the living room, wondering if his little sister really was wiser than him this time.

"Here you go," Jubilee said as she handed the Americano and blueberry muffin to a woman not much younger than her. "Is that all?"

"I haven't had a muffin in six months." The girl inhaled the scent of sugar and blueberries and moaned aloud. "I'm tempted to buy all of them and eat them in one go."

Jubilee laughed. "Maybe just start with one. Although our pumpkin spice muffin is really good, too."

The girl groaned, paid for her food, and left before she could be tempted further. It was mid-morning, and the early morning rush had petered out.

Jubilee drummed her fingers against the counter. She'd already wiped down all the tables and organized the baked goods in the glass case after the usual morning depletion. Megan was currently in the back finishing up a batch of bread, and Jubilee could smell it baking. Even though she'd been working here for two years now, her stomach still rumbled at how amazing it always smelled.

Had it really been two years since she'd moved out of her

parents' house and started this job? It was hard to believe sometimes, while other times, Jubilee itched to do something else. Go somewhere else.

And maybe leave someone behind once and for all.

She blew out a breath. Her acceptance to Avila College remained a secret. She had until the week before Christmas to commit. She hadn't even chosen a major yet, since she'd be taking general education classes at first. Jubilee had considered going into marketing or business, but neither had appealed to her very much.

When she'd been a child, Jubilee had dreamed of becoming a veterinarian. She'd loved animals—dogs, cats, birds, even snakes, to her mother's horror—but when she'd relapsed at age thirteen with another bout of leukemia, that dream had been set aside. Lisa had also never allowed any animals in the home, and by the time Jubilee had moved out, she'd thought that that dream had been put to rest.

But why couldn't she go to veterinary school? The very thought of it sent a thrill through her. To be doing something *real*, to do something that would truly help animals and the people who loved them?

Maybe I should adopt an animal, at least to start. She wasn't home enough for a dog, but maybe she could adopt a cat.

The bell by the front door of the bakery jingled, and in walked a man Jubilee had seen a few times in town recently. He was tall, with sandy-blond hair and a nice smile, although his hair was already thinning on top. He also tended to wear shirts that were a size too small, to the point that if you looked at him from the side, you could see his undershirt through the gaps in between the placket of buttons on his shirt.

"Hi there," Jubilee said. "How can I help you?"

"I've never been here before. What do you recommend?" The man had a bit of a twang, his vowels elongated with each word.

"What do you like? Our cinnamon rolls are pretty amazing, I have to say."

"That's not the only amazing thing in here, I'm thinking."

Jubilee blushed. She thought of Heath's "lesson" a few days ago, and she knew she'd be a fool not to put his advice to good use right now. Didn't she want to date around? Maybe find a boyfriend?

She smiled, making a point to keep eye contact with this latest possible date. "What's your name?" she asked him. It felt strange to flirt with someone whose name you didn't know. "I'm Jubilee."

"That's a pretty name. Mine's not that interesting, I'm afraid. I'm Brian." His eyes gleamed as they scanned her face before landing on her breasts for a long moment.

"Brian's not a bad name. At least you aren't Mortimer. That's a terrible name," she joked.

His lips twisted, and she could've bitten her tongue. "That's my middle name."

"Oh, I'm sorry." When he started laughing, she blushed. "Wait, are you joking?"

"How about you go out with me and find out?"

She didn't know what to say to that. *Say yes, say yes!* her mind screamed. Yet she found herself hesitating. Brian seemed perfectly nice, but he wasn't—

No, she refused to go there. This had nothing to do with *him.*

"How about you tell me your order first?" she replied.

"You choose for me. I trust you."

"All right."

Jubilee pushed her hair away from her neck, just like Heath had told her. Brian licked his lips, which made her feel slightly ill. She grabbed the tongs to choose something—anything—from the food case. In her haste, she knocked a plate of croissants off the shelf onto the bottom of the case, where they covered everything with flakes of pastry.

"Dammit," she muttered. She grabbed one of the pumpkin spice muffins, but not before she hit her head on the edge of the case. Her eyes blurred with tears. "Dammit!"

Brian laughed. "Are you all right?"

"I'm fine." She practically tossed the muffin onto a plate and handed it to him. "That'll be five fifty."

Brian decided to order a cortado before he went to sit down to eat his muffin. Jubilee tried not to dissolve into a puddle of humiliation as she made his drink. *Smooth, Jubilee. Smooth.*

When she gave him his drink a few minutes later, he gestured at her to sit down. "There's no one here, so your boss won't get mad."

"I can't, although I'd like to." She batted her eyelashes, determined that this encounter wouldn't end up another failure. "Does your offer still stand?"

"Of course. I'm new in town, so you should show me around."

She pulled out her notepad and scribbled her number down onto it. "Text me. And I'll try not to bash my head on anything, either."

"Excellent."

As she handed him the note, she made a point to brush

her fingers against his. Brian's eyes lit up. Jubilee did a mental happy dance.

Heath was right. Men are *simple.*

Jubilee returned to the register as more customers came in. Megan bustled in and out with more baked goods, her cheeks flushed but her expression happy. There were few things—and even people—that Megan loved as much as she loved her bakery. Her husband Caleb sometimes joked that he was secondary to The Rise and Shine, at which Megan would joke that as long as he behaved, she'd love him more than baking cinnamon rolls.

Brian gave Jubilee a wave when he left, which prompted Megan to ask her about the gesture when they took a break for lunch.

"His name is Brian. He just moved here," Jubilee explained. "He asked me out."

"He did? He looked kind of old."

"I think his hair is just thinning early."

"Hmm." Megan took a large bite of her sandwich. "Well, he's no Ash Younger, but he'll be good practice. Maybe you can help him with his fashion choices. That shirt was unfortunate."

"Oh, hush!" Jubilee laughed. "This is all part of the plan. Date lots of men for the experience."

Megan grinned. "Sure, but some experiences aren't too exciting at the end of the day."

They chatted after they finished eating. Megan talked about the ultrasound she'd have soon, and how she wanted to find out the gender but Caleb didn't.

"He wants it to be a surprise." Megan rolled her eyes. "But do you know how hard it is to find baby clothes that aren't pink or blue? Besides, I want to be prepared as much as possible. Oh, that reminds me. I'll need to hire someone to help in the next few months, especially when I'm on maternity leave. I want you to be the person in charge, of course."

Jubilee's eyes widened. "Really? Are you sure?"

"Of course I'm sure. You know this place as well as I do. I might still come in to bake, although Caleb might tie me down if I do." She smiled. "Your brother is a pain in the ass, you know."

Jubilee knew she couldn't keep her going to college a secret now, not if Megan expected her to stay to manage the bakery. "I've been meaning to tell you. I got into Avila. I'd start after the New Year."

Megan's eyes widened. "What? Seriously? Why didn't you say anything?"

"Because I'm not sure if I'm going or not."

"Why the hell not? Do you not want to?"

"No, I do, it's just…" Jubilee sighed. "I've never lived anywhere but here, you know? I think I'm afraid it'll be a disaster."

"Now, that's ridiculous. You'll do great."

"What about the bakery? I don't want to leave you high and dry."

Megan patted her on the arm. "Jubi, I'm so glad you're doing this. I've loved having you work here, don't get me wrong, but I've always hoped you'd get out of here. You need to stretch your wings. Seattle will be perfect. Sure, it'll be a lot at the beginning, but you're strong. You've beaten cancer *twice*. If anyone could succeed, you will."

Jubilee was close to tears. She sniffled. "Thank you. Oh, and you're the only person I've told. So don't tell anyone yet?"

"Cross my heart, hope to die." The front doorbell jingled as a customer came in, and then within another moment, they rang the bell at the front. "We better get out there before there's a riot. People need their coffee, dammit."

Jubilee laughed, feeling like a huge load had been lifted off her shoulders for once.

WHEN'S OUR NEXT LESSON? Jubilee texted that afternoon.

Heath had gotten the text while at work, and he'd ignored it until he'd gone home. He then ignored it some more as he made dinner. When he received a second text that simply said, *Stop ignoring me*, he couldn't help but smile.

Not ignoring you, he replied. *How about tomorrow night?*

That works. I have a date this Saturday, so I need some practice.

Heath's initial amusement faded, and he was in a black mood the rest of the evening. Restless, he decided to take a jog around his neighborhood in the hopes that he could burn off whatever this was. Even though it was already dark and cold, the chill felt invigorating.

At least for the first few laps. By the time he returned home, his nose was red and half-frozen, his eyes watering from the blustery weather. Autumn would soon be at an end, and the infamous rainy season in the Pacific Northwest would begin. Days of gray, rain, drizzle, and cold until May.

And soon he'd have to testify against Johnny. Rich hadn't contacted Heath since that first call, but that didn't mean Rich wasn't watching—and waiting. Heath knew his type: they used any weakness you had to get you to bend to their will.

His head pounding and exhaustion swamping his limbs,

he went up to bed, only to wake up even more tired in the morning.

The school day passed painfully slow: two of his students got into a fight at recess that resulted in both of them getting suspended for the rest of the week, while he caught more than one student cheating on the spelling test that day. He also had to deal with Jessie's mom, Lana, stopping by to apologize for Jessie asking him to date her after he'd contacted her about having a parent-teacher meeting. *I don't generally ask my kids to pick up men for me*, she'd joked, although Heath had detected a note of flirtation in her voice. He'd had to shut that down quickly, and Lana had reacted coldly. The encounter hadn't improved his mood one bit. By the time the bell rang, Heath almost bolted from his classroom before his students had even packed up.

When he heard a knock on his front door, it took Heath a second to remember that Jubilee was coming over. His heart did that annoying flip-flop in his chest as he let her inside. Lately, she'd been letting her hair go wavy, and he fought the urge to run his fingers through the silken locks.

"Hi," Jubilee said, her cheeks rosy. "Long time no see."

"Can I get you anything? Let me take your coat."

"Thank you. And no, I'm fine." Jubilee fidgeted, and it melted Heath's frustrated mood to see her. She was like a candle in the darkness, always bright and shining and beautiful. Every time he was around her, he felt like the world could be good and right and lovely. That wasn't something he could say about any other person, except maybe his sister Rose.

"I used your tips a few days ago," Jubilee said in a rush as they sat down in the living room. At his raised eyebrow, she added, "For flirting and catching a man's interest."

"Ah."

"It worked. I have a date Saturday."

"So you said."

She tilted her head to the side, looking like a curious bird. "Is something the matter?"

Of course not. It's not like I want to take whoever this guy is and pummel him for even thinking about going out with you, he thought darkly.

"No, it's just been a long day."

"Okay, well, I wanted to work on something specific. For my date."

His lips twisted. "I figured as much."

Her cheeks turned as red as cherries, and Heath was torn between being charmed and being twisted into knots. It didn't help that Jubilee had put on some kind of perfume that wafted toward him every time she moved. It smelled like jasmine, and it only stoked his desire for her further.

"I need kissing lessons. I don't know how to kiss."

He stared at her, trying very hard to keep a straight face. "You were perfectly good at kissing when we did it," he growled. He didn't care that he shouldn't bring up that night only a few weeks ago.

God, that kiss. That kiss had wrecked him. Jubilee hadn't been experienced, yes, but she'd been eager. Nothing like enthusiasm to make up for any defects in technique.

"Um, thank you." She swallowed. "But we didn't go very far, right? I don't know how to *really* kiss."

Heath wondered if being boiled in hot oil would be less painful than this conversation. Maybe he should throw himself off of the nearest cliff to end this. It sounded preferable to kissing Jubilee so she could kiss *another* man that weekend.

You had your chance, he reminded himself. *She's not for you. If you weren't such an idiot, you'd tell her to go home right now.*

If he were wiser, stronger, better…except he was none of those things when it came to Jubilee Thornton. With her, he was weak. Desperate. Consumed.

And God Almighty, he wanted to kiss her right now more than he wanted anything else in his life.

"Well, then, I guess we better get started." He turned so he faced her. "You'll need to come closer than that."

"Oh! Of course." She scooted closer, their knees bumping. She licked her lips, which didn't help his self-control at all. "Where should I put my hands?"

"How about on my shoulders?"

She settled her hands on his shoulders, her eyes wide. Her perfume enveloped his senses, and he couldn't help but drink in the pale creaminess of her skin. The smattering of freckles on her nose, or how her lips were full and pink.

"Now, you'll tilt your head to the left. Are you ready?"

She nodded, her fingers digging into his shoulders. "Yes."

Heath touched her jaw and pressed his lips to hers. It was a light caress, barely a brush of his lips against hers. She inhaled, and when her eyelids fluttered closed, he smiled.

He didn't deepen the kiss right then. He simply enjoyed the feeling of her lips under his, the way her breathing increased. His cock hardened with every brush of his lips, and it took all of his self-control not to thrust his tongue inside her mouth and have her writhing under him in ten seconds flat.

Steady, steady. He licked at the seam of her lips. When she didn't open her mouth, he traced her cheek.

"Open for me," he murmured.

Jubilee shivered. "I don't know what I'm doing," she complained.

"I'll show you. Just let me lead for now, and then you can kiss me back when you want to. Okay?"

She nodded. "Okay."

She closed her eyes, parting her lips, and Heath's heart thrummed. It was hard to believe she couldn't hear how hard his heart was pounding as he touched his tongue to hers. He tilted her head back as he deepened the kiss. He sucked her tongue and tasted her, loving the way her nails dug into his shoulders.

He just let himself feel: the taste of her, her scent. The silkiness of her lips. When she tentatively touched her tongue to his, he almost exploded. With a groan, he kissed her harder, that self-control snapping in an instant.

Heath tangled his fingers in her hair, and then Jubilee was under him on the couch as he kissed her like he'd wanted to kiss her for ages. That kiss on Halloween had been a cruel tease—he'd needed more. He'd needed everything.

He pressed his hips against her, wanting her to feel how much he wanted her. She shuddered, arching against him. The flames inside him grew and grew, especially as he pushed up her shirt to touch the skin above her jeans.

But then something in his brain told him that he was going too far, that this was way more than kissing. That she wasn't his and never would be, and he was only making it harder for both himself and her.

With great reluctance, he ended the kiss, but he didn't move off her for a long moment. Her eyes opened, and her pupils almost covered the green of her irises.

"Is it over?" she whispered.

He laughed, but it was a bitter sound. He sat up and tried —unsuccessfully—to cover his aching erection.

"I think that's enough. You should go."

Jubilee sat up, and Heath's gut twisted at the hurt in her eyes. "Okay." She pushed her hair off of her forehead. "I need to get up early for work anyway."

It took everything in Heath not to yank her back into his arms and kiss her senseless. Her shirt was still rucked up slightly, and when she bent down to pick up her purse, he got a flash of cleavage that sent a lightning bolt of lust through him.

After they said goodbye, Heath bolted his front door and leaned his forehead against the cool wood.

He was fairly certain he was going to lose this battle against staying away from Jubilee.

An hour into her date with Brian, Jubilee rather wished she'd stayed home. Watching some trashy reality show on TV would've been more exciting than listening to Brian talk about which *Star Trek* series was the best one.

"*Enterprise* is best, but *Discovery* is my second favorite." Brian took a swig of his pale ale, his third one for the night. "Have you ever watched *Star Trek*?"

Jubilee forced a smile. "No, I haven't."

"Oh, then I need to tell you where to start. People think you should start with the first episode filmed, but I totally disagree with that." Brian whipped out his phone and began to text her something. "I sent you the best-watching order, including all of the movies. Except the most recent movie, which was trash."

Jubilee drank her wine and considered if it would really be rude to go to the bathroom and never come back. Brian was perfectly nice, but he was *boring*. He'd barely asked her anything about herself. She had a feeling if she asked him, he wouldn't even be able to remember her name.

He'd taken her to a little hole-in-the-wall Italian restaurant that was mostly famous for serving booze without checking IDs. Jubilee's plate of spaghetti had come out cold and the pasta underdone. She'd eaten all of three bites before she'd given up and decided she'd eat something at home.

"You're not eating?" Brian smiled. "I'm totally fine with women eating in front of me. I know you all think you're not supposed to eat on dates."

Jubilee rolled her eyes inwardly. "I'm just not hungry," she lied.

"If you say so." He took a bite of his own pasta, which he ate with a loud smacking sound that made Jubilee wince. "My ex-girlfriend would always order a salad with no dressing, and then she'd complain about how fat she was. I guess it's a chick thing."

Jubilee blew out a breath. She'd been the one to instigate this whole situation, so she might as well try to salvage at least part of the night. She refused to believe she couldn't find any decent guy to date—any decent guy who wasn't Heath DiMarco.

Her mind drifted to that kiss a few nights ago as Brian droned on about his ex-girlfriend's predilection for leaving clumps of hair in the shower all the time. That kiss had rocked her to her very soul. The Halloween kiss had been just a mere taste, she'd realized after she'd driven home, still shaking from how it had felt to have Heath press her down into the couch cushions.

He'd been hard—for her. She'd never known what it was like to have a man desire you, and it was a heady feeling. It was a feeling she wanted to experience again and again, even if her logical side knew experiencing it with Heath couldn't happen.

They could play at lessons and go their separate ways, because Heath had already made it clear nothing else could or would happen. Jubilee needed to accept this if she was going to avoid getting her heart broken all over again.

"Did you hear me?" Brian asked.

"I'm sorry, no. What did you say again?"

He sighed heavily. "I asked if you wanted to go for a walk after this?"

No, no, and no, she thought. "I can't. I need to get home."

Brian shrugged. "Suit yourself." He finished his pale ale with a belch that cemented Jubilee's opinion of him.

She hadn't planned to let him kiss her when he took her home, but when she stood outside her door, fumbling for her keys, he apparently took that as a sign that she wanted a kiss. He leaned down and pressed his mouth to hers. Surprised, Jubilee froze and then decided to see if maybe Brian's kissing skills were better than his conversational ones.

The way he kissed her could only be described as *nicely.* There was little passion behind the kiss, and when it ended, Jubilee had the absurd thought that it was about as intense as kissing your brother, that kiss. She bit back a laugh, although maybe it was really a sob. Because the contrast between this staid, boring kiss and Heath's soul-burning kisses was so apparent it was physically painful.

"Thanks for tonight," she said, only half-meaning it. "Have a good night."

Before Brian could ask her for a second date or try to kiss her again, she unlocked her door and shut it in his face, hoping he'd get the hint without her having to tell him to his face.

I'm doomed. Totally and completely doomed for the one man I apparently can never have.

⁓

HEATH SWORE as he jogged to his car. The rain had started right when school let out, and Heath had, of course, left his umbrella in his car. Shivering, he almost didn't notice the man approaching until he was only a few feet from him.

"Nice weather, huh?" the man said, like they were enjoying a beautiful sunny day.

Heath looked up to see a nondescript man smiling at him. He was of average height and no older than forty, with only a few lines on his face. His wore a wide-brimmed hat that dripped from the rain and a trench coat cinched at the waist that made him look like some detective from a mid-century noir film. A scar bisected his chin, his front tooth chipped from probably the same fight that had cut his chin.

"Do I know you?" Heath asked, a bad feeling crawling up his spine.

The man grinned. "You don't recognize my voice? Shame. It's Rich. I thought I'd stop by and have a chat."

Heath froze, the cold rain dripping down his collar. Or maybe it was the fear that was making him feel so cold. His umbrella was forgotten as he stared at the man who'd threatened him and stalked him for the last month.

Rain spattered the lenses of his glasses, making the man in front of him look like multiple people from the water's refraction.

The laughter of children drifted to them, only exacerbating the situation. This piece of shit was *here*, at Heath's workplace and at a school. Rage made Heath's vision turn red.

"A chat? Why the hell are you here, where I work? I got your messages. You didn't have to tell me in person."

"I think I did. Because from what I understand, you still plan to testify, so maybe you really didn't understand my message."

Heath gritted his teeth. "I got it. Leave before I call the cops."

"Call the cops if you want, but that'll just make things worse for you. Do you really want everyone in town to know your dirty little secret? Pretty sure schoolteachers aren't allowed to be drug dealers."

"The charges were dropped, and you have no proof, anyway."

"You really want to call my bluff?" Rich's face split into a grin. "Even if you don't care about yourself, I bet you care a lot about your sister."

Rain dripped down Heath's face, soaking his hair, but he couldn't feel it now. Hearing Rich mention Rose was like lighting a match to kindling.

In a swift movement, Heath grabbed Rich by his shirt and shoved him against a nearby car. "Don't ever talk about my sister," he snarled, watching with some satisfaction as Rich tried to free himself from Heath's grip. "Don't you touch a hair on her head. Or I swear to God, I'll kill you myself."

He gave Rich one last shake before letting him go. The only reason he didn't punch him in the jaw was the fact that they were still at school. The parking lot was blessedly deserted right then, but it wouldn't help for one of Heath's coworkers to see him manhandling some guy.

Rich smoothed his shirt. All humor disappeared from his expression. "Threaten me as much as you like. I'm the one who can ruin your life, and your sister's, too. So I'd recommend you make your decision before I make it for you."

Rich got into his car and drove off, his tires screeching against the wet pavement. The rain fell harder, soaking Heath to the skin, but he could only concentrate on his roiling thoughts.

The thought of anyone hurting Rose again sent him into an emotional tailspin. He'd already failed her once, and it would haunt him for the rest of his life. If he didn't do everything in his power this time to keep her safe…

"Are you all right?" Sara Thornton, formerly Flannigan, walked up to Heath and held her umbrella over them both. Heavily pregnant, she was due to give birth at the end of February. Despite Harrison's protests about her continuing to work, Sara wanted to finish this semester before going on leave.

Heath and Sara had become friends when she'd started working at the school, and when she'd gotten together with Harrison, it had only cemented their friendship further.

Heath wiped the rain from his face. "No. You shouldn't be out here. Harrison would kill me if he knew I let you stand outside in the rain."

Sara rolled her eyes. "I'm pregnant, not dying." She patted her belly. "Besides, you're the one soaked to the skin. Did you lose your car keys or something?"

"No—no." He pushed his fingers through his hair and

then tried to dry off his glasses, but his clothes were too wet to make a difference.

Sara took his glasses and dried them herself. "I've never seen you this out of sorts. Now you're really worrying me." She handed him his glasses, her forehead creased. "At least tell me if I can help."

"I wish you could. Really. But this is something I have to deal with myself."

"Well, at least go home and dry off. You'll get pneumonia."

Heath smiled, but it was a brittle smile. "I think that's an old wives' tale."

"And then you're going to agree to come have drinks with me and Harrison. Well, you two can drink. I can't." She sighed, but her eyes sparkled nonetheless.

Seeing Sara so happy and in love, soon to have a baby, sent frissons of longing through Heath. Not for Sara herself—he'd never thought of her in that way. But to have that contentment, the knowledge that when you went home, you'd be with the one person in this world who loved you despite everything. Who wanted to make a family with you.

Jubilee entered his thoughts, and it only made his heart clench. *Don't go there. Don't.*

"Of course I'll come have drinks with you two. Just let me know when. I'll even try not to rub it in that you can't have any booze."

"My hero." Sara patted him on the arm, giving him one last concerned look before she went to her car.

Heath got into his own car, shivering now from the cold, and he waited for Sara to drive off before he did. He didn't want Rich to show up again and threaten someone else. God, just the thought of him going after Sara, or Jubilee, or anyone else he cared about…

He turned his car heater on full blast until the shivering abated enough so he could drive. When he arrived home, he took the hottest shower he could stand, but although his body was no longer cold, it didn't do a damn thing about the icicles forming around his heart.

CHAPTER SEVEN

Fair Haven wasn't exactly a town with a lot of big events like concerts and festivals, other than the annual pumpkin festival in the fall, but when Jubilee saw on Facebook that a local band was playing at a newly opened club downtown, she bought a ticket without hesitation. She'd somehow managed to go twenty-five years without ever going to a concert, other than some school concert as a kid.

She considered texting Megan to go with her, but then she decided that she'd rather go alone. She didn't want to answer any questions. Megan already suspected something was up, especially when Jubilee only told her that her date with Brian had been mediocre at best.

Brian had texted a few times since their date. Jubilee eventually told him that she wasn't interested in a second date, although she wished him well. To her relief, he didn't bother her again. She just hoped she didn't run into him again.

Saturday night, she arrived at the concert and found herself in a mass of people that smelled like sweat and marijuana. The room was hazy, and the alcohol flowed without stopping. Jubilee pushed her way through the crowd to the bar, feeling like she'd climbed Mount Everest just to order a cocktail.

Clutching her drink, she moved back into the crowd. One man with a tattoo on his arm grinned at her. "Hey there," he drawled, taking a moment to drink in her low-cut top that showed off more cleavage than Jubilee was used to.

Smiling flirtatiously, she replied, "Here for the concert, too?"

The man laughed. "Is this a concert? I thought I was going to church."

"If this is your idea of church, I'm a little concerned."

"I'm Peyton. You?"

"Jubilee." Jubilee had to shout over the crowd.

When Peyton was about to reply, the band started playing. He shrugged, but he didn't move away from Jubilee. He and Jubilee swayed to the music, and Peyton made sure that she never had an empty glass.

By the end of the show, Jubilee was giggling and yelling at Peyton's questions, the alcohol making her inhibitions melt away.

"Are you from here?" she yelled, taking a long sip of her cocktail. The alcohol made her lips and tongue feel fuzzy. *I'm drunk*, the tiny part of her brain that was still sober said. But she felt too warm, too happy, to care that in the morning, she'd feel like a train had run over her.

"No, I'm from Spokane! You?" Peyton didn't seem drunk to Jubilee, but he was also pretty tall. And guys could drink more than girls, she thought with an inner sigh.

"That's terrible! I'm sorry!"

Peyton laughed and snaked an arm around her waist. "How about we get out of here? I'm over this joint."

"Okay!"

Jubilee stumbled out of the club, the cold November air hitting her with a slap. She gasped, but her entire body was so warm already from dancing and drinking that it was like the cold was an afterthought.

The beat of the music still resounded outside, but when Peyton spoke, she could really hear his voice. She noticed for the first time that he had a goatee, and she was pretty sure all of his tattoos were tribal designs, save for a barcode on his right wrist.

Jubilee tripped over the sidewalk, Peyton catching her. When he put his arms around her, she had the stray thought that she was getting in over her head right now, but then the thought was instantly forgotten.

"Do you like drinking?" Jubilee blurted before laughing at her own question. "I don't do it much, but I really should."

"I like drinking. I like finding pretty girls even more." Peyton's hands roved further south until they squeezed her ass. "Let's go back to my place."

Jubilee's heart hammered. What had seemed like it was all in good fun was becoming…not quite so fun. Her reaction time was slow, though, and before she knew it, Peyton was pushing up her shirt and about to move one hand to her breasts.

"No, wait—I shouldn't be doing this." She tried to bat his hands away, but it was like a butterfly batting away a python.

"It's fine. You'll have fun. I promise."

"No, stop." Fear started to permeate through the haze of alcohol. She wrenched herself away, almost stumbling again in her haste to get away. She yanked down her shirt as the cold air caressed the bare skin of her abdomen.

"Come on, don't be like that." Peyton pressed closer. "Let's go back to my place."

"I want to go home."

Why had she come out here? Why had she encouraged this random guy? She was an idiot, and she was too drunk to get away.

When Peyton caught her wrist, she felt like a deer, frozen in the headlights.

"I think she told you to leave her alone."

Out of the darkness emerged Heath, his eyes glittering with rage.

"Hey, man, this isn't your business. Fuck off." Despite his annoyance, Peyton let Jubilee go, apparently taking Heath at his word.

"It's my business when some asshole manhandles any woman. Get out of here before I rearrange your face."

Muttering a curse under his breath, Peyton sauntered off without another word.

Jubilee rubbed her wrist, although it didn't hurt. Her heart did a little flip-flop seeing Heath, who always seemed to be in the worst place at the worst time. He always had to see her being stupid, didn't he?

"Are you okay?" He took her hand in his, inspecting her wrist. "Did he touch you?"

"No," she lied, not interested in getting him angry about Peyton touching her. "I was handling it."

"The hell you were." He tipped her chin up. "Are you drunk?"

"No." She tried to walk away, but the sidewalk seemed to

reach up to meet her, and she tripped over her own feet. Heath caught her. She was stumbling into all the men tonight, wasn't she?

"You're drunk. I'm taking you home. Did you drive?"

"Yeah."

"You can pick up your car in the morning, then. Come on."

Jubilee dug in her heels. "Why do you always do this? Swoop in like some hero and then push me away right afterward?"

"Come on, Jubi. Not here."

She bit the inside of her cheek. The hot press of tears threatened, but she cleared her throat. She was drunk, and once she got home and sobered up, she'd be fine.

Except that Heath now stood in the silvery moonlight, and it made him seem more handsome. Like some fairy-tale prince come to take her away as his bride.

"Why are you even here?" she countered as she followed him to his car. "Are you following me?"

He snorted. "Hardly. I was getting drinks with Harrison and Sara. You're lucky they already went home. Harrison would freak."

She silently acknowledged that statement. Harrison, as the eldest of the Thornton siblings, tended to be overprotective of them, Jubilee especially. It didn't help that he still didn't see her as a grown woman instead of the sickly child she'd once been.

"I don't need your help," she said petulantly.

"Maybe, but I'm giving it anyway."

The drive back to her apartment was awkward and silent. Jubilee felt the beginnings of a headache coming on, but she had a feeling it was more from stress than the alcohol.

"You need to drink some water." Heath poured her a glass of water when they arrived, making her down it before drinking a second one.

"Ugh, I want to go to sleep." Jubilee yawned, and after stripping out of her clothes without caring that Heath was only yards away, she collapsed onto her bed. Within moments, she was fast asleep, not noticing when Heath came into her bedroom and tucked the covers around her.

Heath awoke to the sound of something clattering in the bathroom. Bleary-eyed, he groaned at how stiff his neck had gotten after he'd fallen asleep on Jubilee's couch. He glanced at the time and yawned. It was four in the morning, and he should head home.

He'd stayed after Jubilee had gone to bed, telling himself he wanted to make sure she was all right. What if she got sick from drinking too much? Or called up that asshole who'd been manhandling her? He'd decided he'd sleep on her couch until he could be sure she was out of trouble, or so he told himself.

Now, he shivered and wrapped a blanket around himself. Jubilee's apartment was absolutely freezing. He flipped on the wall heater right as Jubilee emerged from the bathroom.

"Oh God, why are you still here?" She groaned and rubbed her eyes. "I thought you went home."

"No, I didn't," he said, rather lamely. "How are you feeling?"

"Like my mouth is the Sahara and I'm not sure if I want to puke or just sleep."

"Come on, you need to drink some more water. Maybe have a piece of toast."

Jubilee didn't protest, which meant she really was feeling the effects of too much alcohol. Heath couldn't help but think of when she'd gotten drunk on her twenty-first birthday and given him that lock of hair. Except now that lock of hair was gone, and Jubilee didn't even remember giving it to him in the first place.

"Drink up, and have some crackers, too. An empty stomach just makes it worse."

Jubilee mumbled something but drank the water in fast gulps. "Ugh. This is why I don't drink much."

"When was the last time you did?" Heath asked, already knowing the answer.

"On my twenty-first birthday. That was way worse than last night, though. I don't remember half of that night. One second I was taking shots, the next I was home, hugging the toilet." She shuddered. "Not my greatest moment."

Jubilee shivered, and he wrapped the blanket already around his shoulders around hers. Her eyes widened slightly, but she didn't pull away. It was a moment of weakness, having her rest her head on his shoulder like this. Maybe it was the darkness or the quiet of the night that made Heath feel like all of his resolutions to stay away from Jubilee were pointless. Or maybe he was just incapable of letting her go.

"I was there, at your twenty-first," Heath said quietly.

Jubilee blinked. "You were? I don't remember that."

"No, you wouldn't. You were very, very drunk."

Red brightened her cheeks. "Oh God, don't tell me what I did. Was it really stupid? Did I maul you?"

"Not exactly." He hesitated, wondering if he was making a mistake in telling her this. "You actually cut your hair."

She pulled away to stare at him. "What? Wait, is that why I had that missing piece of hair? I never knew how that had happened!"

"Apparently you weren't allowed to cut your hair, and you wanted to. You had the scissors in your bag. Luckily, I persuaded you not to cut it all off in one chunk."

Jubilee dropped her head into her hands, groaning. "Oh my God, that's so embarrassing. And *you*! You never said a thing!"

"There didn't seem to be a reason to." He swallowed, his mouth dry. "I kept that lock of hair, you know."

Silence reigned, and the tension was so thick that Heath could almost physically feel it, like it was cinching his chest. Jubilee stared at the couch, and he almost wondered if she hadn't heard him.

"You kept it. You still have it?"

"No, it was lost." *So to speak...*

"Why did you tell me this?" To Heath's surprise, anger flared in her expression. "Why tell me something like this when you've made it more than clear you don't want me that way?"

He'd clearly miscalculated. He raked his fingers through his hair. "I never said I didn't want you. I said that there are things that prevent us from being an *us* in the first place."

"What, are you engaged to some Russian princess? You're actually El Chapo? What kind of secrets does a fifth-grade teacher have, Heath?"

He stifled a bitter laugh. *If only you knew.* "I'm actually engaged to a Hungarian princess, if you must know."

"I'll never understand you. You freak out when you find out I'm dating other men. You pop up and cockblock every guy who gets near me. You kiss me, and then you tell me you kept a lock of my hair." She shook her head. "Am I crazy, or are you?"

He didn't have an answer for that, because she was right. He said one thing and did another. It would drive anyone crazy, and Jubilee deserved better than a man who couldn't give her everything.

"Then I'll leave you alone," he said quietly. "The lessons, everything. Clean break, no more of this back-and-forth."

Jubilee sighed. "You know what's really crazy? I don't want to say yes to that. I don't want this—whatever this is—to end."

They gazed at each other, a seemingly impenetrable wall between them. Heath considered telling her about his past, about Johnny and Rich, Troy and Gregory, but it was like the words were stuck in his throat. Fear always found a way to be more powerful than logic and honesty. Fear that she would no longer want him at all once she knew the truth.

"I think you should go." Jubilee moved so she was no longer under the blanket. "I need to think about everything."

"That's probably for the best."

Heath wanted to protest. He wanted to kiss her until they both forgot every objection against them being together. He wanted to remind himself of what was good and lovely in this world, instead of just darkness and lies. Because to him, Jubilee was all that was good.

"Wait." Jubilee hurried to the door before Heath opened it. "I just—"

Then she stood on her tiptoes and kissed him.

If there was ever an emotional manifestation of tectonic plates shifting, this kiss was it. Jubilee kissed him with an intensity that shocked him and sent desire flaring inside him, but before he could kiss her back, she ended it.

She licked her lips, her breathing only slightly increased. "That's what I needed to know."

CHAPTER EIGHT

When Rose opened the door, she gave Heath a single long look before stating, "You need a drink. Pronto."

Heath wouldn't disagree with that assessment. With a short laugh, he nodded and gratefully took the beer Rose handed him. Callie, Rose's German shepherd, padded after them both before curling up on her dog bed.

"Heath," Seth said as he stood up from the living room couch. Seth and Rose had moved into a bigger apartment together recently, although Heath had given Rose a bit of a talking-to about living with a man before marrying him. Rose had countered that this wasn't the nineteenth century and that she and Seth would get married—eventually.

"Seth. Nice to see you." Heath and Seth had graduated to an amicable relationship when it had once been more heated. Heath had been protective of Rose after everything she'd gone through, while Seth had been falling in love with Rose and struggling to accept that he'd given his entire heart to her.

Seeing Rose now, Heath had to acknowledge that Seth Thornton was good for her. Rose smiled and laughed, the strain in her features gone, and Seth would often look down at her with a smile just for her.

It was strange, seeing Seth and recognizing some of Jubilee's features in his. They had the same coloring, which all of the Thornton siblings had, but otherwise, they didn't really look much alike. But sometimes Heath saw it in the way Seth smiled: he could see Jubilee with that same smile, too.

"Long day at work?" Rose asked Heath. "Did those students of yours finally break you?"

"Not yet. It was a good day at school, actually. Nobody set anything on fire or got into a fight. And everyone seemed to have studied for the history test, which is pretty much a miracle."

Seth grunted a laugh. "Please, let's not talk about tests. You're giving me flashbacks."

Rose patted his arm. "Don't worry, we won't make you write an essay." A timer dinged from the kitchen right then. "You two go set the table and I'll get the lasagna."

Seth and Heath obediently shuffled to the small dining room, setting the table for the three of them as Rose finished cooking.

"You let her cook?" Heath whispered. "And nothing burned down?"

"This time. She's gotten better, so I'm taking it in stride. You'll eat every bite and like it, got it?"

"I won't say a word."

The lasagna was, admittedly, somewhat underdone, the middle pieces of pasta a bit crunchy, and Heath thought the sauce desperately needed salt. But it was edible, and Rose looked pleased, so everyone ate without complaint.

The food and the conversation weren't enough to distract

Heath from his thoughts, however. After school, he'd gotten a call from the DA's office about his upcoming testimony against Johnny Porter. Heath had asked about potential retaliation if he did testify, although he couldn't get into specifics. The DA would contact the police, which would result in Rich more than likely fulfilling his threat against Heath and, even worse, against Rose.

"Baby, what is this?" Seth skewered something on his fork and held it up. "Is this a vegetable?"

Rose peered more closely at the lump covered in red sauce. "Oh, that's garlic. I didn't have time to cut it up, so I just put in whole cloves."

"Huh." Seth considered the garlic, looked up at Rose's expectant face, and took a bite, only slightly grimacing. "It's good," he lied.

Rose bit her lip and then burst out laughing. "Oh God, it's terrible, isn't it? No, don't keep eating it. Eat the salad instead. It's from a bag, so I couldn't ruin it."

Heath snorted with laughter, and then all three of them were laughing until their eyes watered. Heath went into the kitchen and snagged another bottle of wine as they ate salad and the more edible parts of the lasagna.

"I don't know why I'm so bad at cooking," Rose bemoaned. "I'm good at other things. But cooking? I always mess up."

"Seth could always cook." Heath smiled at Seth's dark look.

"I don't cook because I don't want to poison anyone." Seth gave Rose a quick kiss. "I'll get the dessert. You bought that already baked, didn't you?"

Rose stuck out her tongue as Seth chuckled. When silence

settled on Rose and Heath, she set her chin in her hand and asked, "So, are you going to tell me or just sit there brooding?"

"I never brood."

"You and Seth brood like nobody I've ever met. You should start a club for brooding men. You could get together every Wednesday to sit in the dark and think about your life and your choices."

Heath smiled, but it felt false. He needed to tell Rose what was going on, if just for her own safety.

"After we finish eating, there is something I need to talk to you and Seth about."

Rose's eyebrows winged upward. "That sounds serious. Are you okay?"

No. Yes. Maybe. "I will be."

Seth came in with a cake that read *Happy Birthday Steve* on it in red icing.

"Who's Steve?" Heath asked.

Rose shrugged. "It was on sale. I guess Steve didn't want to celebrate his birthday, so they put it out for anyone to buy."

"Too bad for Steve, then." Seth started cutting pieces and handing them out. "Who doesn't pick up a birthday cake they ordered?"

"Maybe he was abducted by aliens," Rose offered.

Seth and Rose bantered, each giving more absurd reasons why Steve hadn't wanted his birthday cake. Heath picked at the cake, the frosting so sweet it made his teeth ache.

Sensing Heath's mood, Seth and Rose went quiet as they began to clean up dinner. Rose motioned for Heath to follow her into the living room, where Seth joined them some minutes later.

"I wanted to talk to you guys about something," Heath began. "It's about Johnny."

Seth tensed, while Rose paled. With a growl, Seth asked, "What about him?"

"Well, it's not about him, exactly. It's Rich." Heath blew out a breath. "He's been threatening me if I testify against Johnny."

Seth and Rose stared at him. Heath could see a vein pulsing in Seth's forehead, and Heath had a feeling the only reason Seth didn't explode into a rage was because he needed to stay calm for Rose.

"When did this start?" Seth asked, his voice hard.

Heath told them everything—even about his involvement in Troy's drug dealing and Gregory's death.

"I never told you this, Rose, because I thought it was over. And it was my mistake to deal with."

"Oh, Heath." Rose took his hands. "You should've told me. I'm always here for you, just like you've always been there for me."

Heath pulled his hands away. "That's the thing: I wasn't there for you when you needed me. We both know it. If Rich wants to destroy my life, fine. I'll do whatever it takes to keep you safe from any further threat."

"You need to go to the police. Talk to my brother Caleb. We can't let Johnny and his bullshit keep fucking with us," said Seth.

"I want to. I do. But Rich has threatened to reveal what Rose did. The deal she made with Johnny." Heath sighed as Rose's shoulders slumped. "I'm sorry. I didn't want to tell you, but I thought you had a right to know."

Rose wiped her eyes. "No, I'm glad you did. You shouldn't

be going through this alone." Standing up, she motioned for Seth to stay. "I just need a second, okay?"

Seth watched her go, his expression etched with concern. Water ran in the bathroom, and Heath hoped he'd done the right thing in telling Rose about Rich.

"I'll keep her safe," Seth vowed. "I'll never let those assholes get close to her. Not after what happened this summer."

Stuck between a rock and a hard place, Rose had met with Johnny, only to have him kidnap her. Heath had been the one to warn Seth of Rose's disappearance, and Seth had saved Rose in the nick of time.

"I know you will. And I don't care about my own reputation. But I won't let Rose get dragged through the mud."

"I still think you should talk to Caleb. It doesn't even have to be an official investigation." Seth blew out a breath. "I don't want Rose hurt again, either, but if she testifies against Johnny, too, her story will be put out there regardless."

Heath paled. "I thought she wasn't going to talk about what Johnny did to her, except for the kidnapping."

"It's recommended that she tell everything, although that doesn't mean the judge will allow the evidence in court." Seth rubbed his forehead. "What a fucking nightmare."

Heath's heart pounded. His mouth dry, he said, "I'll give Caleb a call. But I'm afraid that smashing one will only cause three more to show up. That's how Johnny and his crew are: they're like roaches."

"Don't I fucking know it."

Rose returned then, her eyes red but dry. She sat down next to Seth, and he wrapped an arm around her.

"Heath, whatever you need to do, I support you." She smiled sadly. "We'll stop Johnny once and for all."

Heath's heart twisted at his sister's bravery. Taking her hand, he squeezed it, hoping he was doing the right thing for once.

JUBILEE WATCHED as her family chatted and laughed as they waited for dinner to be ready. After much persuasion and nagging, Lisa had gotten all of her children—and their various significant others—to agree to come for family dinner. Jubilee wasn't sure how they'd all fit, but she shouldn't have doubted her mother. One of Lisa's talents was throwing a party.

All of Jubilee's five siblings were either married or attached. As the youngest, Jubilee knew she shouldn't feel like the odd one out, but she did. Her brothers and sister were moving on with their lives: marriage, babies, new jobs, new experiences. And what was Jubilee doing?

Working at a bakery. Kissing a man who didn't want her.

"Oh, the baby kicked." Sara smiled as she rubbed her very pregnant belly. "He gets active this time of night."

James, Sara's eight-year-old son from her first marriage, said, "He's probably hungry. I'm starving. When are we going to eat?"

"Soon, buddy." Harrison ruffled James's hair. "Didn't you have a sandwich earlier?"

"That was *two hours* ago." James rolled his eyes at his stepfather's obviously stupid question, the adults laughing at his response.

Megan and Caleb were having a baby, too, due in June. Mark, Jubilee's third-oldest brother, was happily married to Abby. Lizzie and Trent had their daughter, Bea, who was currently on the carpet playing with blocks and laughing at her father's weird faces. Even Seth, with everything he'd gone through, had found Rose.

Jubilee sighed inwardly. *I might not have a boyfriend, but I have my own news.* Tonight she'd tell her family about her acceptance to Avila College and her intention to move to Seattle. She knew they would most likely react with surprise and concern.

For so long, Jubilee had been the sick little sister. Sick from chemo, pale and bald and thin. Sick from tests and medications and hospital stays. She'd had two bone marrow transplants—both from Lisa, although Lisa never talked about it—and although she'd been healthy for a decade now, it was like that memory of her being sick had yet to disappear from her family's collective memory.

Rose whispered something into Seth's ear before getting up to sit beside Jubilee. Jubilee forced herself to smile, even though it was difficult to look at Heath's sister without seeing Heath.

"The first time Seth brought me here, I almost peed my pants," Rose confided. "Your parents are terrifying."

Jubilee laughed. "You don't have to tell me that. All of my siblings give our mom a wide berth. Our dad isn't as bad, though."

"The first time we met, she asked me about my entire life and choices. 'Where did you go to school? What are your political beliefs? What are your thoughts on public schooling versus private?'" Rose's eyes widened comically. "I think I said something about private schools being totally fine for rich people. Oops."

Lisa was chatting with Lizzie right then, probably asking Lizzie everything about Bea. Lisa meant well—usually. To Jubilee, she'd been an attentive, protective parent who'd been at her side through every treatment and hospital stay. To her siblings, Lisa was overbearing and meddling. It wasn't until Jubilee was older that she'd realized her brothers and sister had a very different idea of the woman who'd raised them all.

"Did you know my mom was my bone marrow donor?" Jubilee didn't know why she was saying this now, of all times, but sometimes she felt the need to defend Lisa. To show another side of her that wasn't the one that tried to keep Harrison and Sara apart for seemingly shallow reasons.

"No, I didn't. Seth told me you had leukemia as a kid."

"I did. Twice. When I was five, then again at thirteen." Jubilee smiled wryly. "It sucked."

"To say the least."

"But you know what sucked the most?"

"What?"

"The fact that my family wrapped me up in a cocoon and hasn't let me out since." Jubilee tried to mask the bitterness in her voice, but it crept through. "Now I'm twenty-five and I've done nothing with my life."

Rose bumped her shoulder against Jubilee's. "Don't be so hard on yourself. You'll get there." In a lower voice, she added, "And for what it's worth, I've told my brother he's an idiot."

Jubilee felt a blush creeping up her cheeks. Had Heath talked to his sister about her? How embarrassing. The last thing Jubilee needed was her entire family knowing what was going on with Heath.

At dinner, Jubilee ate in silence, trying to find the right moment to announce her news. Her palms sweaty and her heart pounding, she waited until there was a brief beat of silence before clearing her throat.

"I have some news," she said.

Her family turned toward her, almost like they were surprised she'd spoken at all.

"What is it?" Lisa asked.

Megan gave Jubilee an encouraging smile, since she already knew Jubilee's news. *You can do this. It'll be fine.*

"I got into Avila College. I'm going to move to Seattle after New Year's."

No one said a word at first. Harrison frowned at Jubilee across the table, while Lisa looked like she'd just found a rotten fish sitting on her dining room table. Dave Thornton, for his part, finally broke the silence. "Where will you live?" he asked.

Jubilee hadn't gotten that far yet. "I'll probably find someone who needs a roommate, or sublet. I'm working on that."

"Seattle, though? Jubi, you've never lived in a big city. How will you get around? What happens if you get lost?" Lisa asked.

"She has a car, Mom," Caleb interjected. He patted Jubilee on her shoulder. "Great job, kiddo. What are you going to study?"

"I'm focusing on general education for now, but I think I'd like to apply for veterinary school."

At that announcement, the entire table erupted with questions, some more supportive than others. Jubilee couldn't help but notice that Lisa had fallen silent, except for the occasional shake of her head as she finished her meal.

When the family returned to the sitting room after dinner, Harrison pulled Jubilee aside. "Are you sure about this? You've never been on your own."

"I'll be fine. It's Seattle, not Mars."

"That being said, what about doing online classes? You haven't been in school for a while. Managing classes and living on your own is a huge step."

Jubilee knew Harrison meant well. As the eldest, he'd watched over her. He'd gone to medical school to become a pediatric oncologist because of her bouts with leukemia.

But she'd also acceded to her family's wishes for so long that the thought of giving this up, this chance at finding out what she really wanted to do with her life, only made her want to do it even more.

"Jubilee, may I have a word?" Lisa gave Harrison a wordless look. Harrison hesitated, but then with a sigh, he nodded, allowing Lisa to take over.

"Jubilee Christina, what has gotten into you? When did you decide all of this?"

Jubilee and Lisa were about the same height, although where Lisa was willowy and almost fragile, Jubilee was curvy and rosy-cheeked. So many times as a child, Jubilee had cowered before her mother's disapproval, which she could give with just a heated glance. She struggled against giving in to keep the peace like she always had. If she just stayed in Fair Haven, her mother would leave her alone.

"I made the decision on my own, because I think it's for the best," Jubilee said slowly. If she lost her temper, Lisa would use that against her. "I need a change."

"But to move all the way to Seattle? Jubi, you don't know how to live on your own. Not really. Having an apartment here is one thing, but in a city? And college is so stressful. What if you make yourself ill?"

That had always been the fear, really; that Jubilee would get sick again if she pushed herself too hard.

Don't jump, Jubilee. Don't run, Jubilee. Don't get too excited, Jubilee. Your health isn't good. You have to be careful.

She never jumped. She never ran. She never got too excited. Yet for once, she didn't want to be careful. She wanted to jump until her knees hurt, or run until her lungs burned.

"I won't get sick again. And even if I do, how can I keep living my life doing nothing with it?"

"You are doing something with it. You're working. You have an apartment. Eventually you'll get married like your siblings and have a family—"

"Maybe I want something different." *Liar.* "Maybe I want to get out of Fair Haven."

Lisa paled. "What's gotten into you?"

It was like a tether snapped inside her. The frustration bubbled up and over until she couldn't contain it any longer.

"What's gotten into me? What do you think? Mom, I've never been allowed to *live*. I've been stuck here because you and everyone else are so afraid of me getting sick again. But it's not about keeping me healthy, is it? It's about keeping yourselves free from worry, my own life be damned."

Jubilee had never said anything like that to Lisa, and Lisa looked as shocked as Jubilee felt. It was only when Caleb laughed loudly from the sitting room that they both jumped, like they'd been frozen.

"If that's how you truly feel, then go. But know that all I've ever done was try to keep you safe and well. Because I'm your mother."

Jubilee refused to apologize, despite the guilt building inside her. She *hated* conflict. She'd always avoided it. Swallowing her apology, she returned to the sitting room, safe from her mother's continued reproofs for the time being.

As Jubilee drove herself home, her mind buzzing, she couldn't help but think of Heath. If she was truly committing to Avila, then she needed to step up her game. She needed to cross off the most important thing on her list before she left for Seattle.

When she arrived home, she opened her laptop and paid her deposit for Avila before she could rethink her decision.

And then she vowed that tomorrow night, she was going to change the bargain she'd made with Heath and rid herself of her virginity once and for all.

CHAPTER NINE

Jubilee swore as she searched through her jewelry for the pair of earrings she needed. It didn't help that her hands were shaking and her heart was pounding like crazy. Her nerves were close to getting the best of her.

She finally gave up looking for the earrings and decided it wouldn't matter anyway. She was planning to get naked, right? She blushed at the mere thought.

Tonight she would up the stakes: she and Heath wouldn't just be doing flirting or kissing lessons. This would become a full-scale seduction.

With one last puff of hairspray and check for a shiny nose, Jubilee headed out, teetering on heels she'd worn all of once. She couldn't exactly go to a man's home, telling him she wanted him to take her virginity, wearing yoga pants and no makeup, right? She had to seem serious, even if that meant her feet would complain about it later.

When Jubilee was at Heath's door, she hesitated, her fist raised to knock. What the hell was she doing? She was crazy. Heath would take one look at her and send her packing.

Then she thought about his confession regarding the lock of her hair he'd kept, and it gave her courage. *He isn't as disinterested as he'd like to pretend*, she told herself for the millionth time. And anyway, sex didn't mean a relationship.

This would solely be a friends-with-benefits fling. Nothing more, nothing less.

Heath opened the door on her second knock. This time, he wasn't surprised at her sudden appearance. He smiled wryly and ushered her inside.

"You look nice," he said.

Jubilee had her back turned to him, but she swore she could feel the heat in his gaze as he took in her appearance. Her skirt was absurdly short; she forced herself not to keep trying to pull it down.

"Are you going on a date tonight?" Heath folded his arms, an eyebrow raised. He sounded annoyed. "If so, I don't see why you needed to stop here first."

"I wanted another lesson." Jubilee's voice was raspy, and her face flooded with color.

"I think we've had enough lessons. Did you bring a coat? You'll freeze."

"I…" Jubilee suddenly felt the chill on her arms. "I forgot."

Heath sighed and pulled a coat from his hall closet before settling it over her shoulders. Except, unlike when he'd done the same thing at Halloween, this time, he didn't step away. He kept his hands on her upper arms. Jubilee shivered at the heat in his touch and his eyes.

"Why are you really here?"

All of the words Jubilee had practiced vanished. She'd had

an entire speech prepared, with reasons to overrule Heath's objections.

Now, she felt like she would melt into a puddle at his feet. It didn't help that his face was shadowed with a beard, his hair falling across his forehead. Despite his auburn hair, his beard was darker, not blond like a lot of men with his coloring.

Reaching up, Jubilee touched his cheek. "I don't have a date tonight. I came here because I wanted to change our bargain."

"Change it? Or end it?"

"Change it." She took a deep breath, steadying herself. Then, before her courage left her, she said, "I want you to take my virginity."

Heath stared at her in astonishment before digging his fingers into her arms. It didn't hurt, but it kept her from moving away.

"What the hell are you talking about? We agreed to kiss— nothing more than that. While I found you a real man to date."

Jubilee shook her head. "I don't want another man. I want *you*."

"Jubilee…"

"No, I already know what you're going to say. I'm not talking about a relationship." She swallowed. "I'm talking about a friends-with-benefits thing. I'm tired of being a dried-up old virgin."

That made him laugh dryly. "You're hardly old or dried-up." He looked down at the cleavage overflowing her top. "Not even slightly dried-up."

"So you just don't want me?"

He stepped away, although it seemed like it pained him to

do so. "Jesus, how can you even ask that? I *burn* for you. I've wanted you for years. Haven't you seen it? Felt it? But that doesn't mean this can—or should—happen."

"Let me see. My brother, your sister, the president, the universe at large, etcetera, etcetera. They're all reasons."

His lips twitched. "Pretty much."

She let his coat drop to the floor. "What if I don't care what they think? What if I say, fuck the universe? They don't get to tell me what to do." She pressed her hands against his heart, which thumped as hard as hers did. "What if for the first time in my life, I stop being afraid and stop listening to people who think they know what's best for me? What if I let *myself* make that decision?"

Heath didn't say anything. His breathing increased, and as Jubilee moved closer, she knew he was aroused.

She snaked a hand around his neck and pulled him down for a kiss. When their mouths touched, he groaned in surrender, especially when she pushed her tongue inside. He wrapped an arm around her waist and kissed her so hard she felt dizzy.

"Wait, wait." He was panting, shaking his head. "I need to tell you something first."

"I don't want to talk." Jubilee felt like she was going to come out of her skin if she waited a second longer. She wanted to strip naked and feel him press her into his bed, muscular and hot and dominating. She wanted to give herself to the man she'd never been able to get out of her head.

"I don't want to talk, either, but I need to."

Jubilee kissed his throat, licked his collarbone. Heath swore and pushed her away.

"Talk. Now." He pointed a finger to the living room and, rolling her eyes, Jubilee marched inside.

Whatever he had to tell her, she didn't care. She wanted him regardless.

Matching his pose from earlier, she crossed her arms, still standing. She heard him riffle through something before returning with a piece of paper.

"What is it?"

He handed it to her. "I found it that day at The Rise and Shine. I should've returned it. I'm sorry."

Jubilee took her missing list. She opened it to read the words she'd written what seemed like ages ago.

"You had it?" She frowned. "Why?" Slowly but surely, the pieces clicked together. "That's why you decided to do—all of this. The lessons. Vetting the men."

"I'm sorry," he said again. "When I read it, I just…lost my mind. The thought of you with any other man." His jaw clenched. "It tore me up."

Jubilee knew she should be angry. He'd read something extremely personal and then used it to get her to do what he wanted. Yet, she couldn't find the anger inside herself because this only confirmed what she knew: Heath cared for her. He wanted her. And he'd wanted her enough to keep her away from other men.

She sidled closer as she crumpled up the list. "If you're sorry, then you should make it up to me." She licked her lips. "Make love to me and help me strike something off my list."

He cupped her cheek. "I don't give two shits about that list, but I do care about you, Jubi. You understand what this means? Just sex. Nothing else."

She knew that—she'd said as much herself—but it still

stung. Forcing a smile onto her face, she said, "I get it. Now, are you just going to talk or are we going to get this show started?"

"Oh, we're getting started, but there's no pleasure in rushing, especially when it's your first time." He considered her, tracing her jaw with his thumb. "What experience do you have? Besides kissing?"

She blushed. "None, really. I've never dated any guy. There was never anyone worth the trouble."

There was never anyone like you, she wanted to say. Heath seemed to hear those words in her voice, though, because his forehead wrinkled.

"Then we'll need to go extra slow." He took her hand and led her to his bedroom in the back of the house.

The butterflies in Jubilee's stomach threatened to overwhelm her, but when Heath smiled at her over his shoulder, she felt calm take over. And then she felt the butterflies flutter for an entirely different reason: excitement.

"Can I turn on a light?" Heath asked quietly.

"Oh, sure. If that helps."

He chuckled as he clicked a nearby lamp on, bathing the room in a dim golden glow. "I've found it helpful, yes." He didn't say anything for a long moment, which made Jubilee want to fidget.

"Should I take off my clothes?" she blurted. Her cheeks turned bright red, and when Heath laughed, she blushed even harder.

"Do you want to take your clothes off?"

"Um...don't you have to?"

Now he was moving her into his embrace, and she rested

her head on his shoulder. "We can do whatever we want. I think tonight, though, I'd rather focus on you."

She inhaled his spicy scent. "Me?"

"Yes, you."

She narrowed her eyes at him. "Are you backing out?"

"No." He tipped her chin up to meet his gaze. "I'm just not going to jump on top of you and get things over with, either."

"Well, I figured that. If I wanted that, I could find any guy down at The Fainting Goat—"

He pinched her lips closed. "No more talking, except to tell me how something feels. Got it?"

She nodded, and he pushed her hair to the side, exposing her neck. He kissed her in that spot: softly, slowly. The warmth of his lips sent a frisson of want through her entire body. He kissed up her throat until he reached her mouth.

"I think some kissing is in order."

"Didn't you just say no more talking?"

That made him grin. "Right. No more talking."

He swooped down to capture her lips, and Jubilee gasped. He ravished her mouth with deep kisses that made her body pulse. Her blood heated with every stroke of his tongue. Reaching up, she tangled her fingers in his hair, trying to get as close as she could.

She felt his hardness then, against her belly, and despite everything being so new, it didn't scare her. It only made her want him more.

"I'm going to make you come tonight," he whispered against her ear, "until you beg me to stop."

"Is that a threat?"

"It's a promise."

As he kept kissing her, he palmed one of her breasts, stroking her nipple through the fabric of her blouse and bra. He played like that until she wanted to rip off her clothes and demand that he kiss and touch her everywhere. When he pushed her blouse up and exposed the pale skin of her belly, she struggled to keep breathing.

"Are you nervous?" he asked. "Don't be. You're beautiful. I'll make this so good, Jubi. I will."

"You're still talking." She laughed breathlessly.

"I lied, then. I can't stop talking to you. About you." He caressed her abdomen before tugging on the hem of the blouse. "I want to see you."

Jubilee froze, suddenly unsure. She'd never been naked in front of a man, of course, and it seemed overwhelming right then. What if he hated what he saw? She wasn't exactly the skinniest woman. She was curvy, her stomach soft, her hips flared. She also had totally forgotten to shave *there*, and now she couldn't let Heath see her like that—

Heath tapped her nose. "Stop thinking. You don't have to do anything you don't want to."

"It's not that I don't want to…"

"Then what?"

"I'm afraid you won't like what you see."

His eyes flared. "That's not possible. Everything about you drives me insane because you're gorgeous. Seductive."

"Seductive?" She giggled. "Even when I dumped water in your lap that time?"

"Even then." He kept caressing her belly, tracing the waistband of her skirt. "Even when you're drunk and trying to cut off your hair. Or when you make ridiculous lists that make me lose my damn mind."

"I didn't make that list for you," she said with a sniff.

He pinched her ass, making her yelp. "Then why are you here? Tell me that."

She gazed into his eyes, feeling her heart turn over in her chest. Deep down inside, she knew why she was here. She *knew*. But right then, she didn't have the courage to tell him, let alone admit it to herself.

"Because I want to be here," she whispered.

"Then let me see you."

Jubilee began to unbutton her blouse, her hands shaky. It seemed to take an eternity, and by the time she reached the last button, she was tempted to tear off the blouse in sheer frustration. It fell to her hips, exposing her fanciest bra, which was a taupe color and not really all that fancy. Jubilee had always bought comfortable underwear—not the kind you'd wear to seduce a man.

She almost apologized, but the heat in Heath's eyes made her bite her tongue.

"Beautiful." He kissed her right above her heart. "You're amazing."

"So are you." At his grin, she blushed for the thousandth time.

Why couldn't she be smooth about this? Smooth and calm and collected? She blew out an annoyed breath. Clearly, this seduction was going to be anything but seductive if she kept saying and doing stupid things.

"Stop thinking so much," said Heath as he began to push one bra strap down her arm. "Just enjoy."

"Easier said than done."

He tapped her nose. "Try it. How about you close your eyes? And take deep breaths."

Jubilee gave him a skeptical look but finally obeyed. She closed her eyes and waited.

"Count. Breathe in, three, four, five, breathe out, three, four, five."

Jubilee breathed in slowly, counting out loud, but she couldn't concentrate when Heath began to push her other bra strap down her arm.

"Keep counting," he said as he reached behind and unhooked her bra.

The cool air made her nipples harden, almost painfully so. She desperately wanted to open her eyes to see what Heath was doing, but at the same time, it only increased the excitement.

"One, two, three, four, five," she said on her next breath, right as Heath cupped one of her breasts in his hand.

He kissed her neck as he rubbed her nipple with his thumb, circling and circling until Jubilee was about to come out of her skin. She struggled to keep counting, and she kept repeating the same numbers over and over each time Heath touched her.

"You're terrible at counting. My fifth graders count better than that." Heath chuckled as he pinched one of her nipples. "Keep counting or I'll stop."

She counted as Heath touched her breasts, making them ache, the nipples swollen. Jubilee had never paid much attention to her breasts beyond being annoyed when they'd gotten bigger and she'd had to buy a new bra as a teenager. Now, though, all of her pleasure was centered there, the heat of Heath's palms and the calluses on his fingers pleasuring her beyond anything she could've imagined.

But it was when Heath bent down and took one nipple

into her mouth that she forgot all about the counting. Gasping, her eyes flew open.

He swirled the tip of his tongue around one peak, his lips and mouth relentless, and all Jubilee could do was hold on to his shoulders. *I never knew*, she thought, dazed. *I never knew it could be like this.*

When he kissed the scar above her right breast, though, she wanted to crawl away in embarrassment. She didn't know why; it wasn't as if he didn't know she'd had leukemia.

"It's from the port," she blurted before he could ask the obvious question. "From the bone marrow treatments."

He rubbed his thumb across that small scar. "I'm glad you're here, for what it's worth. Scars and all."

"As long as you don't say that you're sorry. I hate when people say that. Why apologize for something you had nothing to do with?"

His lips quirked. "Good to know." He kissed her over her heart, which effectively banished all thoughts of ports and transplants and cancer from her mind. *Thank God.*

"You taste like spun sugar," he muttered. Standing, Heath pushed her blouse and skirt down her hips until all she wore was her tights and panties. Like he couldn't wait a second longer, he cupped her sex, rubbing her clit with the heel of his hand.

"Oh my God." Jubilee tipped her head back as he licked down her throat.

"You stopped counting," he admonished, but he didn't stop touching her. Instead, he pulled her tights down to her ankles before delving below the waistband of her panties, spreading her, groaning at the wetness he found there.

Jubilee felt like she was about to explode. She trembled

and gasped as Heath circled her entrance as he continued to rub her clit with his palm like before. Her world tilted on its axis, and when he pressed a finger slowly into her sheath, it was like fireworks exploded inside her. She bit her lip to stifle her scream as she came, shudders wracking her frame, her knees giving out.

It was only Heath's arm around her waist that kept her from slumping to the floor like a puddle of mush. Jubilee felt Heath backing her toward the bed, where she landed with a thump before he lay down next to her.

She kept panting as Heath rubbed her back in slow circles. Finally, she opened her eyes to see him looking down at her with a satisfied smile.

"Like I said," he said, "you're terrible at counting."

She stuck her tongue out, which just made him laugh harder. Jubilee felt languid and sleepy, and when she yawned, Heath wrapped her in a throw blanket and kissed her forehead.

"So we're not doing anything else tonight?" Jubilee couldn't help but ask. She'd come here to lose her virginity, which remained no matter how hard she tried to get rid of it.

"Not tonight. You should be seduced. And a good seduction takes time."

She wrinkled her nose. "Spoilsport." Except she found herself yawning a second time, and she struggled against falling asleep in Heath's very warm and cozy embrace.

"I want you, Jubi. Don't ever think otherwise. But your first time should be special."

He kissed her nose as he whispered, "So let me make it special."

CHAPTER TEN

The week before Thanksgiving—and days after her first seduction lesson—Heath sent Jubilee a text saying that he had to go out of town that weekend. *A teacher training in Seattle*, he wrote. *Super boring. I'd rather stay in town with you.*

That last line made her heart flutter. She hadn't been able to stop thinking about that night, or how amazing Heath had been. And they hadn't officially had sex yet! She had a feeling when they got to the actual sex, she might not survive it.

I wish you had stayed here, then, she replied after she arrived home from The Rise and Shine that Friday night. *What am I supposed to do tonight? Netflix and chill by myself?*

Don't you have twenty siblings you can hang out with? :)

Jubilee laughed. *No, thanks. I see them enough as it is.*

Besides, she thought, the last thing she needed was for one of her nosy older brothers to see how happy and distracted she was and put two and two together. Especially Harrison. He was still suspicious of Heath, and he'd tried more than once to get Jubilee alone to tell her how he disapproved.

Okay, then what are you going to do tonight? Watch a movie? Read?

Jubilee chewed her bottom lip, considering. Normally, she would do one of those things. Sometimes she cooked something nice for herself, or organized her closet. Something boring, usually. But tonight she was restless, her blood heating just from texting with Heath, and as she began to drink her glass of wine, she realized she didn't want to organize her shoe collection tonight.

I think I want to do something new, she sent.

Like what?

Taking a deep breath, she slid the strap of her tank down her arm, exposing her bare shoulder. With a seductive smile, she took a few photos, trying to find the best one. Then she sent the photo without any caption.

Then she waited.

And waited.

Finally, Heath replied, *You're going to kill me.*

That made her laugh. *Do you want to see more?*

Jesus Christ, yes.

Then send me something in return.

Instead of a photo, her phone began to ring.

"A phone call isn't a photo," she admonished upon answering.

"I needed to hear your voice." His own voice was almost a growl, and it made her shiver in anticipation. "Now, here's a classic question: what are you wearing? Describe it to me."

"Couldn't I just send you a photo?"

"Tell me, Jubi."

She sighed, but it was a happy sigh. "Well, I'm wearing a purple tank top. It's not very exciting—"

"Come on, now."

"But underneath, I'm not wearing anything. No bra."

Heath groaned, and she heard what sounded like him falling onto his bed. "Send me a photo."

Jubilee had never taken a topless photo of herself, and she'd never thought she would. Yet right then, she wanted to be daring. To do something new. She pulled her tank top off, cupping one of her breasts as she took a few photos from different angles. Her nipples peaked, and she could almost feel Heath's hands and mouth on them like when he'd touched her that night.

She sent the photo and waited for Heath's response. He swore.

"Baby, are you sure you're a virgin? Because you don't take photos like one."

She snorted. "How should a virgin take topless photos? I didn't know there were specific directions involved."

He chuckled, the sound warming her through and through. "Every night since that one we had together, I've thought about you. Under me, over me. Calling my name."

"What am I doing?" she asked, her voice breathy.

"Everything. You're riding me until I explode inside you. Or I'm pounding inside you as I hook my arms under your knees. Or I make you go onto your knees and take you from behind, your delicious ass pink from a spanking."

Jubilee was melting from head to toe. A flush began from her chest and climbed up into her cheeks, and she felt herself growing wet just from Heath's descriptions. Closing her eyes, she trailed her fingers down her belly and below the waistband of her pajama bottoms.

"Are you touching yourself?" he asked.

She nodded before realizing he couldn't see her. "Yes."

"What does it feel like?"

She pushed her panties aside and found her curls drenched. "Wet," she whispered, blushing harder. "Oh God. And hot."

"How do you like to touch yourself? Do you like to rub your clit?"

"Yes." She gasped as she began to circle her swollen clit with her thumb. "Sometimes I like a finger inside me, but sometimes it's too much. Like it won't fit."

"What are you doing now?"

His voice washed over her as she began to touch herself in earnest. She could feel the edges of her orgasm gathering in her belly. She was no stranger to touching herself, but with Heath's voice egging her on, it made it more intense. Wetness coated her palm as she rubbed faster and faster.

"Are you close?" he growled.

"Yes! Oh God, yes."

"Keep touching yourself, but imagine it's me. That I'm pushing a finger inside you as I massage your clit. And then I'll get on my knees and put my mouth on you until you scream and come against my lips."

She panted, rubbing harder, until her orgasm slammed into her. She let out a little screech of surprise and collapsed back onto her living room couch. When she realized she'd knocked her phone onto the floor, she laughed.

"Are you still there?" She wiped her hands on her pajamas as she picked up her phone. "You got dropped on the floor. Sorry."

"The only thing you should be sorry for is how hard I am right now and you not being near to do anything about it."

"Why can't I do anything about it? I want to see you. Show me."

He was silent for a long moment. "Are you sure?"

"Of course I'm sure. Fair is far. Show me the goods, Heath DiMarco. Otherwise I'm going to assume you're too much of a scaredy-cat. And here I am, the actual virgin."

"Then turn on video chat. I want this to be live."

SITTING up on his hotel room bed, Heath pushed away the voice in his head that said this was a bad idea. All of it was a bad idea. He'd said he'd leave Jubilee Thornton alone, and here he was, sexting with her and looking at topless photos she'd sent him. If Harrison found out about this, he'd skin Heath alive.

Jubilee's face came onto his phone. "Can you see me?" she asked.

"Yes. Can you see me?"

"Yes. But I didn't think I was doing this just to see your face."

He chuckled. He should've known that Jubilee would be a force to be reckoned with, no matter that she was, technically, still a virgin. Seeing her now, her cheeks flushed and her eyes glassy from her orgasm, his cock hardened until it was painful. He unzipped his jeans and grasped his cock.

"What are you doing?"

He gritted his teeth. "What do you think?"

He smiled as her blush increased, but undaunted, she said, "I want to see you. Please?"

Heath wasn't sure the logistics of video sex—holding the phone in his hand was awkward as it was—so he set his phone against a stack of books.

"How about that?" he asked as he palmed his cock once more. "That enough of a view for you?"

"Oh, yes."

She fell silent, and he worried that he'd scared her. Cracking an eyelid open, he saw that she was watching him intently, her lips parted.

"Baby, you're gonna have to keep talking. Otherwise I'm worried you're not enjoying yourself," he rasped.

She let out an embarrassed giggle. "I'm sorry. I am. I just wish I were there with you, right now. What do you want me to say?"

He groaned. Sweat beaded on his forehead, and God Almighty, he was already so close. Jubilee crying out in her own orgasm had been enough to drive him completely crazy.

"Say whatever you want." He swirled his thumb over the tip of his cock, which made him shudder.

"Then I'll tell you that the first time I met you, I thought you were gorgeous."

That startled a laugh out of him. "What?"

"It's true. I loved your smile, and how kind you were. You didn't treat me like I was a little girl."

"Jubi, I appreciate everything you're saying, but this kind of talk isn't what I meant."

"Then I'll say that you're even more gorgeous—no, handsome, how about that?—than you were then. I love the way your hair falls across your forehead. I love your hands. I love watching your hands right now."

Considering his hands were wrapped around his cock, he could appreciate that statement. He closed his eyes and let Jubilee's voice wash over him in a heated, sensual wave.

"I wanted you to touch me with those hands for ages. I

dreamed about you, you know. That you'd strip me and then you'd tease me. I had a dream once where you bent me over the arm of my couch and took me—"

With a muffled shout, he came, jerking and shuddering for long moments. His heart pounded in his ears, and he could just make out Jubilee, still talking.

Finally, he turned and picked up his phone to see Jubilee smiling like she'd won first prize.

"Enjoyed that, did you?"

She nodded. "I've never seen a man do that before." She licked her lips. "It was…good."

"Good? It was fucking amazing, at least for me. I'm just annoyed I'm stuck here, without you."

"Heath," she whispered, "when do you get back into town?"

"Tomorrow afternoon."

"Come see me right when you get in. *Right when you get in.*"

He didn't need a translator to understand what she meant. Swallowing, he nodded, his mind whirling with the mere thought of finally taking Jubilee Thornton to bed. Really taking her. Seeing her naked, parting her legs, and plunging inside her tight, wet heat.

Just the thought made him hard again.

They said their goodbyes, Heath promising he would drive straight to her place when he got into Fair Haven.

You should leave her alone. You told her you would. What happened to that promise?

He argued that she'd approached him. She'd made it clear this was nothing but sex, anyway. If they kept to that understanding, nobody would get hurt, and nobody would have to get overly involved. If Jubilee was just a fling, there was no reason she needed to know about all of the details of Heath's murky past.

The following morning consisted of a last training session before Heath could get on the road. As he drove back to Fair Haven, he practically vibrated with anticipation.

By the time he was only a few miles from Jubilee's, his phone rang. To his surprise, it wasn't Jubilee, but Seth. Frowning, he answered the call.

"Hello?"

"Where are you?" Seth practically barked. "I need you to come to my place—now."

"What? Why?"

"Because Rose was attacked by none other than your guy Rich."

The bottom of Heath's stomach dropped out. "Is she okay? What happened?"

"She's shaken but unhurt. I stopped him before he could do anything, but he ran off. Rose wants to talk to you. God only knows why, but I told her I would get a hold of you."

"Of course. I'm on my way." Heath swore when someone honked behind him, and he realized he'd been sitting at a green light. He drove without seeing, his mind in chaos.

Rich had tried to hurt Rose—again. His vision went red with rage, his fists clenching around his steering wheel.

He only remembered his promise to Jubilee when he arrived to find Seth, grim-faced and enraged

Something came up, Heath texted. *Sorry, need a rain check. Talk to you later.*

He didn't stop to wait for Jubilee's reply. When he saw Rose sitting on the couch, dry-eyed but pale, he embraced her.

"What the hell happened?"

"Rich attacked her." Seth stood over them both. He looked like a grim specter, and Heath knew the only reason Seth wasn't out there hunting Rich down was because Rose needed him to stay close by.

"I was walking Callie," Rose said, the dog in question lying at her feet. "She started barking right when Rich tried to —" She swallowed. "I don't even know. Kidnap me? Scare me? He tried to drag me away, but Callie attacked him. She bit him in the leg right when Seth arrived. I'd left my gun at home. Stupid. I know better."

"Not your fault. You should be able to walk home without being afraid." Heath wrapped an arm around Rose, although he wondered if he was comforting himself more than he was comforting her. "What happened to Rich?"

Seth narrowed his eyes. "He ran. Only reason I didn't break his fucking neck was because Rose told me not to."

That caused Rose to smile slightly. "I'm so sorry I stopped you from murdering someone."

"For you, I'd kill anyone who'd try to hurt you."

Heath silently agreed. Rose had been hurt enough, and the thought of Johnny trying to mess with her through Rich sent waves of anger flowing through him. If Seth wouldn't break Rich's neck, Heath would. With relish.

"Before Callie got him, Rich said that he wanted to send a message. To you, Heath." Rose turned to look him in the eye. "This is about the threats you've been getting, right? Rich must've wanted to hurt you by hurting me."

Guilt threatened to overwhelm Heath, but he swallowed it. Guilt wouldn't keep his sister safe. *And if Rich goes after Rose, who's to say he won't go after other people I care about?* Jubilee's face came into his mind right then, and the mere thought of her getting hurt because of him almost broke him in two.

"He's a cowardly piece of shit," Seth growled as he started pacing like a caged predator. "He thinks that if he scares us enough, we won't tell everyone what his boss has done. God knows Johnny probably put him up to this."

"Then this just means I need to testify against Johnny more than ever." Heath squeezed Rose's hands. "I don't care what Rich does to me."

"What is he saying he'll do? I don't understand," said Rose. "What are you not telling us?"

Heath hesitated, but he knew that he needed to be honest with his sister about his involvement with Gregory's overdose. With a deep sigh, he recounted the story in halting tones: Troy selling drugs while Heath turned a blind eye; Troy selling those drugs to Gregory, which caused Gregory's death. How that guilt had weighed on him for years, and he was tired of living half a life.

"So you see, I wasn't totally innocent like you thought. I deserved to go to prison. I shouldn't have let Johnny get me off." He dropped his head into his hands, his fingers digging into his eyes under his glasses. "I shouldn't have cared more about my career and my reputation than you."

"No, Heath. You didn't know about Johnny because I didn't tell you. We were both stupid by being silent." She took his hands from his face. "You know who's fault this is? Johnny's. And Troy's."

"And I'm not going to stay silent anymore." Heath touched Rose's cheek. "I just don't want to hurt you. Testifying means telling your story, and I won't have you go through that kind of pain again."

"Now you're being ridiculous. I'll do whatever it takes to put Johnny—and his cronies—away for good. Even if that means telling everyone what he did to me." Seth came to her then and took her hand, squeezing it with a silent look of pride. "We'll take Johnny down together."

After a moment of silence, Seth sat down next to Rose, his forehead creasing. "Who tipped the police off to get you arrested, Heath? Was it your roommate?"

Heath shook his head. "I never found out, since it was anonymous."

Seth drummed his fingers against his knee. "That sounds like a mystery right there. Why do I feel like it has Johnny's name written all over it?"

"What? He'd get Heath arrested only to have him set free?" Rose frowned. "That makes no sense."

"It does, if you think about what he wanted." At Rose's confused look, he said softly, "You, Rose. He wanted you. What better way to bind you to him than to get you to agree to stay with him to save your brother?"

Heath's throat closed. He wanted to deny the idea, but it

made a twisted kind of sense. Johnny had been obsessed with Rose since he'd first met her. Why wouldn't he ruin both of their lives to get what he wanted?

"If that's true," Rose said, her voice harder than Heath had ever heard it, "then I want him to pay. I'll snap his neck in two if I have to."

Seth's mouth twisted in a grim smile. "I'll be right behind you, hummingbird."

Seth followed Heath to his car afterward.

"Whatever you decide to do," Seth said, "I'm behind you. That being said, you realize that you could lose your job over this if your story comes to light? I don't think you get much leeway being a teacher."

Heath blew out a breath. "Don't I know it. I hate the thought of having to leave my students and my school. But this isn't about me. Not anymore. It's about Rose, and doing the right thing."

Seth gave him a searching look, which Heath felt in the pit of his stomach.

"Do you think Rich will go after anyone else?" Seth finally asked.

"Like who?"

"Anyone you care about. Anyone vulnerable." Seth rolled his eyes. "Look, I know about Jubilee. I mean, I have some hints and I know about the lock of hair. Rose told me."

Heath was glad it was dark out; otherwise Seth would have seen the embarrassed flush crawling up his neck. He did not want to talk about Jubilee with her older brother— especially not an older brother who was a former Marine who could take Heath out back and shoot him if he wanted to.

"Jubilee and I..." His voice trailed away. "It's complicated."

Seth snorted. "Isn't it always?" He shrugged, looking away. "I don't need details. I'm just saying that if you care about her, be honest with her. Oh, and if she gets hurt, I'll come for you myself."

After Seth returned to the apartment, Heath drove home, his thoughts tangled. He couldn't bear the thought of Rich coming after Jubilee, too, but the thought of her disgust if he was honest with her...

They weren't serious, though, so why tell her? It would only cause heartache for her. He didn't need to put all of this on her, too. It wouldn't be fair.

He should leave her alone. He recognized that. The sooner, the better, and then he wouldn't lead Rich straight to her.

When he got home, he realized that Jubilee had texted him multiple times, asking if he was all right. He almost replied before he shook his head.

He needed to let her go—no matter how much he didn't want to.

～

THANKSGIVING CAME AND WENT, and Jubilee heard nothing from Heath. She'd texted and called, but the only response she received was a terse *Sorry, something came up.* After that, it had only been silence.

Had their phone call spooked him? Jubilee couldn't understand why, considering he'd seemed totally into what they'd been doing. She'd been tempted to go to his place and demand answers, but the cowardly part of her didn't want to hear him reject her a second time.

The Sunday following Thanksgiving, Jubilee reluctantly agreed to get lunch with Harrison and Caleb after Harrison had badgered her at Thanksgiving. She loved her older brothers, truly, but they were nosier than a bunch of old church ladies. It didn't help that Harrison and Heath were good friends, either. She knew the stupid rule that friends didn't poach on younger sisters. Harrison had always been overprotective in regard to Jubilee.

"Don't you two have enough leftovers from Thanksgiving to feed yourselves for weeks?" Jubilee asked as she sat down across from Harrison and Caleb at one of the few greasy diners in town.

Caleb grinned. "Megan ate all of it already. Apparently pregnancy makes a woman hungry."

"Don't tell her you said that," said Harrison. "Especially since Sara's done the same thing."

Harrison and Caleb looked like Jubilee, with their dark hair and green eyes, although both were much taller than her. Caleb was taller than Harrison, although Harrison was stockier. When Caleb had surpassed his older brother in the height department, he'd crowed about it for months.

"Do you have names picked out?" Jubilee asked Harrison before adding, "That question is for you, too, Caleb."

"We have names, but Sara has sworn me to secrecy." Harrison smiled. "She doesn't like people giving opinions on baby names."

"Megan's the same way, although she's terrible at keeping secrets, so we'll see how long she holds out," said Caleb.

After all three of them ordered, Jubilee continued to ask

them questions, mostly so they didn't ask *her* questions. Harrison was still skeptical about her plan to go to Avila in January, and despite her best efforts to avoid the subject, he'd brought it up at Thanksgiving.

How will you live on your own in a big city? Are you taking out loans? You shouldn't go into debt unless you really need to. Believe me, I'm still paying off my medical school loans.

Caleb had been more supportive, but with a baby on the way and his focus on his wife and his career in the police force, he didn't exactly have the time to dedicate to getting every single family member on board with Jubilee's plan.

After they got their food, Harrison frowned down at his phone before shaking his head. "Have you heard from Heath?" he asked Caleb.

Caleb popped a fry into his mouth. "Not really. He bailed on Thanksgiving this year but he didn't say why." He shrugged. "Can't say that I blame him. It's not like he's obligated to hang out with our crazy family."

"Hmm." Harrison tapped his fingers against the tabletop. "He's been acting weird lately." His gaze landed on Jubilee, and she tried her hardest to act nonchalant under that assessing look. "It's almost like he has a secret. Or two."

Jubilee took a big bite of her burger to avoid saying anything in reply.

"So?" Caleb countered. "What's it to you? We all have secrets, and we even have things going on in our lives that you don't know about." With a sly grin, he added, "You're worse than Mom."

Harrison looked genuinely offended. "I don't *meddle*. Don't be a dick. Jubi, do I meddle?"

"Um." With a laugh, she said, "You do. Meddle, that is, although you're not as bad as Mom."

"Oh, thanks for that," said Harrison. They chatted and joked for the remainder of their meal, the topic of Heath not brought up again. Jubilee breathed an inward sigh of relief. She was a terrible liar. If either of her brothers asked her point-blank if something was going on with Heath, she was fairly certain she wouldn't be able to avoid answering truthfully.

"Oh, I need to head out," Caleb said as he answered a text. "I need to pick up Megan to go crib shopping." He rolled his eyes, but Jubilee could see how happy her brother was. "I'll see you two later." He slapped Harrison on the shoulder and kissed the top of Jubilee's head before heading out.

Harrison waited all of five seconds after Caleb's departure to ask, "So what's really going on with you and Heath?"

Jubilee flushed. *Please just take me out back and shoot me,* she begged the powers that be.

"Who says anything is going on?" she asked weakly.

Harrison cocked an eyebrow. "I know when a man is interested in a woman. I've seen how Heath has looked at you. It's been going on for a while. I've also known you've had a crush on him for a long time. I just never thought Heath would act on it."

Jubilee wanted to sink into her chair and melt into a puddle. She felt all of six years old right then, like when she'd tried to go out for a bike ride with friends when she should've been home and recovering from another surgery. Harrison, almost an adult by then, had stopped her with a stern lecture.

You aren't like other kids, he'd explained. *You have to be more careful.*

But I don't feel sick, she'd countered. *I've been feeling a lot better today.*

That's good, but that doesn't mean you can do things that might make you feel bad. That means you need to stay home.

Sometimes she wondered if he could see that she wasn't that little girl anymore. This time, it wasn't about risking her delicate health, but her delicate emotions, she supposed. Did Harrison think she'd disintegrate like sugar in water if Heath broke her heart?

When she didn't reply to Harrison's question for a long moment, he said quietly, "What's going on, Jubi?"

She was torn between telling her big brother all her troubles and being annoyed that he thought he could direct her life. Shrugging, her heart twisting in her chest, she said, "It's complicated."

"Try me."

She blew out a breath. "Not that it's any of your business, but I won't lie and say you aren't right about me. About the crush on Heath." Her cheeks turned red again. "But it doesn't matter, because he doesn't feel the same."

"How do you know?"

"Because he told me," she snapped. "More than once."

Harrison blinked before narrowing his eyes. "I'll break his legs. That son of a bitch——"

"No, no. It's not your problem. It's mine. I get that you're trying to help, but I'm not a little girl, Harrison. Can't you see that?" She put her palms up, pleading. "This is something I have to deal with myself."

Harrison's expression was stormy, and Jubilee knew very well that her brother would go beat the stuffing out of Heath if she said the word. Growling under his breath, he paid their tab and walked her to her car, his gaze far away.

"I know you're not a little girl anymore. Sometimes it's hard to believe, but you've grown up a lot in the last two years." He smiled, the smile a little sad, as he chucked her under her chin. "But you're still my baby sister, okay? I'll beat up anyone who even thinks about hurting you. Never doubt that."

"Oh, I know. You, Caleb, Mark and Seth will beat up any guy who so much as looks my way. It's a miracle Lizzie ever managed to find a guy willing to put up with you jerks."

"Love you too, Juju-bee." His expression turned serious. "Be careful, though. Heath is one of my best friends, but he has secrets. Secrets I don't know about. I have a feeling any woman who gets too close will get burned."

Fear spread like ice around Jubilee's heart at those words. Hadn't she sensed as much? Yet she didn't want to believe it. She wanted to believe that Heath would be honest with her. *Except you two aren't serious, so why should he tell you what's weighing on him?*

"Don't worry," she said, trying to convince Harrison as much as herself, "There's nothing between me and Heath anyway."

earing footsteps behind him, Heath whirled, only to see the last person he expected to come for him at Fair Haven Elementary. Harrison Thornton stalked toward him, his expression stormy, and Heath was only surprised he didn't get a punch in the jaw from Harrison right then.

"What's going on with you and my sister?" Harrison demanded. He wore a shirt and slacks under his coat, so he must've come straight from work at his private practice.

Heath looked up at the sky: gray and gloomy, and apparently there was a chance of snow in the forecast. Just what he needed, although it reflected his own mood.

"Hello to you, too. Did you want to get a drink after work?" Heath crossed his arms. Although they were in the school parking lot, there were enough people around to keep Harrison from decking him.

Hopefully.

"I don't drink with men who hurt my sisters. Either tell me what's going on between you and Jubilee, or I'll make you tell me."

Heath rolled his eyes. Harrison had been a good friend to him, but he could get melodramatic when it came to his siblings. "What, are you going to beat me up? At an elementary school? Sounds like a good way to have your brother arrest you."

Heath headed to his car, Harrison following. "Hey, I'm talking to you!" Harrison caught up to him and grabbed his arm. "Don't walk away from me."

"You're drawing attention."

It was true: a number of parents and teachers were looking their way. Heath wondered if Sara was nearby; he doubted she would've agreed to let Harrison approach Heath like this.

"I don't give a damn who's watching," Harrison growled, but he let go of Heath's arm and lowered his voice. "Tell me nothing is going on between you and my sister, and I'll leave."

It would be easy to lie. Technically, nothing was going on, since their relationship was just a fling. A brief thing. Something they'd forget in a year and maybe look back at fondly.

What a load of shit.

"I don't know if you're aware of this, but Jubilee is a grown woman. She's not a child. What business is it of yours?"

That answer made a red flush crawl up Harrison's cheeks, and Heath was glad he'd been impulsive enough to confront him in public like this. As a physician and upstanding citizen of Fair Haven, Harrison wasn't about to get into a brawl in front of kids.

"It's my business when I think someone *older* is taking advantage of her. Jubilee is an adult, yes, but she's been sheltered for most of her life. She's never dated, to my knowledge, and considering your age and hers—"

"I'm not that old!"

"No, but if you consider that Jubilee has never been to college, never lived outside of Fair Haven, you'd see she's much younger than she seems." Harrison's forehead creased. "Her health is delicate. I don't want additional stress to make her sick."

Heath swallowed, a lump in his throat. "Is something wrong with her?"

"No, but that could change. She's been in remission for a decade, but she's had leukemia twice in her life." Harrison's gaze looked far away then, remembering things that Heath could barely imagine. "You didn't see her when she was sick, Heath. Her hair gone. Pale and in pain and so sick. I remember her crying when she had to get more tests because she was too young to really understand why she kept being poked and prodded and cut open. When other kids her age were busy playing and going to school, she was stuck in a hospital. She went into remission when she should've started second grade, only for the cancer to return when she was in seventh grade."

Heath had known all of this, but he hadn't been there. Not like Harrison and the rest of the Thorntons had been. At the time, Harrison had been almost an adult, and Heath had gleaned from the few conversations they'd had about Jubilee that Harrison had taken on a fatherly role in regard to the rest of his siblings when his parents had been consumed with caring for Jubilee.

"Harrison, I get it. I'd do anything for my sister, but I also had to let her make her own decisions. I told her to stay away from Seth in the beginning."

"Seth's a good man," Harrison countered, offended.

"He is, but it took me a time to see that because Rose had been hurt before. Sometimes our own desire to protect clouds our judgment."

"Maybe, but that doesn't change the fact that you're too old for Jubilee, and if you hurt her, I'll rip you limb from limb."

"I'm aware," Heath said dryly. "Besides, there's nothing between us. Not really."

Harrison leaned against Heath's car, arms crossed. "Funny you should say that, because I just talked to Jubilee yesterday. She confessed that she's had a crush on you for ages, which I'd suspected for a while. But the one person in the equation I can't make out is *you*. So, are you going to take advantage of my sister's infatuation, or are you going to be the bigger person and let her go?"

Heath barely heard Harrison's words beyond Jubilee confessing her feelings to Harrison. It wasn't that Heath hadn't *known*, but hearing the words out loud struck a painful kind of clarity inside of him. You didn't tell your brother these things unless you meant them, and he knew deep down that her proposal of them being friends with benefits had just been a front.

Let her go. Let her go before you really hurt her. Don't make this worse than it is.

As he looked at Harrison and saw bits and pieces of Jubilee's features in Harrison's face, Heath knew that he couldn't let her go. He'd wanted her for years, hadn't he? He'd dated a few women here and there, but none had been able to hold a candle to Jubilee. She was all that was lovely in this world to him.

"If Jubilee tells me it's over," Heath said finally, "then it's over. But I'm not making the decision for her."

"Dammit, man—"

"Keep your nose out of our business. You're going to turn into your mother, you know."

Harrison gaped at him before bursting into a hearty laugh. "Caleb said the same thing. Fine—fine! Do what you want, but my warning stands regardless. Hurt Jubilee, and you're dead."

"Oh, I believe you. Although I'm not as worried for myself as I am for you." Heath pointed over Harrison's shoulder, where Sara stood, tapping her foot. "Hi, Sara."

"Hi, Heath. Is my husband bothering you? I hope you know I'd never tell him to do something so *stupid* and *childish* and I *hope* he realizes he's an *idiot*."

"Sara, this is between men—"

"Oh, please. Go measure your dicks somewhere else, preferably not in a school parking lot."

Heath sputtered a laugh while Harrison glowered. Taking Harrison's arm, the very pregnant but very tenacious Sara said to Heath, "See you tomorrow!"

Heath drove home, but by the time he arrived, he didn't want to stay there. He wanted to find Jubilee. He wanted to tell her—oh, he didn't know. He wanted to tell her about Rich, about Troy and about Gregory, but then he imagined her disgust at his cowardice and his courage shriveled up inside of him.

He told himself he would tell her everything if she wanted to make this relationship more than a fling. That would raise the stakes, certainly. Until then, he wasn't going to burden her with his problems. She had her own burdens: namely her family that seemed determined to keep her in a protective bubble the rest of her life.

He looked at the clock. Jubilee wouldn't be off work until after five o'clock. He was tempted to wait outside her apartment until she came home, but considering he'd avoided talking to her at all since he'd broken off their meet-up a week ago, he knew he'd need to come up with an explanation. And he needed to grovel and apologize.

I'd like to see you tonight, he texted her. *I'm sorry for ghosting on you. I'd like to explain.*

He waited for what seemed like an eternity before she replied. Finally, she sent him a text that said simply, *Okay. Come over after you get off work.*

He blew out a relieved breath and waited.

JUBILEE WASN'T able to say a word to Heath before he embraced her and kissed her with a desperation that shocked her. Confused and aroused, she kissed him back before pushing him away.

"What was that?" She shook her head in astonishment. "One second you freeze me out, the next you kiss me like we haven't seen each other in years?"

He had the decency to look sheepish. "I owe you an explanation."

"Uh, to say the least." She was halfway tempted to send him packing, but he looked so handsome, wearing a dark blue shirt that brought out his eyes, the sleeves rolled up and exposing his muscled forearms once he took off his winter coat.

"I'd ask if you wanted something to drink," she said as she led him into the living room, "but I'm too annoyed with you to be polite. You can't just show up and kiss me, you know."

He smiled. "You're beautiful when you're angry, you know."

"Don't flatter me." Despite her words, she couldn't help but preen under his compliment.

She'd missed him—not just his kisses, but his conversation. The way he pushed his glasses up the bridge of his nose when he was thinking. How his laugh made her feel warm inside and out. How he looked at her like she was the only woman in existence, the only woman for him.

Now you're being ridiculous, she admonished herself. *You can't let him keep giving you whiplash like this.*

"Are you going to tell me what happened? Or am I going to have to guess?"

Heath rubbed the back of his neck. "I shouldn't have ghosted on you like that. I'm sorry. It's just that the upcoming trial has been holding my focus. It's difficult on Rose." He seemed like he would say more, but to Jubilee's disappointment, he didn't elaborate.

She knew all about what had happened with Rose and Johnny this past summer. Rose had told Jubilee later that Johnny had tricked her into thinking that he'd kidnapped Jubilee. Jubilee had been shocked that Johnny had even known who she was, to say nothing of how creepy it was that a criminal like him would somehow use her to get to Rose.

If Johnny hadn't been caught and tossed in jail, Jubilee

knew she'd be looking over her shoulder all the time, afraid that he'd try to come after her.

"Heath," she said quietly, "I know our…relationship isn't a conventional one." That admission made her blush scarlet, but she powered on. "But you can talk to me. I hope you know that."

To her dismay, he grimaced. She almost wished she could take back her words. Feeling foolish, she fidgeted, wishing things didn't always end up being so awkward between them. They could be so good with each other, but the times that were awkward or painful? Sometimes Jubilee wasn't sure if the good times outweighed the bad in those instances.

"I appreciate that. I do. I need to make it up to you somehow."

"Well, I do have a list that still has some things to be checked off."

Heat flared in his eyes. "I haven't forgotten—not for one minute."

"I should send you home, you know. For ignoring me like you did." She couldn't mask the hurt in her voice as she added, "I'm tired of this back-and-forth, Heath. I can't figure out what you want. Sometimes I wonder if you're doing this out of some weird obligation."

"Never." His voice was fierce, and he cupped her cheek as he said roughly, "I've wanted you for ages, Jubi. You have to know that. It's just that there are so many ways and reasons this could go wrong—"

"But it could go so right."

"Could it? I don't know. Except being away from you only made me realize that I don't care. I don't care about your damn brother or anyone else. I don't care about what's responsible or wise. I care about *you*."

She saw truth in his gaze, and her heart squeezed. She covered his hand that still rested on her cheek with her own.

"I want it to be you. I always have." Jubilee swallowed. "I want my first time to be with you and no one else."

Heath stared at her, his nostrils slightly flared, a flush on his cheeks now. She could practically feel him vibrating with want, and her own body echoed that desire. It was like every time he was near her, her body unfurled like a flower drinking in sunlight.

He brushed his thumb across her bottom lip. "Then let's go to your room," he rasped. Before she could react, he stood up and picked her up, carrying her to her bedroom like a bridegroom crossing the threshold.

Jubilee trembled, but it wasn't out of fear. It was out of anticipation and sheer need.

Thank God for ridiculous lists, was her last, giddy thought before Heath kissed her.

CHAPTER THIRTEEN

J ubilee had imagined this exact moment so many times
that it was difficult to believe it was really happening
now. She almost pinched herself to make certain she
wasn't dreaming.

But in her dreams, she couldn't feel how warm and solid
Heath was, and she had to admit, he didn't kiss like this in her
dreams. He'd kissed her sweetly in her dreams.

In reality, he kissed her like she was necessary to his very
being—nothing sweet about it.

"Are you sure?" Heath asked. He searched her face. "You
want this?"

She smoothed her hands down his shirt, and he shuddered. "I want you more than I've ever wanted anything else."

Groaning, he pressed his forehead to hers, but he didn't
ask her again if she was sure. He kissed her temple before
capturing her mouth in a kiss that made her entire body yearn
for his.

She knew that losing your virginity could be painful. She'd

always been a little afraid of it, if she was being honest. What if it were awful? She'd heard enough horror stories that she couldn't help feeling a little trepidation.

Heath must have felt her stiffen, because he tipped her head back to look into her eyes. "What's wrong?"

"Nothing. I mean, I'm just a little jittery, is all." She laughed, but it sounded choked. How did she explain she was excited but also afraid?

She hoped she wouldn't make a complete fool of herself. Heath was experienced. What if she couldn't compare to the other women he'd been with? And then the thought of him being with another woman nipped at her with jealousy.

"We'll take things slow. There's no rush." He kissed her cheek and down her throat, not pushing, but simply enjoying.

Eventually, Jubilee felt herself being led to sit on the bed and then she was on her side with Heath still kissing her. When she gasped for air moments later, she laughed when she saw that Heath's glasses had fogged up.

He grinned as he took them off, setting them on the nearby bedside table. "I think I'll manage without them."

Jubilee waved a hand in front of his face. "Can you even see me?" she teased.

"I can see you just fine. I'm not that blind." Pulling her shirt up to expose her belly, he growled, "But I need to see more of you. All of you."

Jubilee nodded and helped him get her shirt off and then her bra. She thought of when he'd made her come at his place, and anticipation was heady in her veins.

Heath touched her like she was both delicate and strong, his mouth creating heated paths down her stomach, across her breasts. When he took one of her nipples into his mouth and sucked, hard, Jubilee arched off the bed with a small cry.

"I dreamed about doing just this," Heath confessed as he licked the tight peak of her nipple. "I'd kiss your breasts until you yelled my name, but then I'd wake up and realize it had all been a dream."

"I had dreams, too." At his eyebrow raise, she blushed.

"Tell me."

She shied away from voicing those things aloud, but Heath was relentless.

"Tell me, tell me," he whispered as he nipped at her hip, laughing when she tried very halfheartedly to stop his nips. "You don't have to be ashamed of what you dream, Jubilee."

"I had one recently…" She swallowed and said in a rush, "That you kissed me. Down there."

His smile was slow and blinding. "'Down there'? You mean here?" He touched her knee, making her giggle. "Or here?" He stroked the back of her thigh. "Or maybe here?" he asked as he traced a circle on her pelvis.

"Close, but not quite."

"Then tell me where you meant, exactly. I'm a literal guy. I need specific directions."

She burst out laughing, rolling her eyes, but when he continued to tease her and kiss everywhere but where she wanted him, she finally told him exactly where she wanted his mouth. The flush on his cheeks confirmed that he wanted that as much as she did.

"Naughty girl." He spanked her ass lightly before stripping her of her jeans and panties. "Good thing I was wanting to do exactly that."

Except now that she was completely naked, he moved

downward to kiss her ankle. She groaned in frustration before laughing. Why was he determined to drive her absolutely insane?

"Do I want to know what's so funny?" Heath asked as he kissed her knee, then her calf. He tickled the arch of her foot, which just made her laugh harder as she tried to get away from him.

"No, no! Oh God, stop!" Breathless, she launched herself at him, which only made him rise over her on the bed, pinning her wrists down.

"Be good, or you'll have to wait longer." His actions belied his words, though, and he traced his fingers down her torso to her thighs before parting them.

Jubilee trembled. It was so strange to have anyone *look* at her there, and she forced herself not to snap her legs closed out of embarrassment. It was even stranger seeing the stark desire on Heath's face—strange, yet it only stoked the flames in her belly further.

She took a deep breath, closing her eyes. She let herself simply feel instead of overthinking every action, every small movement. The tips of Heath's fingers were callused, and it only heightened the sensation of him touching her.

He kissed the insides of her thighs, his tongue licking patterns on the silky patch of skin. He kissed her hip, her lower belly, before he finally kissed the top of her mound. She gasped his name when he parted her folds and licked her center.

Jubilee couldn't describe how she felt: it was simultaneously strange and wondrous. Her body hummed with every stroke of his tongue against her sex.

"You taste amazing. So sweet." His voice was guttural, and

Jubilee's eyes flew open at the sound.

He looked up at her, and she could just make out his sensual smile before he began to circle her clit with his thumb. Just like he'd done the last time he'd touched her. Her hips bucked, especially when she just needed him to rub a little harder, a little longer…

"Look at me, Jubilee," he commanded. "I want you to watch as I make you come."

She sat up on her elbows, gripping his hair as he began to kiss her harder, thrusting his tongue inside her as well. The moment was so erotic that Jubilee felt like she'd been transported elsewhere, like it couldn't possibly be happening to her.

Heath growled, and his own enjoyment only heightened her own. When he began to flick her clit as he pushed a finger inside her, she bit her tongue to keep from screaming. Just a second later, the coil inside her belly exploded into her release, and she cried out from the sheer joy of it. Trembling, she had to grip Heath's shoulders to keep herself from collapsing onto the bed, her bones and muscles melted.

"God, you're amazing." He kissed her, and she tasted herself on his mouth. She moaned, and then moaned again when he broke away.

He began to strip in hurried movements. "Wait," she said, standing up. "Let me. I want to see you."

His eyes darkened, but he didn't stop her. Smiling, she helped him out of his shirt, her heart fluttering when his bare chest and abdomen were revealed. He was a work of art, muscular and lean, with probably next to no fat on his frame. If she weren't so distracted by how much she wanted him, she'd tease him and ask him how an elementary school teacher managed to stay so fit. Weren't they supposed to be gawky and pale from sitting behind a desk all day?

She trailed her fingers down his torso, loving the way he sucked in a breath at her touch. He had a smattering of dark hair on his chest that was a similar auburn shade to his hair. Leaning forward, she kissed him over his thumping heart. His skin tasted salty, the crispness of his chest hair in contrast to the smoothness of the skin at his waist, his hips.

"You're trying to drive me insane, aren't you?" He swore when she kissed him right below his belly button. "Dammit, Jubi—"

"Fair is fair." She unbuckled his belt and pushed his jeans down to reveal his boxers. He was obviously hard, and her mouth watered when she saw how hard he was—and how big.

She wasn't entirely sure this would work, but she didn't want to voice that fear out loud. The last thing she wanted to do was seem like some spineless ninny, though, and before she could lose her nerve, she dipped her hand below the waistband of his boxers to grasp his cock.

"It's soft," she said wonderingly. At his wry look, she giggled. "I mean, the skin is. It's definitely hard. It's soft-hard." She knew she was blathering, and she blushed scarlet.

"You're adorable," he said, a bit wonderingly. Then he enclosed his hand around hers. "Like this. You won't hurt me."

She squeezed him, and he groaned. Her heart thrilled at that sound. It was one thing for him to please her—for her to be able to reciprocate made her feel like the sexiest woman alive. Even if she didn't always say the right things.

There was something so unbearably erotic about making a man tremble and moan your name as you touched him. Jubilee's heart pounded, and with every stroke of her hand around his cock, her heart pounded faster and faster.

Heath hissed out a breath when she squeezed him a bit harder, and when she drew away, he laughed, breathless. "You didn't hurt me, but you better stop that. Otherwise this will be over before it ever began." He stripped his boxers down his hips, leaving him completely naked.

Jubilee inhaled deeply. He was beautiful—there was no other word for it. His skin was lighter in color on his hips and buttocks, but her gaze remained on his iron-hard cock that seemed to twitch before her very eyes. Touching him was one thing; seeing it in all of its glory was something else entirely.

She moved back toward the bed. "What are you waiting for?" She batted her eyelashes, which made Heath growl and pounce on her. They rolled onto the bed until Heath lay on top of her.

His chest pressed against her breasts, his legs tangling with her own, and they kissed deeply and without reservation. Jubilee opened her legs and when she felt his hardness brush against her sex, she shivered.

Would he fit? She wasn't entirely certain he would. She didn't have much basis for comparison, but he *seemed* large. Then again, as a virgin, she didn't really know. She floundered, trying to regain her bearings, and once again, Heath seemed to sense her unease.

"Are you nervous?" He smoothed her hair from her forehead.

"Yes. I mean, what if it…doesn't work?"

"What do you mean?"

She could tell he was trying to hold back a chuckle, although that didn't help her embarrassment. It wasn't that she was afraid of pain—God only knew she'd experienced enough physical pain in her lifetime already—but that it wouldn't be *good*. That she wouldn't be any good at it.

"What if it's terrible?" she whispered.

"Has it been terrible so far?"

"No, but that doesn't mean anything."

"Jubi, there's no way in hell it would be terrible." His expression was serious now. "Do you know why?"

She shrugged.

"Because it's *you*. Experience doesn't mean the sex will be good. It's already been amazing. The best I've ever had."

Her heart lifted at his words. "Really? You're not just saying that?"

"Jesus, no. I mean it. You're—" He shook his head, like he didn't have the words to explain it.

Jubilee understood. Sometimes you couldn't find the words to explain something that was simultaneously complex and simple, and she and Heath were both of those things. When she was with him, it felt right, yet there were reasons why they couldn't be more than a fling. Reasons that seemed to be melting away with every time he kissed her, every time he looked at her, every time he said things like this to her.

"Then I want to find out how good it really can be," she said with a shy smile.

He kissed her, his tongue tangling with hers, before he abruptly stopped.

"You wouldn't happen to have condoms, would you?"

Jubilee shook her head. "Should I?"

"No. I didn't even think." He blew out a breath as he sat up next to her. "Damn. I'm usually more prepared than this."

She sat up as well. "Do we need condoms?" At his look, she flushed. "I mean, are you clean? I am. Virgin and all that."

"There's still a chance for pregnancy."

"Pull out, then." At his surprised look, she giggled. "I'm a virgin, not a nun. I know about the logistics, Heath." She pressed her hand against his thumping heart. "No more delays. Make me yours."

Heath didn't need any more encouragement than that. He tumbled her back onto her bed, his weight resting on his arms so as not to crush her.

"Tilt up for me. There you go." He kissed her cheek, her jaw, as he took hold of his cock and began to slowly push inside her. "Relax, babe. I'll go slowly."

She wanted to snap that she was trying to relax, but it wasn't easy when something as big as his cock was pressing into her. He moved in small increments, letting her adjust, but when he finally was completely inside her, she felt like it was just too much. It took her a moment to get used to him.

Heath was inside her. She wasn't a virgin anymore. She was both thrilled and terrified at the same time.

"Okay?" He touched her cheek. "Want to keep going?"

She arched a little, his cock sliding deeper somehow. They both moaned. "Yes," she whispered. "Yes, please."

He started a slow but steady rhythm, and Jubilee knew he was holding back. Sweat broke out on his forehead as he thrust. The initial discomfort faded until she felt that magical coil in her belly that signaled the beginning of her release.

"Move with me. There you go." His breath was hot against her ear. "God, you're amazing. So tight and wet. It's like a dream."

She flushed with pleasure, and when she moved with him, he started thrusting faster. She moaned as he filled her, and it was exquisite. She couldn't catch her breath. Her orgasm tightened and tightened inside her with each stroke of his cock, and then her release burst upon her. She cried out and clutched at him, like she was being tossed into the waves, and he held her close as her orgasm seemed to go on and on.

"God, Jubi—" He groaned and pulled out just as his own release hit him. The heat of his seed splashed onto her belly right as she reached up and grabbed him for a kiss.

Jubilee tingled from head to toe, and when Heath moved off her, she groaned at his absence.

"Are you okay? I didn't hurt you?"

She smiled languidly. "No, you didn't hurt me. That was…" Once again, she didn't know how to describe what had just happened.

I just slept with Heath, and I think my heart exploded.

"Mind-blowing?" he supplied. He yawned. "Do you mind if I stay the night?"

She didn't even get a chance to reply before he fell into a deep sleep. Shaking her head, she got up to go clean up and put on her pajamas.

When she looked at herself in the bathroom mirror, she wondered if she looked any different, no longer being a virgin. Her hair was mussed, her cheeks flushed, but she looked the same. She rubbed the small scar on her chest from where she'd gotten her bone marrow transplants, a small reminder of her former life.

She thought of Halloween, how she'd stood in front of a mirror like this and vowed to get over Heath DiMarco. Now, standing there looking at herself, she knew that she'd never get over him.

Because how could she get over the man she loved?

CHAPTER FOURTEEN

J ubilee smiled as Heath gave her more pancakes on her plate the following morning. They'd both woken up starving, and although Heath had been tempted to go a second round, their rumbling stomachs had been so distracting that he determined they needed breakfast before any more sex.

It didn't help his self-control one bit to see Jubilee wearing his shirt and nothing else, her hair still mussed from his running his fingers through it. She was flushed and happy, and she kept giving him looks from under her lashes.

Heath decided he'd cook them breakfast, mostly to give himself something to do that didn't involve pouncing on Jubilee. *She's probably sore. Give her a break*, his mind said, but his mind had very little influence over his libido at this point.

His gaze was far away as he flipped pancakes and scrambled eggs for them both. Last night had been…mind-altering. When he'd told Jubilee that the sex had been the best he'd ever had, he'd meant it. And now that he'd been the one to take her virginity…

The caveman inside him gloated at that. That same caveman very much would like to toss her over his shoulder and carry her back to bed, especially when he turned to see the silky curves of her pale thighs peeking from under the hem of his shirt.

"I'll make coffee," Jubilee said as she began to riffle through his cabinets. "Too bad you don't have an espresso machine. Otherwise I could make you your usual latte."

His heart did that annoying squeezing-thing when she said that. He could easily imagine her being at his place all the time.

Hell, he could imagine her living here with him, making coffee, smiling at him, her scent permeating his sheets and pillows, hair ties scattered across the bathroom counter along with all the other little accouterments that went with being a woman. Soaps for every part of your body; lotions that smelled like flowers; various implements for making one's hair straight or curly. He could see her shoes kicked off at the front door next to his own, or imagining her taking a bath at night, her skin gleaming, dewy, and warm.

He swore when he realized one of the pancakes was burning. Taking it off the heat, he gave Jubilee a wry look. "I don't usually burn breakfast," he said.

"Of course you don't." She stuck her tongue out at him, and he couldn't stop himself from curling an arm around her waist and pulling her in for a deep kiss that made her tremble.

After they'd finished eating and drunk four mugs of coffee between them, Heath leaned back in his chair and asked, "What are your plans for today?"

"I have to go into work this afternoon. I know, lame. I'd much rather stay here with you."

"I agree. You should call in sick."

"And leave Megan on her own on a Sunday?" She clucked her tongue. "You're a bad influence, you know."

At that, he picked her up, making her squeal, and placed her on his lap. His cock came to attention at the feeling of her in his arms, and he could tell by the redness in her cheeks that she'd noticed, as well.

"You know who I think is a bad influence?" He kissed her jaw. "You are. Writing that list of yours. Leaving it where I could find it."

Jubilee mock-gasped. "I did not leave it on the ground for you to find it! That was an accident."

"Sure it was." He smiled, nipping her collarbone as he skimmed his hand up her thigh. "And I'm sure you just *forgot* to wear panties this morning, didn't you?"

She bit her lip as he caressed her mound. "I didn't think I'd need them," she whispered.

"You're a naughty girl. You act innocent and sweet, but I know deep down you're not." He parted her, her wetness coating his fingers within moments, and he kissed her roughly as he stroked her.

She trembled and moaned, and he could feel her tightening around him with each movement of his hand. God, he couldn't get enough of her. She was so sweet, so sensual, and she was all his—only his. She could only ever be his.

His mind whirled at the possessiveness of his thoughts, so much so that he didn't hear his phone ringing from his bedroom. He ignored it, letting it go to voicemail, only for it to ring again. And again.

"You should get that," Jubilee said, sitting up. "In case it's important."

He wanted to say that nothing was as important as bringing her to climax, but she was probably right. What if something had happened to Rose again? After washing his hands at the kitchen sink, he went to the bedroom to see that his principal was calling him. On a Sunday.

He frowned as he answered the call finally.

"Heath?" Principal Anderson said, his voice harried. "Good, I'm glad you finally picked up. I need to speak with you. In person."

He heard Jubilee come up behind him. "Today? Is everything okay?" He couldn't imagine what this was about.

"Yes, and no. I'm sorry to be so vague, but I'd rather speak with you before the school week starts tomorrow. Can you meet me at my office this afternoon? Would one o'clock work?"

"I can do that. I'll see you then." He hung up, staring at his phone in confusion. Fear began to coil in his belly right then.

Had Principal Anderson found out about his past? Had he found out about Troy, Gregory, and Heath's involvement with Johnny?

"What is it? What happened?" Jubilee touched his arm. "You've gone white as a sheet."

He wanted to tell her everything, but the words died in his throat. Rose being understanding was one thing; he didn't expect that from Jubilee. She'd been so sheltered, so protected, that he couldn't bear to shatter her innocence right then.

Or you just don't have the courage to tell her the truth and have her despise you.

"It's just a work thing," he explained. "I need to get ready, and you need to get to work, right?"

"Heath, what is it? That wasn't some normal call. And why would you have a work thing on a Sunday? That makes no sense."

He wanted her to stop talking, and shame poured through him. He gave her a tight smile. "Sometimes my principal wants to have staff meetings on weekends. It's weird, but we put up with it." He gave her a quick kiss. "Get dressed. You don't want to be late."

Jubilee stared at him, her eyes narrowed, before she shook her head. She grabbed her clothes and headed to the bathroom. He almost expected her to slam the door, but when it closed with a quiet click, he flinched.

Coward. You're a coward, DiMarco.

Jubilee arrived at The Rise and Shine fifteen minutes past one o'clock. Expecting Megan to be annoyed with her, she braced herself, only to find not Megan waiting for her, but her mother.

Jubilee couldn't remember a time Lisa had ever graced The Rise and Shine with her presence. Lisa hadn't eaten sugar as long as Jubilee had been alive, and she preferred green tea over coffee. Confused, Jubilee approached her like you'd approach a wild animal: with extreme caution.

Luckily, there was a family eating muffins only feet away. If Lisa wanted to reprimand Jubilee for something, she wouldn't do it in public.

"Mom, what are you doing here? Have you seen Megan?" Jubilee went around to the register and took down the sign that said to ring the bell for service. "Did you want to get something?"

"You know I don't eat sweets. I wanted to see you." Lisa lowered her voice, although Jubilee felt the chill behind it regardless. "You've been ignoring my calls since Thanksgiving."

Guilt filled Jubilee, but she refused to apologize for wanting to move to Seattle and go to college.

Her heart sank at the realization in front of her: how could she move away and leave Heath? She loved him; she wanted to be with him. She couldn't expect him to give up his job to follow her to Seattle. They could always have a long-distance relationship and see each other on weekends, but if he wasn't willing to have a relationship with her when they were in the same town, why would he say yes to one where they lived hours apart?

It was such a depressing thought that Jubilee didn't hear Lisa's next question.

"Jubilee, are you listening to me? You've been acting so strange lately. What's gotten into you?"

Jubilee forced herself to push her thoughts of Heath to the side. "Nothing's gotten into me. I'm sorry I didn't tell you earlier about going to Avila, but I wasn't sure how to tell you or the family."

A customer approached the register, and Lisa stepped aside, but not before giving the man a cold look. The man hurried through his order and grabbed his coffee like he was afraid Lisa would knife him if he didn't move quickly enough.

"This isn't just about you running off to Seattle," Lisa said when they were somewhat alone again. "I've heard that you've been running around with Harrison's friend. The teacher."

Jubilee flushed to the roots of her hair, almost dropping a can of coffee beans in the process. Swearing, she set the can on the counter before she spilled the beans all over the floor.

"I can see it's true, based on your face." Lisa shook her head. "I can't say that I approve of my children's choice in spouses, but I thought that you would have better sense. You always did what was right. Besides, he's too old for you, Jubilee. He'll break your heart without a second glance."

"You don't know that. You don't really even know him."

"I know that he has a past of his own. I'm assuming he hasn't said a word to you about it." Lisa wrinkled her nose. "Men like him never do."

Jubilee had to act normally as more customers approached. She filled their orders without even seeing what she was doing, her heart pounding a mile a minute. Of course Heath had a past—they all did.

But then she thought about what had happened this morning when he'd gotten that call. He'd refused to tell her what was going on, and she'd sensed that he'd been lying to her.

Jubilee hated a lot of things in life, but she *hated* when people lied to her, ostensibly to protect her. Everyone thought she was too delicate, too sickly, to hear the truth. So they'd kept her in a bubble her entire life, and if her family had its way, they'd keep her in that bubble forever.

Megan came out with a tray of blueberry muffins. Seeing Lisa, she raised her eyebrows. "Lisa, how are you? Did you want anything? It's on the house, my treat."

Lisa waved a dismissive hand at her daughter-in-law, her gaze still fixed on Jubilee. "We'll talk again. Don't forget what I said."

"Well, that was fun," Megan said wryly after Lisa had left. "What did she mean? What did she say to you?"

Jubilee shrugged. "What else? Me going to Seattle. She's not happy about it." It wasn't precisely a lie, but Jubilee couldn't tell Megan her fears regarding Heath.

Because if what her mother had said was true, Jubilee didn't know if she could bear to know that Heath was just another person who wanted to keep her trapped in a life she desperately wanted to be free of.

PRINCIPAL LEWIS ANDERSON, a middle-aged man with a shiny pate and a generally calm demeanor, met Heath at the door of his office with a look that Heath could only describe as *concerned*.

"Come in, come in." He gestured for Heath to sit down. "Thanks for coming in on such short notice, and on a Sunday." Lewis gestured at his casual clothes, a cotton t-shirt and jeans, with a wry smile. "Don't tell the kids about this."

Heath had never seen Lewis in anything but a suit and tie, and seeing him dressed like this was jarring. It didn't help that Heath's nerves were tangled, his mind going over every possible reason why Lewis would've asked to see him like this.

When Lewis sat down at his computer before turning the monitor toward Heath, it took Heath a moment to understand what he was supposed to be reading.

Allegations Brought Against Elementary School Teacher with Shady Past

The article had been published on the website for Fair Haven's single, tiny newspaper. Heath's stomach dropped into his toes and he struggled to breathe. He read the entire article, which included anonymous sources that told the entire story of Heath's arrest years prior.

"I can see by your face that you haven't seen this yet," Lewis ventured. He turned the monitor back toward him. "When I first saw it, I assumed it was ridiculous. Of all the people in this school, *you*, a drug dealer? Clearly you'd have a case for libel on your hands. And who authorized something like that to be published at all? But then I got this." Lewis pushed a letter toward Heath, although Heath didn't need to read it to know what it contained.

It was from Rich. He'd made good on his threat, hadn't he? He'd warned he'd ruin Heath's life and career, and he'd done it.

At Heath's expression, Lewis sighed. "Is it true?"

"Yes, but the charges were dropped and expunged. Nothing came of it."

"Clearly, and I don't judge you for this. That being said, once this gets out to the public, I doubt they'll be as understanding, especially with their kids' education."

"It's already out, though. That article—"

"I contacted my brother over at the newspaper to get it taken down. It's not a perfect solution, but better to nip this in the bud as quickly as possible."

"Thank you." Heath swallowed, his heart hammering. "But you don't know the full story. I'll hand in my resignation tomorrow to avoid putting you and the school in a difficult position."

"No, you won't. You'll stay until winter break, at the very least. Like you said, the charges were dropped, so legally, you've done nothing wrong and there's nothing we should do. I'm just worried about the court of public opinion."

Heath wanted to argue, but he also hated to leave Lewis in a bind. Nodding tightly, he agreed to stay for the next few weeks, although he knew it was unlikely he'd be able to keep his job in the long run.

Bitterness filled him at the thought, but at the same time, he felt oddly…free. He would testify against Johnny, and he'd have the last word anyway. Rich's threats wouldn't hold him back from doing the right thing—not anymore.

As he drove home, he dialed Caleb Thornton's number. "Caleb," he said, "can I come talk to you down at the station? I need to report something."

CHAPTER FIFTEEN

J ubilee took out the infamous list and crossed out *Lose my virginity*, smiling widely. She'd been able to accomplish a handful of things on this list already, hadn't she? Except for one, which now glared at her with seemingly neon letters.

Go skinny-dipping

Considering it was now December, she wasn't sure how she'd pull that off without freezing off her bits and pieces. She could always wait until summer, but then she'd be in Seattle, wouldn't she?

If only she could find a hot tub in town to use instead…

She sent off a quick text to her sister Lizzie, who would be the most useful person for accomplishing this. Lizzie texted back readily, and then Jubilee found herself waiting outside one of the swim clubs in Fair Haven for Heath to show up. This particular club sat on a hill overlooking Fair Haven, which made it feel private.

Heath did show at the appointed time, giving her a wry look as they stood outside the gates that were closed for the winter. "Are we breaking and entering to swim?" he joked.

"Kind of." Jubilee flashed a swipe card and within moments, they were inside. It was helpful to have a sister who not only was a singer, but who had fans who would do her favors for free tickets to her upcoming show. Lizzie had made Jubilee promise that they would "leave things the same as when they came inside."

Simple enough, really.

"I'm impressed." Heath followed her inside.

The pools were covered, of course, and the lights were off, but there was enough illumination from the streetlamps from downhill. When they reached the hot tub, which was also covered, Jubilee began to pull the cover from it. Lizzie's contact had said they'd turn on the Jacuzzi a few hours before to warm it up, and she breathed a sigh of relief to see it bubbling away.

"All of this to sit in a Jacuzzi?" Heath helped her get the cover all the way off. "I could've asked my neighbor if we could've used his."

"Except I didn't want your neighbor to see us." Jubilee grinned as she began to strip. When she revealed that she wasn't wearing a bathing suit under her jeans and shirt, Heath's eyes looked like they'd fall from his head.

"Oh God, it's freezing!" She jumped into the hot tub and sighed in relief as the hot water flowed around her. She swam toward Heath, who still stood over her. "Are you coming in or not?"

He stripped out of his own clothes in record time. Setting his glasses on top of his clothes on a nearby chair, he slid into the hot tub next to her with a low, rumbling growl.

He pulled her toward him until he squeezed her ass. "This

was one of the things you wanted to do, wasn't it? On your list?"

"Originally I wanted to do it in a lake, but I didn't want to wait until summer." Her heart dropped into her toes as she explained, "I got into Avila, in Seattle. I'm going to move there to start classes in January."

Heath stilled, and she expected him to—what? Be upset? Surprised? Instead, he just said, "I'm glad, Jubilee. You need to get out of this town. Live your own life." He stroked her cheek, but unless she was imagining things, she thought his smile looked sad. "What are you going to study?"

It was hard to talk about studying with him touching her like this, his hardness pressing against her belly. "I'm not sure yet. I think I'd like to go to veterinary school, though. It was always my dream as a kid. I just had to give it up, for obvious reasons."

"Do it. I'll support you." He kissed her forehead, and she laid her head against his shoulder. She hadn't realized how much she'd needed someone to say those words to her. Her entire family was still convinced she couldn't do it, that she'd come home in a few months with her tail between her legs, the big city having beaten any dreams she might have had out of her.

It was in that moment that she knew she needed to be completely honest with Heath.

"I love you," she said, before she could lose her courage. "I lied when I said I just wanted this to be some fling. I think I've loved you for a long, long time."

He didn't say anything but took in a shuddering breath. His eyes were inscrutable. Jubilee trembled, waiting for his answer. Would he push her away? Laugh at her? She was close to pushing *him* away, only so as to preserve the tattered remains of her stupid, lovesick heart.

"I don't deserve something like that from you." His voice was hoarse, strained. "But God, I'm not a good enough person to say no to it."

He kissed her then, and although her heart ached from his lack of answer, she knew that he felt more for her than he could say. She could taste it in his kiss, which was desperate for her. It was almost like he was saying goodbye to her in that kiss. Whimpering, she clung to him, the whir of the hot tub's water jets barely covering the sound of their moans and heated whispers.

He cupped her breasts, flicking her nipples, and she ran her fingers through his damp hair and down to his broad shoulders. His skin was slick and hot, and when she licked his shoulder, she tasted salt and chlorine.

Heath moved them both toward the perimeter of the hot tub so he could press her against the wall. Jubilee giggled when one of the spouts of water hit her right on her left ass cheek.

"I've always heard using one of these is a great way to get off," she mused as she moved a few inches away from the spout. "That, and a detachable shower head."

Heath groaned. "Don't put that image in my mind. You're killing me."

"Oh, we wouldn't want that." She dipped below the water to wrap her hand around his cock. She smoothed her thumb over the tip, which made him shudder.

"You're way too good at that. You sure you were a virgin just a few days ago?"

"Flatterer." She squeezed him like he'd shown her how he

liked it, which made him dip down and take her mouth with a searing kiss.

His hands were everywhere on her at once, it seemed like. He cupped her breasts; he pinched her aching nipples. His fingers caressed her belly and then he was delving down to find her already wet for him. She quivered as he stroked through her folds, finding the aching bud of her clit at the crest of her sex.

He worked her body like a musical instrument, and she was on the edge of climaxing when he stopped. She whimpered.

"Don't stop," she groaned as she tried to get him to keep touching her. "I'm so close—"

"I need to be inside you. God, Jubilee." Heath sat on the step that ran around the circumference of the hot tub and placed her in his lap. His cock bobbed between them, rubbing against her lower belly.

"I don't know what to do," she admitted, blushing a little.

"I'll be here. Sit up and take me in your hand." His nostrils flared as she did as he instructed, placing his cock at her entrance.

Slowly, she sat back on him until he was fully seated inside her. She gasped. It didn't hurt, but he was so big that she felt almost too full of him. It took her a moment to adjust. Heath didn't push her, even though she could feel the tension running through his body as he kept himself from taking over.

Jubilee rose up and back down. Holding on to Heath's shoulders, she rode him in a tentative rhythm at first before quickening her hips. Heath kept his hands on her hips, his fingers digging into the bones of her pelvis.

She loved the bite of pain from his hands, the feeling of

his cock stretching her. Moaning aloud her pleasure, she rode him faster, chasing her release once again.

Everything overwhelmed her, and it was like a flood of emotions coupled with physical sensation boiling inside of her. She wanted to tell him again how much she loved him, how she couldn't imagine doing this with anyone but him, how she loved how he kissed her and touched her and made her come. Mostly she wanted to beg for him to come with her to Seattle, or for him to beg her not to go—at this point, she didn't care where she went, as long as Heath was with her.

Heath tipped his head back, his jaw tense. As Jubilee got closer to her orgasm, he grunted something under his breath before hoisting her up and against the wall behind him. Hitching her legs around his hips, he thrust inside her and took over completely. Her eyes widened as he pounded into her, and she loved that he didn't treat her like she was something breakable.

Who else in her life had ever thought of her as strong and capable? *Only Heath. It's always been him.*

Jubilee dug her nails into his shoulders as he thrust. The water in the hot tub splashed over the edge with each stroke, and if Jubilee weren't so preoccupied, she'd laugh at the mess they were making.

This time, she wasn't nervous about doing something stupid. She moved with him, chasing her own pleasure, desperate to find that release she'd been denied earlier. Heath increased his rhythm until Jubilee could barely breathe, her body tightening until it was almost painful.

"Come for me, baby. I can feel you tightening around me." Heath reached down and thumbed her clit as he filled her.

Jubilee's eyes flew open, and they watched each other come. Crying out, she writhed in his arms, her orgasm slamming into her. She felt Heath's cock twitch inside her before he came, too, his pupils blown so wide that his eyes were almost black.

The water undulated around them and slowed down as they clung to each other. Jubilee felt tears prick her eyes—stupid, foolish tears. *I love him so much, but he doesn't feel the same.*

He cared for her, that was for certain. He lusted after her. But did that mean he loved her? She didn't think so. She also knew she wouldn't be able to keep doing this without getting her heart trampled on in the process.

Right then, however, she wrapped her entire body around him, unwilling to let go. *Just this one night. Let us have this one night before it's all over.*

HEATH STRUGGLED to catch his breath, especially as Jubilee curled up next to him in the hot tub. The night was calm, but his mind hardly was.

I love you. I think I've loved you for a long, long time.

He didn't deserve her love. That didn't mean he didn't drink it up like finding water in a desert. Hearing those words…they were everything.

Jubilee hummed under her breath before looking up at him. Her eyes sparkled in the low light, her cheeks flushed.

But she was leaving Fair Haven, wasn't she? Seattle wasn't that far, not really, but it would be a parting regardless. She would most likely meet someone more suited for her: someone her age, someone without a past like his. His stomach twisted at the thought of her with someone else. He didn't know if he had the strength to let her go, even if he knew it was the right thing to do.

"How did you manage all of this?" he asked, gesturing at the hot tub. "Should I be worried?"

She wrinkled her nose. "I have friends in high places."

"Really? Like who?"

"Okay, my sister knows people who are easily bribed with concert tickets. Happy?"

He kissed her, a loud and smacking kiss, which made her giggle.

"Deliriously," he admitted. And it was true. Jubilee made him happier than he could remember being.

Suddenly, the words he knew he could never say hovered on the tip of his tongue. Did he love her? *Oh God, I do. I love her.*

The realization should've stunned him, but it only filled him with an odd sense of peace. It was a melancholy feeling, knowing he was going to let her go, but perhaps being honest with oneself was almost as important as being honest with someone else.

"What happened with your principal?" she asked. "You never said."

The thought of Principal Anderson, the newspaper article, Rich—it was like a bucket of cold water on the entire evening. Just because Lewis had been able to get the article taken down didn't mean it wouldn't come out some other way, and Heath knew very well he needed to tell Jubilee.

He couldn't tell her he loved her. He could tell her the truth about himself, though.

"Get the hell away from my sister," a voice commanded right before a bright flashlight blinded Heath.

Jubilee gasped, and it took Heath a second to realize that Harrison Thornton stood over them both, looking like he'd happily tear him limb from limb.

"I didn't want to believe it. Goddammit, Heath. And you." He turned to Jubilee before looking away. "Get some clothes on," he growled as he stalked away to give them a second of privacy.

Heath helped Jubilee from the hot tub, and he thanked Jubilee's good thinking in having brought two towels for them both. They dried off quickly, their hair dripping onto the collars of their shirts as they approached Harrison.

Heath had known Harrison for seven years now, but he'd never seen his friend this angry before. It was in the way his jaw clenched, his eyes narrowed. How he paced, and how he kept clenching his fists, like he desperately wanted to punch someone—how he desperately wanted to punch Heath.

"I told you to stay away from her," Harrison said. "I told you, but you went behind my back and did this."

Before Heath could reply, Jubilee stepped forward. "You told him to stay away from me? Why?"

"Because you're too young for him! Because he lied to me about leaving you alone, and now I've found you two breaking into a pool in the middle of the night, skinny-dipping!" Harrison swore under his breath as he pushed his fingers through his hair.

"I shouldn't have lied to you," Heath admitted, "but this isn't any of your damn business, either. Jubilee's a grown woman."

"And did you tell her the truth about you? Huh?" At

Heath's silence, Harrison laughed bitterly. "Of course you didn't. Do you know that he was arrested for drug trafficking? Did he give you that little tidbit, Jubilee?"

Heath watched as the blood drained from Jubilee's face. "What is he talking about?" she whispered.

"You lying scumbag. You put your hands on my sister, lie to her, and then have the audacity to act like you did nothing wrong? What the hell is wrong with you?"

It was like getting caught in an avalanche. Heath tried to find his footing, except more snow and ice plunged him down the mountain until he couldn't make heads nor tails of anything. He was drowning—and he was angry. A red haze covered his vision, and all he wanted to do was deck Harrison so hard that he crumpled at his feet.

"The charges were dropped. I was never convicted of anything."

"And who got the charges dropped?" Harrison shook his head. "Who was it, Heath? Be honest now."

"Don't do this. Don't." Heath didn't know if he was saying those words to Harrison or to himself.

Harrison got into his face right then, his nose only inches from Heath's. "Tell her. Tell her who got you off. Tell her that you let your own sister take the fall for you so you could walk free—"

Before Harrison could finish those words, Heath slammed his fist into Harrison's jaw. Jubilee cried out as Harrison staggered back, breathing hard. His eyes glittered, but as he rose up to continue the fight, Jubilee stepped between them.

"Stop it! Just stop! That's enough." She shoved her brother —or tried to, as he was much taller and muscular than her.

"This isn't any of your business and never has been. Go home."

"I'm just trying to protect you." Harrison's voice softened. "You're so young, and you don't know men. I do. He'll use you and set you aside, and then you'll be brokenhearted."

"Then that's my risk to take. Not yours. I'm tired of being kept in a bubble because you and everyone else think you know what's best for me." Her voice rose, and along with it, Heath's pride in her for standing up to her family. "You'll keep me in a tower because it makes *you* feel better, not me. It hasn't been about me in a long time. I may have been sick, yes, but that doesn't mean I shouldn't get to live my life. You don't get to make my choices for me!"

"Juju-bee…"

"Just, leave me alone. I don't need you. I've never needed you. I'm so tired of this family I could scream."

Heath couldn't help but notice the hurt on Harrison's face, but he was smart enough to surrender when he'd lost.

As Harrison walked past Heath, he said, "Tell her the truth. Or I will."

The sounds of the night floated around them, the hot tub humming merrily yards away. Jubilee had her back turned to him, and when he went to touch her, she pulled away.

"I'm going home. And if you're smart, you'll come with me and tell me everything."

She didn't wait for him to reply but stalked off into the night, her hair still dripping onto the concrete.

CHAPTER SIXTEEN

Jubilee stared straight ahead as she sat in the driver's side of her car, Heath silent in the passenger seat. She'd initially thought they could talk at her apartment, but the thought of going there, where Heath had first touched her and shaken her world, seemed unbearable right then.

Jubilee shivered despite the heater going full blast. She'd tried to get the water out of her hair, but then it had seemed so pointless in the grand scheme of things.

Heath had lied to her. When she'd asked him if something was going on, he'd lied to her face without flinching.

So she waited, hoping he had an explanation she could understand, if not swallow so they could move on.

"I should've told you everything a long time ago," Heath admitted. He sighed. "I didn't know how to tell you, Jubilee. And I didn't want to lay that burden on you."

She flinched, but she said nothing. She knew well enough that one of the best ways to get people to talk was to wait. The words inevitably spilled out in an attempt to fill the endless silence.

"This happened a long time ago, but it's one of those things you never forget." He blew out a breath. "I had a roommate in college. We were friends, although we were never close. I hadn't thought I'd ever go to college, not after my parents died. But I scrimped and saved, and I was so close to getting my teacher's license that I couldn't imagine letting anything get in the way of that."

Finally, Jubilee looked at him and saw the anguish in his expression. Her heart softened. "What happened?"

"My roommate—Troy—he was struggling to pay tuition, and he started dealing drugs. I looked the other way. I thought it was temporary, you know? It wasn't right and it was definitely illegal, but I didn't have the money to find a new place on such short notice. And I was afraid if I snitched on Troy, the police would look at me and then everything would be over.

"But of course, things did end. A neighbor of ours, Gregory, who'd just gotten sober, became one of Troy's clients." Heath smiled bitterly. "He overdosed and died. Because I didn't say anything. Then Troy and I were arrested, and I was suddenly facing drug trafficking charges. At the very least, aiding and abetting a criminal."

"Oh, Heath." She couldn't stop herself from squeezing his hand. "You made a bad decision, but you weren't the one who sold those drugs to your neighbor. You can't blame yourself. And the sad thing is that people who want to get drugs will find them regardless."

"I know. Yet that doesn't stop me from wishing I'd done something to stop it." He returned her hand squeeze. "I was facing these charges, and then suddenly, I was free. They were dropped and that was that. I only found out later that Rose's ex-boyfriend Johnny had done it all."

Jubilee's eyes widened. "Why would he do that? He tried to kidnap Rose just a few months ago!"

"I didn't know then what a piece of shit he was. I also didn't know that Rose had made a deal with the devil: she'd agreed to stay with Johnny in order to set me free."

Jubilee's heart clenched at the pain in Heath's words. She couldn't imagine the amount of guilt he felt over all of this. And he'd kept it inside all of these years? She couldn't imagine.

"Rose suffered for me. She shouldn't have done that. I wished to God she hadn't." His fists clenched, and he seemed like he would burst from the car in anger. "I was a coward, Jubilee, and I was a coward not to tell you the truth. I wanted to protect you."

At that, she pulled her hand away and looked straight ahead again.

"And now this guy who's one of Johnny's cronies is doing his best to ruin my life and my career. That's why my principal called me in. There was an article in the newspaper about my arrest, although they didn't know about Gregory's death."

Jubilee wanted to comfort him; she wanted to rail at him. She heard his words over and over in her mind—*I wanted to protect you*—and she wasn't sure she'd be able to forgive him for lying to her. Her family had coddled her, lied to her, told her half-truths, for years. Harrison still thought she couldn't make her own decisions.

What did it say that the man she loved thought she couldn't cope with what he was struggling with? How could they base a relationship on a complete lack of trust and openness?

"What article? I didn't hear about anything."

"It was taken down fairly quickly, but we all know nothing can be deleted from the Internet entirely," he replied. "I should've told you all this. I'm sorry."

"You lied to me." She felt tears forming, and she swallowed hard, trying to keep her composure. "You lied to my face. I asked you what was wrong and you said it was nothing. I mean, it was really none of my business, I guess, but——"

"That's not it. Jesus, I wanted to tell you. I hated keeping you in the dark. But you have your own life, your own burdens. What good would it have done to lay that on your shoulders?"

She gave him a bitter smile. "Because I'm so fragile, right? You sound like Harrison."

She could tell her words shocked him. He reared back, his brow creasing, and she wanted to apologize. Except she was right: he was acting like Harrison, and her mother, and all of her siblings combined. She'd thought Heath was different. He'd believed in her; he'd thought she could stand on her own two feet.

"There were so many things my family kept from me," she murmured, almost talking to herself. "No one told me about Caleb almost dying in a car accident; no one told me that Lizzie had miscarried a baby. No one told me *anything* because they thought, 'Jubilee is so delicate that if she's stressed, she'll get sick again.' I've lived in a bubble my entire life. I can't even go to Seattle to college without everyone going against me, telling me I'm making a mistake. I'm not even allowed to make mistakes!"

Her voice rose, and she sounded shrill to her own ears. "And you, *you*, were supposed to be different. You were supposed to be the one person who saw me not as some sickly kid, but as an adult. As a woman." At that, the tears overwhelmed her, and she couldn't say another word.

"I wanted to protect you. I know you're an adult, but you haven't been in the world, either. You don't know what it's like. You've never seen the darker side of life, and for that, you're lucky. Believe me."

She sobbed. "Are you serious? Do you think I haven't seen how shitty life can be? Tell me, did you think you were going to die from cancer when you were six? Did you spend months in a hospital room undergoing bone marrow transplants because they were the last resort? Did you hurt so much but you didn't understand why everyone kept poking and cutting and hurting you? You have no idea what I've been through. Just because I haven't been arrested like you have doesn't somehow make me some innocent little girl, either."

"I'm sorry," was all he said. "Maybe this is for the best."

Another sob crawled up her throat. *Why won't you fight for us?* she wanted to scream. *Is this it, then? You're just giving up?*

"Maybe it is." She wiped her face, although the tears kept flowing regardless. "I'm leaving soon. I didn't expect you'd follow me. So we should end things now to avoid any more hurt."

Heath was stricken, and she couldn't help but notice that he swiped a hand across his eyes, under his glasses. "Then I think we have our decision. This is over. It was supposed to just be a fling, wasn't it? We should stop now before it gets nasty."

Jubilee's bottom lip quivered. She heard the anguish in

Heath's voice; she saw the tension in his shoulders. She knew he wasn't saying these things lightly, and she wondered if he loved her, too. Would he have been so upset about her reaction to his lying if he didn't care for her?

"I love you, Heath," she whispered, "but that doesn't mean I'm going to let anyone lock me up in a tower. I'll never be that girl again. I'm going to live my life how I want to live it."

"And you'll be amazing. You'll go on to be a veterinarian, Jubilee, I know you will. For whatever it's worth, I believe in you."

He leaned over and kissed her on the cheek, and she wanted to beg him not to leave. The only thing keeping her from flinging herself at him was the ragged remains of her pride.

Heath got out of her car without another word. When she heard him turn on his car's engine and drive away, Jubilee finally gave in to her tears, crying for Heath, for herself, and for the love that had just not been meant to be.

CHAPTER SEVENTEEN

Jubilee stared at the bowl of batter in front of her. She'd completely forgotten what she'd been making. Banana bread? Pumpkin bread? She knew most of the recipes Megan used at The Rise and Shine by heart, so she couldn't just read what she'd need.

Staring at that bowl of nondescript batter, Jubilee felt tears rising. It was stupid, really, how anything could make her cry lately. It had been two weeks since she'd broken things off with Heath, and she missed him. She missed him like she missed a severed limb—or a piece of heart.

She still loved him. She wished she could push that love aside and move on, but her heart wouldn't let her. Every night, she dreamed of him. Every time she heard the bell jangle at The Rise and Shine, she looked up, hoping it was him.

But it never was. He didn't come to her apartment to beg her to come back; he didn't stop by her work to tell her he was an idiot. He didn't call her to say he'd been a coward to let her end things.

She'd wanted him to fight for them. Instead, she'd realized he didn't *want* to fight for them.

Tears dripped down her face, falling into the bowl below. Annoyed with herself, she threw out the batter with a bit more force than necessary. In a fit of pique, she threw the plastic bowl and plastic utensils into the sink. The loud bang only satisfied her for a moment before she felt the seemingly endless sensation of sadness creep back inside her.

"Good lord, what's happening back here?" Megan poked her head into the kitchen, her hair a bright flame on top of her head. "Are you okay?"

Jubilee's lip wobbled. She needed to pull herself together. After that night with Heath, Jubilee had gone home and cried the entire night. The morning after, she'd gotten out of bed and tried her hardest to push everything she felt deep inside. She hadn't talk to anyone about Heath because it had just been too painful.

"I'm fine," Jubilee replied, swiping the errant tears from her eyes. "What did you want me to make? I forgot."

Megan clucked her tongue as she came into the kitchen. "Banana bread, hun, but it doesn't matter. I put up the sign in case anyone comes in, so you have no excuse not to tell me what happened. Is this about Heath?"

Hearing his name made her face crumple, and to Jubilee's humiliation, she started crying right then. Leaning against Megan, she felt Megan stroke her hair as she said soothing nothings.

"Well, that explains why you've been a zombie these past few weeks," Megan said. "Do you want to tell me what happened? Or do you just want me to send Caleb to break his legs?"

That made Jubilee giggle. "No, but I appreciate the offer. I've already had enough issues with my brothers."

Harrison hadn't talked to her since that night, either, and Jubilee hadn't wanted to talk to him. Sometimes she didn't know who she was angrier with: Heath or Harrison. Was it her fate to be surrounded by men who thought they knew what was best for her?

"Hmm, Caleb may have mentioned as much to me. Harrison told him some things, but not the whole story. Now, tell me what happened so we can make a plan to ruin his life."

Jubilee told Megan the entire story in a halting voice: Heath getting in between Jubilee dating other men; his offer to vet the guys; Jubilee's counteroffer of kissing and flirting lessons. Then how everything had gotten so complicated and tangled together before it had fallen apart.

"I love him, and I hate him, too," she said in a choked voice. "How can I feel two different emotions for the same man?"

"Oh, believe me, you can hate and love a man in equal measures. Been there, done that, wrote the book. So you love him?"

Jubilee nodded miserably. "I don't want to. He's the worst." She sniffled, laughing a little. "He's also kind, handsome, funny…and he believed in me. Until that night, that is."

"I think he still believes in you. I don't think he ever stopped." Megan considered her. "I went through something similar with Caleb, you know. He wasn't honest with me, and it broke my heart. But in the end, I realized his dishonesty was more about fear than it was about keeping me in the dark. Because you know what truly terrified him?"

"What?"

"Losing me. And I bet you everything it was the same for Heath."

Jubilee nodded. "He said that, but it doesn't help that he tried to do what everyone else in my family has done. He wants to keep me locked up in a tower, coddled and in a bubble. I can't do that anymore."

"Jubi," Megan said, "think for a second. He didn't do those things. Would a man who wanted to keep you in a bubble agree to give you flirting lessons? Or help you with your list? And when you told him you were leaving for college, he didn't say you shouldn't go. He said you'd succeed and he wanted that for you."

Jubilee knew Megan spoke the truth. Heath had lied to her, that was true. She hated that, but had she been looking for an excuse to push him away?

"He never said he loved me," Jubilee said with a deep sigh. "So I think it's all moot at this point. If he can't love me, then I need to move on."

Megan frowned. "I don't believe he doesn't love you, but he might just need time to get his head out of his ass. Men tend to do that." She slung an arm around Jubilee and hugged her. "It'll all work out. And like I said, if you need Caleb to bash in his kneecaps, he'll do it in a heartbeat. Actually, all of your brothers will."

"Oh God, please don't get my brothers involved. They've already stuck their noses into my business. Harrison especially." Jubilee growled under her breath. "I don't know if I'll ever forgive Harrison for what he did."

"I can't blame you there. Sara told me that he told her what he did, and she was so angry for you he was in the doghouse for a week."

"Then why hasn't he tried to contact me, either? It's not like he doesn't have a phone, or know where I work or live."

Megan wrinkled her nose. "I have a feeling Harrison is lying low. He's not *that* stupid. He doesn't need another woman twisting his balls off."

When Jubilee arrived home, she received a text from none other than Harrison. *Can we talk?* was all it read.

Jubilee's head hurt, and at that moment, she wasn't in the mood to forgive her older brother for treating her just like their mother. Maybe it was harsh of her, or petty, but she could only reply, *I'm done with talking.*

She almost expected Harrison to show up at her door, but he eventually just sent back a single text saying: *I understand. I'll be here, though.*

And for whatever reason, that text made her heart clench in pain, and she wished more than anything else that she could lay her head on Heath's shoulder and tell him all of her troubles.

But you and Heath are over. You need to move on.

She knew that. It was a shame that logic could never be the ruler of one's heart.

Despite Principal Anderson's best intentions, the newspaper article detailing Heath's arrest was seen by a handful of Fair Haven Elementary parents. The weeks leading up to winter break were a maelstrom of five parents in particular demanding that Heath resign while Heath's principal and coworkers stood by him. The loudest parent had been Jessie's mother, Lana, who had apparently taken his rejection of her harder than Heath had realized. Other parents were more understanding, countering that an arrest didn't equate with a conviction. But those five parents' protests were loud enough for the school board to hear, and it was with a heavy heart that Heath handed in his resignation.

And Rich? Caleb and the police force had immediately gone to work, but Rich had somehow managed to disappear into thin air without a trace. Heath didn't even know if Rich was his real name.

Today was the last day before the kids went on winter break. Heath wasn't naive enough to think his students hadn't heard rumblings of what was going on, although they were young enough not to fully understand what it all meant. At the moment, though, they were more preoccupied with going on winter break, already restless and inattentive despite there being three more hours in the school day.

Heath had decided the day would be a fun one, full of art projects and games. His heart twisted in his chest every time he thought about how this was going to be his last day with these kids. Like Jessie, who'd brought him homemade sugar cookies that morning; or Stevie, who never followed along during read-aloud but never failed to make Heath laugh when he told some wild story; or Madison, who'd been so shy at the start of the school year but who now directed an entire group of fellow students on the best way to paint Christmas ornaments.

Bitterness curled in his gut as he watched his class. It wasn't fair, but he knew he'd done the right thing. He had no idea what he'd do from here on out, although he would still receive a pension from the school, so he wouldn't be strapped for money right away. Perhaps he could change careers;

perhaps he could travel, go somewhere far, far away, instead of looking for Jubilee Thornton around every corner.

"Everyone, I have an announcement," Heath said near the end of the school day. At his unexpectedly serious tone, his students gave him their attention. Even Stevie stopped doodling to look up in anticipation.

"I've really loved having you in my class this year," he began, emotions welling up already. He cleared his throat. "It's been an honor to be your teacher. It really has. But I won't be coming back after winter break."

His class erupted with surprised exclamations, multiple students asking why simultaneously.

"Where are you going? Are you moving?" Jessie asked. Her eyes shone with tears. "Why?"

"Sometimes in life, you have to give up some things because they just aren't working out." He knew it was a vague non-answer, but what else could he say? *A few of your parents demanded I leave or they'd drag the entire school through the mud?* His jaw clenched just thinking about it.

His students deflated before his very eyes, and a few started crying. Guilt filled him.

"I'm sorry I won't be here when you come back from winter break, but you should know that I'll be rooting for you all from the sidelines. You have to promise me that you'll behave yourselves with the new teacher, okay?"

"Okay," the class mumbled.

When the bell rang, Heath stood by the door and hugged each of his students, giving each one a bit of advice or encouragement. Jessie hugged him so hard he was a bit worried she'd cracked one of his ribs.

Heath sat at his desk after all of his students were gone.

He needed to pack up his things, but he couldn't find the energy to do so right then.

Johnny had taken everything from him: his job, his reputation. He wanted to blame Johnny for taking Jubilee away from him, except that had been his own fault. He'd been so afraid to tell her the truth that he'd driven her away.

He put his head in his hands, wishing he could simply sink into the ground and never come out again.

This was how Harrison found him. "Am I intruding?" he asked, knocking on the door frame. "Sara told me you were still here."

Heath looked up in surprise. He hadn't talked to Heath since their fight that night after the hot tub escapade. The bruise on Harrison's jaw had faded to a light yellowish-green. To Heath's greater surprise, Harrison seemed sheepish. He'd never seen his friend be anything but confident.

"So, you really resigned?"

"I did. It was for the best," Heath replied.

Harrison grimaced. "This is my fault. I should've kept my mouth shut. If there's anything I can do—"

"It wasn't your fault. You didn't get that article published; Johnny's crony did. And somehow I feel like this would've happened eventually, anyway." Heath sighed. "What are you doing here?" His anger toward Harrison had dissipated in the intervening weeks, although he'd wanted to blame Harrison for Jubilee ending things between them. After a lot of reflection with a healthy dose of whiskey, Heath had grudgingly realized that he probably would've acted just as stupidly if it had been Rose.

"I'm asking myself the same question. Well, really, Sara told me if I didn't make things right, she'd never talk to me ever again." His mouth twisted wryly. "Never cross a pregnant woman, Heath."

"I'll remember that."

"Look, I messed up. I did. I should never have tried to interfere like that, and I never should have told Jubilee about your past. That was for you to tell, not me."

Heath rubbed the back of his neck. "I won't say I'm sorry for punching you, because you deserved that. But I should've been upfront with Jubilee from the beginning. I should've been honest with you, too." He frowned. "Shouldn't you be saying this to Jubilee?"

"Oh, believe me, I've tried. She won't return my calls or texts beyond to tell me she never wants to speak to me again. I've been tempted to show up at her apartment, but Sara told me I'd be a huge idiot to force things."

Heath felt a pain in the center of his chest from just hearing Jubilee's name. God, he missed her. He hadn't stopped thinking about her since that night. He'd been filled with regrets. He'd wanted to go to her, to tell her how sorry he was, but at the same time, he wanted to respect her wishes. She'd ended things. He would do what she asked and leave her alone—even if it was like a small death every day he lived without her.

Harrison grimaced. "I won't say I'm thrilled about my baby sister dating you, or any man. To me, she'll always be that little girl who was so sick. So very, very sick. You didn't know her when she couldn't walk from the pain, or when she lost all her hair, or how she'd beg our mother to make it all go away." He swallowed hard. "I know she's an adult now. I know she's healthy. That doesn't mean it's easy for me to reconcile the two different versions of her."

He narrowed his eyes at Heath. "I saw the way Jubilee looked at you. We all knew how she felt about you. And although she won't talk to me, I've heard enough from Sara to know she's hurting ever since you two ended things."

Heath almost told Harrison to stop talking, yet the other part of him rejoiced in hearing that Jubilee still cared for him. He wanted to go to her more than he'd ever wanted anything in his entire life.

"She told me she couldn't trust me again," Heath explained with a deep sigh. "I don't think she'll forgive me."

"Do you love her?"

It was stupid, but a flush crawled up Heath's cheeks. Probably because he was talking about this with her *brother*. Except he couldn't ignore Harrison's question—and at this point, he could no longer lie to himself.

"I love her," he said quietly. "I always will."

Harrison blew out a breath. Slapping Heath on the shoulder, he said, "Then why the hell are you standing here talking to me? Go to her. Tell her your feelings. Jubilee loves you, man. Believe me, one of the stupidest things you can ever do is let love slip through your fingertips. It's a gift."

Heath's heart lifted at those words. He wanted to drive straight to her apartment, to tell her he loved her, that he wanted to be with her. He glanced at the clock—then groaned.

"She's at work right now. I can't exactly confess my undying love for her as she's getting people cinnamon rolls."

Harrison grinned. "Probably not. Want help packing up? Then maybe we can get drinks until Jubilee gets off work."

"It's a deal."

CHAPTER EIGHTEEN

Jubilee shivered as her car very slowly heated up. After a lot of persuasion (or, in Jubilee's mind, nagging), she'd agreed to go to her parents' place for dinner. Lisa had told her she wanted to talk, which Jubilee knew really meant listening to Lisa lecture her about whatever she'd decided Jubilee had done wrong.

She'd never understand why Lisa was so set on keeping Jubilee from living her own life. She'd always be grateful for everything Lisa had sacrificed for Jubilee during her treatments, but when would Lisa finally realize that she had to let go?

Jubilee had found an apartment in Seattle and had begun packing up her things for her move. Although it was tinged with sadness and loss, it also provided a distraction from thinking about Heath every hour of every day. Last night, though, she'd read her infamous list for the thousandth time before taking a lighter and burning it until it was nothing but ashes.

At least she wouldn't be stuck in Fair Haven, running into

Heath all the time and trying to act like he hadn't broken her heart. She'd start over in Seattle. Maybe she'd even find another man—one who wouldn't lie to her.

If all else failed, she'd get a cat. Or five. Living as a crazy cat lady spinster held a lot of appeal in that moment.

"Why aren't you working?" she grumbled at her car's heater. It was currently blowing what she'd call lukewarm air, and although it generally didn't get too far below freezing in Fair Haven, it had gotten cold enough for there to be some ice on the streets. A wicked wind blew, shaking the trees and making Jubilee's car wobble when a particularly strong gust caught the vehicle.

When she looked up from fiddling with her heater, she saw in her rearview mirror that a car tailed her. Not in the mood to deal with some asshole driver, she sped up, but the car only sped up, too, keeping on her tail. Considering the car could easily pass her in the left lane since there was no one around, Jubilee didn't understand why the driver wanted to tail her. Besides, she was going at least ten miles per hour over the speed limit. This guy needed to chill.

Her phone rang. "Hello?"

"Good, you picked up." It was Harrison. "Are you coming to Mom and Dad's for dinner?"

Jubilee was tempted to toss her phone away, but she didn't need Harrison hounding her even more at their parents' place. "Yeah, I'm driving there now."

"I know you've been avoiding me—"

"More like ignoring you."

He grunted a laugh. "And you're very talented at it, I have to say. Maybe even better than Lizzie. Can we talk tonight, though? To clear the air? I'm sorry, Jubi. I messed up. I shouldn't have interfered like I had."

"That's the understatement of the year." Her anger, though, melted at his sincerity. She'd missed Harrison, her entire family. They drove her crazy, but they loved her.

She wanted to say no. She wanted to tell her brother that he was the worst and that she hated him, but right then, it all seemed so petty. At the very least, she could hear him out. It didn't mean she had to offer him forgiveness.

"If you can keep Mom from bugging me, we can talk."

"It's a deal." He paused, and then he said, "I saw Heath, you know."

Her breath caught. "How is he?" Then she cursed herself for sounding so eager.

"He resigned from his job."

At that, she inhaled sharply. "What? Why? And in the middle of the school year?"

"Apparently some parents got wind of his arrest and essentially forced him out. He thought it was best if he went quietly."

"That's bullshit."

"I agree. He's a great teacher."

Jubilee's heart ached for Heath. What would he do now? Would another school hire him? He loved teaching, and she knew it had been his dream for a long time. He'd made a mistake in not telling her the truth, but that hadn't meant that she'd wanted him to lose his job.

"I can't believe it," she said. "Will he stay here in town?"

"I don't know. I doubt it." Harrison blew out a breath. "Hey, Sara's calling me, but we'll talk more when you get here. Oh, and Jubilee?"

"Yeah?"

"Heath loves you. If you feel the same, don't let him go. Believe me: you'll regret it."

She mumbled a goodbye. She tossed her phone onto the front seat right as she came upon a curve in the road. The Thorntons lived up in the mountains above Fair Haven, and the road to their place was twisty and often deserted.

When Jubilee came around the corner, she heard an engine revving and the car that had been tailing her began to pass her. He sped past her, making a point to drive right next to her for a moment, as if to be as annoying as possible.

Except the car wasn't passing her. He stayed in the left lane—going the wrong way—and Jubilee glanced over at the driver in confusion. She saw a man she didn't recognize. He grinned at her, and her heart stopped.

As they came to another curve in the road, he inched forward, and she thought he'd finally pass her. Lights flashed, and a car coming the opposite direction honked. Jubilee's breath caught, expecting a head-on collision, but the driver cut in front of her just in time. The other car's horn echoed into the night.

Jubilee slowed down, hoping the driver would drive on and leave her alone. There were no exits to take, and since this was such a narrow road, turning around was nearly impossible, especially in the dark. Her palms were sweaty from fear, her heart thumping a jagged rhythm. She didn't want to stop and make herself even more vulnerable. At least her car offered her some amount of protection.

If I can just get to the next exit, I can lose him. It's not far.

The driver slowed down again and got into the other lane a second time. Instead of simply driving next to her, he swerved toward her. Jubilee was barely able to keep him from hitting her. She righted the car and pushed on the gas. She had to get out of here—now. This guy was trying to kill her.

The driver wasn't giving up. He swerved toward her a second time, and again she avoided colliding with him. But when she yanked the steering wheel to the right, her tires skidded on a patch of ice. Her car quickly careened out of control, spinning like a top before it began to fall down the nearby embankment. Its momentum flipped it over, and it rolled down the hill like a tumbleweed.

Jubilee screamed as she was carried down the hill, upside down, right side up, upside down again. Glass shattered, bursting around her, and the noise deafened her.

She knew in that moment that she was going to die. She wished she'd told Heath she loved him one last time. She wished she'd let Harrison explain his actions. She wished she could've hugged her mom and told her that she'd be okay, that she didn't need her to protect her like she had when she'd been a sick little girl.

It was Heath's smile she saw before pain exploded inside her skull and then the world went dark.

When Heath needed to think, he sometimes drove to the highest hill in Fair Haven and stared out over the town. Tonight, the sky was clear, and he could make out a number of constellations despite the lights below. It was freezing cold, and his breath fogged in front of him. He didn't care. The cold kept him awake, and it forced him to keep feeling.

At least one hundred feet below was a twisting, winding

road, although few people drove on it, especially if it was remotely icy. Heath had counted on this. No sounds of traffic or cars to disturb his thoughts.

He didn't know where he would go or what he'd do now that he no longer had a job. He could go to Seattle, or one of the suburbs. Maybe Olympia. He could even move to Portland if he really wanted to get far away.

He smiled grimly. He knew very well that no matter how far he moved, he'd never forget about Jubilee.

Harrison's words today had stuck inside him like a burr, and Heath wanted to scratch at it until he bled. Did Heath still have a chance with Jubilee? Or had he ruined it?

She loves you. Heath wanted to believe that so badly it hurt. He wasn't sure he deserved a love like that from Jubilee, but he wanted it. He wanted to show her how much he loved her. He wanted to make things right; perhaps they could at least part as friends.

I need to see her, at least. One last time. I can't leave things like this.

He felt better, just from making that promise to himself. He loved Jubilee with all of his broken, desperate heart. She'd been the missing piece in his life, a piece he hadn't even known he'd needed. Her sweetness, her courage, her beauty. Everything about her had been like a balm to his soul, and he almost couldn't blame himself for falling for her as hard as he did.

"Where are you right now, Jubi?" he whispered into the cold night. He imagined her curled up on her couch, reading, her hair dark and shining. She'd smile up at him when he came home, and she'd whisper his name right before he kissed her.

The sound of a car engine, and then tires screeching,

caught Heath's attention. He heard what sounded like a second car, and he got up from where he'd sat on the hood of his own car to see what was happening. He watched as one car tried to force another car—a red one with a missing hubcap on the back right tire—off of the road.

He knew that red car. He'd know it anywhere: it was Jubilee's.

The two cars turned a bend right before the red car began fishtailing and spinning. Heath screamed, "Jubilee!" knowing it wouldn't make a difference. The other car had driven off without stopping.

Heath dialed 911 as he drove back down the hill to where Jubilee's car had tipped over and rolled down the embankment.

"Yes, Route 91. North side. Please come quickly." He stuffed his phone into his pocket, parked his car and got the flashlight he always carried in his trunk. He then sprinted down the embankment after Jubilee, flashlight bouncing off of the ground as he ran.

He followed the trail of smashed bushes and trees, trying not to trip over his feet in his haste and go tumbling onto his face. The trees were smaller saplings that had snapped from the impact of the car, but they also slowed down the car's momentum.

Along with the flashlight's glare, the light from the full moon was enough to illuminate where the car had finally rolled to a stop. The car was upside-down, and when Heath finally got a good look at Jubilee, he was sure she was dead.

"Jubilee! Jubilee, it's me, Heath. Can you hear me?" She dangled upside-down, a cut on her forehead that dripped blood down her face.

She stirred at the sound of his yelling, but she didn't awaken. He sobbed a breath of relief: she was alive.

He didn't know when help would arrive. They were out in the middle of nowhere. What if Jubilee was bleeding from a serious injury? Flashing the flashlight across her, he didn't see any more blood beyond the cut on her forehead. But it was difficult to tell, with all the debris, not only from all the glass, but from the trees, grass, and dirt that had flown inside as the car had rolled down the hill.

Jubilee moaned, and her eyelids fluttered. "Heath?" she murmured. "Where…?"

"Don't talk, baby. Help is on the way. I saw everything."

He knew it was Rich who'd done this, and he vowed to find him and break his neck. Guilt also filled him, because he'd put Jubilee in danger. Rich must have figured out their connection. *I'll kill him slowly. He won't live to see another day.*

Jubilee kept moaning. "My head hurts." She reached up and touched the blood on her forehead.

"Just stay still. Please."

Their gazes locked, and Heath reached a hand inside the window where the glass had blown out to squeeze her hand. "I love you, Jubilee. No matter what happens. I want you to know that. I'm the biggest idiot in the entire world. I'll never have enough time to make it all up to you, but if you let me—"

She squeezed his hand, rolling her head back and forth. "Stop. It doesn't matter." She took in a shuddering breath. "I love you, too. Nothing else matters."

As Heath's heart soared, he realized that there was smoke coming from the hood of Jubilee's car. Panic threatened to overtake him. He couldn't wait for help to arrive to get Jubilee out. He knew smoke meant they needed to get away from here as fast as possible.

Adrenaline made his movements ragged, but a sort of calm also settled over him. It was like watching someone else do this from far away, and Heath was watching, cheering himself on.

Jubilee fell unconscious again. Using the butt of the flash-light, he smashed in the window before reaching up to open the driver's-side door. He breathed a sigh of relief when the door creaked open.

"Jubilee, listen to me," he said as calmly as he could, shaking her. "I have to get you out of here. Can you hear me?"

She stirred. Smoke began to fill the car, and Heath knew they only had minutes. When he reached to unbuckle her seat belt, he realized that the locking mechanism had somehow gotten mangled, and he couldn't get Jubilee free from it without some kind of tool to break it open. He swore colorfully.

Jubilee's eyes opened again as he took off the shoulder strap and, catching her under her armpits, he began to pull her from the car. Smoke choked him, making him cough, and Jubilee cried out when she landed on the ground.

But she was free. Heath bent down to pick her up, jogging as far away from the car as possible for cover. Only seconds later, an explosion shook the ground, and Heath covered Jubilee with his body as it seemed like hell itself at begun raining down upon them.

Heath vaguely heard sirens, but he only had eyes and ears for Jubilee. She was crying—from fear or pain, he didn't know—and he brushed the tears away with gentle fingers.

"I have you, I have you. You're safe. I love you. I love you so much. Don't you dare leave me or I'll never forgive you."

She sniffled and laughed a little before moaning in pain. "I'm—not—going—anywhere," she gasped in halting breaths. "I'm going to make your life hell for lying to me."

Tears filled his eyes. He kissed her softly. "It's a promise."

When the EMTs and firefighters filled the area, it took all of Heath's strength to let them see to Jubilee. Someone took his arm, saying something about getting him checked out, but he could only watch as Jubilee was placed on a stretcher and carried up the embankment to the waiting ambulance.

CHAPTER NINETEEN

"Are you sure you don't want me to stay with you tonight? I don't think you should be alone."

Jubilee bit back a sharp reply, knowing all too well that her mother meant well. Lisa Thornton hadn't left Jubilee's side from the moment she'd found out about her car accident. Not only Lisa, but the entire Thornton clan had shown up at Fair Haven Memorial, demanding to know what had happened.

Jubilee knew she'd been lucky. Despite everything, she'd only suffered a cut to her forehead from flying glass, which had only needed some stitches, along with a minor concussion. She'd been released from the hospital after forty-eight hours. The attending physician had said that she should take it easy and come back to the ER if she suffered any kind of dizziness or nausea, but so far, all Jubilee felt was tired.

"Mom, I'll be okay. Really. I just want to sleep."

Lisa looked like she wanted to protest, but then she just sighed deeply. "All right. Please call me if you need me. I'll come straight away."

Jubilee hugged her mom tightly, and after a moment, Lisa

returned the hug. They hadn't always understood each other, but Jubilee knew without a shadow of a doubt how much her mother loved her.

The moment Lisa closed Jubilee's apartment door behind her, Jubilee texted, *She's gone.*

And then Heath was there in her doorway and she was finally, *finally*, in his arms.

"I thought she'd never leave," he muttered, cupping her cheek. "I was waiting for hours."

Jubilee grinned. "It was maybe a half hour." She poked him in the chest. "You could've come inside, you know. My family loves you now, since you saved me from certain death. I'm pretty sure my dad would've given you my hand in marriage if you had asked."

He didn't laugh at her joke. His expression turned serious, and she noticed the dark circles under his eyes.

Heath hadn't left her side from the moment she'd arrived at the hospital. He'd been her guardian angel, saving her like he had. She didn't want to think about what would've happened if he hadn't seen the accident and pulled her from the wreckage. Her car had exploded and burned down to little more than scrap metal.

"I don't care about your family," he said. "I care about *you*. Just you."

Stepping away, he pushed his fingers through his auburn hair. Jubilee's heart twisted. She'd wanted him to say that he loved her, that he wanted to be with her. Sometimes she wondered if she'd dreamed that he'd told her he loved her during the accident. Had he stayed by her side simply out of duty? The thought depressed her so much she wanted to sink into the floor.

He started pacing. Unsure and suddenly exhausted, she sat down on the couch and waited for the inevitable. *He's going to say it's over—for good. He's just trying to figure out how to tell me.*

Had she known all along this would happen? That despite what she felt for him and what he felt for her, it could never go anywhere? Tears pooled in her eyes, but she blinked them away, feeling foolish.

"I'm sorry for everything," he began. He kept pacing, and it made Jubilee a little dizzy. "I put you in danger. I hold myself responsible for what happened. Rich would never have targeted you if it hadn't have been for me."

While Jubilee had been in the hospital, Caleb and the entire Fair Haven Police Department, along with the police forces of a few nearby towns, had gone on a manhunt to find Rich. They'd gotten a tip two days ago, and they'd caught him at a seedy motel fifty miles outside of Seattle. He'd surrendered immediately and currently sat in jail. He'd end up going to prison just like his boss, and for that, Jubilee was thankful.

"It wasn't your fault. How could you have known he'd do something so crazy?"

"I did know, though. He tried to hurt Rose. He threatened me, made me resign from my job. All because we dared to say something about Johnny and his crimes." His voice rose with each word. "I was angry when I heard that Rich had been caught because I wanted to take him down myself."

She smiled, but it was a sad smile. "And then what? You'd get your revenge and move on? Justice will be served. Rich will be locked up for a long, long time. I think that's a pretty decent punishment for any person."

Heath stopped pacing, not saying anything. He seemed to

be at war with himself. His shoulders tensed, his forehead creased.

Jubilee's heart pounded from nerves, and in a burst of frustration, she said, "Will you just tell me already?"

He blinked. "What?"

"Tell me we're really over? That you don't love me anymore?" Her voice cracked, but as she spoke she rose from the couch to stand before him, she refused to crumple at his feet. "It's fine. I appreciate that you saved my life, and I'll always be grateful to you. But you don't have to hang around just because you feel guilty or because you think it's your duty or something."

She was breathing hard by the end of her speech, and Heath still hadn't said anything. *Why is he silent?*

Waiting for the ax to fall was the worst feeling of all. Close to begging, she opened her mouth to say something else when he held up a hand. She bit her lip.

"You think I'm here just because I feel guilty? No other reason?"

She squared her shoulders. "Aren't you? You won't touch me. You won't even talk to me—"

"Because you almost died!" he burst out. His face was anguished, and finally, some emotion other than anger seemed to crack its surface. "Jesus Christ above, Jubilee, I almost lost you. If I hadn't been there, if I hadn't pulled you out of that damn car, you'd be dead. I wouldn't be standing here talking to you. I'd be at your fucking funeral, watching you be buried six feet under as your family blamed me for your death." He panted, a flush staining his cheeks. "I do feel guilty. I'll always feel that guilt, but that's not why I'm here."

Her throat closed up, and she suddenly couldn't find the words she needed.

"I'm here," he said slowly, decisively, "because every time I look at you, every time I think of you, I know that you are vital to my very being." He closed his hands around her biceps, and despite his gruff tone, his touch was gentle. "I love you, Jubilee. I meant what I said three days ago. I love you so much I don't think I could survive if something happened to you. You are my everything."

She trembled, a sob bursting from her, before she started laughing. She was laughing and crying at the same time, her vision blurred with tears, and she could only bury her face in his chest and cry so hard that it wracked her whole frame.

He soothed her, whispering her name, stroking her hair. She felt like her heart had broken and then mended all in the same moment, and it was a strange sensation of both terror and elation.

"You love me?" she whispered, looking up at him. "Even after everything I said to you?"

"Yes, I love you." He stroked her cheek. "But what about you?"

"Oh, Heath. I think I fell in love with you the first time you ever smiled at me. I tried to move on. I did. I told myself it was just a crush, that it would pass—"

Growling, he wrapped his arms around her and finally, *finally*, kissed her. She moaned and, tilting her head back, she reveled in the feeling of his mouth moving against her own. His embrace made her feel safe and loved, and then she felt him bend down and pick her up in his arms.

"I'm never letting you go," he vowed as he laid her down onto her bed, crawling on top of her.

"But what about Seattle? I'm moving soon. And your job? Harrison told me what happened. You shouldn't have had to resign. It wasn't fair at all."

"It doesn't matter, because we'll figure it out. I loved my job, but I love you more. A job can be replaced. You, though?" He kissed her forehead, below where the stitches had been placed, then kissed her cheeks, her nose, her chin. "You can never be replaced."

"And neither can you." She arched upward, needing him to touch her, to feel the warmth of his skin against her own. "I need you," she moaned when he did nothing but kiss her.

"You're too sore."

"No, I'm not, but you'll be sore if you don't make love to me right now."

He chuckled. "Then your wish is my command."

HEATH FELT like his heart would burst in his chest. Seeing Jubilee in that car, so close to death, and then so pale and fragile in her hospital bed, had made him realize how much she meant to him. The mere thought of losing her had been like an arrow to the chest.

He struggled against wanting to wrap her up in wool and never letting her go anywhere without him. He knew she'd only hate him if he coddled her like her family always had. She'd resent him for it, and he wouldn't have their love dissolve into something so bitter.

Smoothing the hair from her forehead, careful of her stitches, he said, "I don't want to hurt you."

"You won't. I'm tough." She smiled. "I beat cancer twice and now a car accident. I'm invincible."

He wanted to shout that she wasn't, that she was human and vulnerable and he needed to protect her from all that life would try to throw at her, but he swallowed the anxiety.

"Do you know how precious you are to me? When you were lying in your hospital bed, I prayed. I never pray, but I made a deal with God that if he let me have a second chance with you, I'd do whatever he wanted."

Her eyes widened. "*Anything?* Are we going to be missionaries in the wilds of the Amazon now?"

That made him laugh. "Hardly." He bent down to kiss her, slow and sweet. "As you can see, my thoughts are hardly pure at the moment."

"I can see that." She cupped his erection as she said it. That mere caress had him wanting to strip her bare in five seconds flat and push inside her, but he forced himself to be slow. She might not have gotten seriously injured, but she was bruised and battered. He brushed his fingers across a vivid bruise on her forearm, just below a cut from the shattered glass.

"Are you afraid? Because you shouldn't be. I won't break, Heath."

He realized that he was afraid, in a way, and it only showed him how much he truly loved her.

"I don't know if I can be gentle," he admitted as he pushed her shirt up her belly, exposing the pale, smooth skin. "I need you so badly. It's like a fever in my blood."

"Then have me. I trust you."

It was like a switch went off in his brain. With a low moan, he stripped her out of her shirt, pushing her bra down so he could kiss and suck her breasts. She inhaled, her stomach turning concave, as he licked the pink nub of one nipple before sucking it into his mouth.

He hummed under his breath, worshiping her breasts, loving the way she said his name and tugged at his hair. She was so responsive to his touch that it only sent his desire for her into a frenzy. His cock pulsed, his breathing increasing as he kissed down her body.

It wasn't long before he had her naked and splayed on the bed like some kind of erotic offering. Her eyelids were heavy as he stood up and took off his own clothes, and when he stroked his cock, she licked her lips in anticipation.

Jubilee sat up and closed her hand around his own, and they stroked him together. With her looking up at him through her dusky lashes, her cheeks flushed and her lips parted, she was so beautiful it took his breath away.

"May I?" she asked. "I want to taste you."

As if he would say no. Nodding, he let her explore, her fingers closing around his cock as she bent to swirl her tongue around the tip. His toes curled into the carpet, and he tipped his head back on a groan when she licked him from root to tip. She licked him like that for a time until she made a frustrated noise in her throat.

"I have no idea what I'm doing. What should I do?"

He swallowed. "Take me in your mouth. Go slowly. Oh God, Jubilee…"

He couldn't speak after that as she sucked his cock, swirling her tongue around him. She couldn't get all of him inside, but it didn't matter. Seeing the woman he loved hum in pleasure as she gave him the greatest blowjob he'd ever had? He'd never forget this moment for the rest of his life.

When she began to bob, her mouth hot and wet, he groaned as his balls tightened. He let her continue for a few more minutes until he gently pushed her away and onto the bed.

"You're going to kill me," he muttered, kneeling on the floor on front of her. He pushed her legs apart until he could see her dewy pink center, already so wet for him. God, he loved her, and as he licked through her folds, those were the only words he could think.

I love you. I love you. I love you. He buried his face in her sex, and she cried out when he sucked the swollen nub of her clit. She strained and panted, moving as he made love to her with his mouth, and when she screamed with her first orgasm, he couldn't stop the pleased grin from crossing his face.

"Don't look so smug," she said as she rolled her eyes.

"Oh, I'll be smug if I want to, and I'll go to bed dreaming about you coming under my tongue like you just did."

She blushed scarlet. He chuckled as he rose and hooked his arms under her thighs, pulling her toward the edge of the bed.

"Are you ready for me? Because I don't think I can wait another second."

She nodded, her hair a dark circle around her head. "Yes, yes, now."

He pushed his cock inside her in one smooth thrust, making them both moan simultaneously. Her delicious wet heat almost sent him over the edge right then. Gritting his teeth, he slowly pulled out, only the tip of his cock still inside her, before he thrust into her again. He continued with that rhythm, loving how her moans got higher-pitched with each stroke.

"I love you." Sweat beaded on his forehead, and God Almighty, his glasses were getting steamed up. He'd laugh if he weren't about to lose his damn mind. "I love you."

"I love you, and I need you to go faster. Don't hold back."

He did as she wanted, pounding into her, the sound of their bodies slapping together filling her room. He panted, sweat now dripping down his chest as he watched her writhe on the bed. She was so gorgeous, so dear to him, and he could hardly believe she was truly *his*.

"Heath," she gasped right before her release slammed into her. She bowed upward, the tendons in her neck showing, and it was only a millisecond later that he felt his own orgasm gather in his lower back and burst inside him. He came in endless waves, filling her with his hot seed, his vision going black. He was fairly certain he'd died and gone to heaven right then.

He fell onto the bed, groaning, and she laughed.

"I can't move," he said. He rolled her onto her side to see her face. "I think you killed me."

"But what a way to die." She kissed the tip of his nose before giggling. "Your glasses are all foggy. Oh dear." She took them off and wiped them on the comforter before sliding them back onto his face. "There you are."

It was a small gesture, but it only made him love her more. Kissing her temple, he whispered, "You're the best thing to happen to me. I'm never letting you go."

"I'm glad we agree, because I'm not letting you go, either. You're mine, Heath DiMarco, and you'll just have to get used it."

He snaked an arm around her, his heart completely full.

J ubilee woke up to sunshine and birdsong. It was ridiculous, really, how gorgeous it was going to be today. Then again, after a rainy winter *and* a rainy spring, any sunshine was welcome.

"Good morning," she said as she passed her roommate Renee on the way to the bathroom. Jubilee had found Renee's listing online for a roommate, and after a few emails back and forth, Renee had asked her to move in. Two weeks after New Year's, Jubilee had packed up everything she wanted into her new car and driven to Seattle to start her new life as a college student.

Her family had wanted to help her move, and it had taken all of Jubilee's powers of persuasion to convince her brothers she didn't have enough things to warrant all of them coming with her.

"Heath is helping me, anyway. I'm not even taking much furniture with me."

Harrison, though, had convinced her he'd like to help, and Jubilee had finally agreed. During the Thornton Christmas get-together with all of her siblings and their significant others, he and Jubilee had finally been able to have that talk.

"I'm so sorry," Harrison said, the anguish plain in his face. "We almost lost you, and if I hadn't been able to tell you how sorry I was—"

"But I'm here." She sighed, shaking her head, but she smiled, too. "It's all water under the bridge. But it also means you have to be civil to Heath. We're together now. I love him."

Harrison enveloped her in a hug. "Jubi, I'll never love the idea of you going far away, but I'm happy for you." He kissed her forehead. "I'll miss you."

Her throat closed, and she nodded. She was excited to move to Seattle, but she'd miss her family—no matter how annoying they tended to get.

"And if Heath hurts you, I'll break his legs," he said, his voice way too cheerful. "Although Caleb, Mark and Seth might get to him before I do."

Jubilee snorted. "Love you, too, Harrison. Now, I hope you got me that tablet I wanted, because that's really all you needed to do to make up for being a total jerkface."

He gave her a noogie as they returned to the sitting room. Heath gave her a searching look, and she smiled.

"Everything okay?" he asked as she settled next to him.

"Everything's perfect."

A few days later, Heath told her he'd gotten a call from Principal Anderson. "He says he wants me to finish the school year," Heath said. "Apparently the school board reassessed and realized they didn't want to be bullied by a few over-bearing parents."

"That's great! So you get your job back?"

"I told him I would need time to think about it." At her

surprised expression, he added, "I wanted to see what you thought."

"I'm sad you won't be moving to Seattle with me," she admitted. "I am." Taking his hand, she squeezed it. "But I know how much your students mean to you, and it would mean the world to them to finish out the year with their real teacher. We can make it work. I know we can."

"I love you." He kissed her, pressing his forehead against hers. "You're way too good for me, you know."

She'd snorted at that statement and had made a point to show him exactly how very naughty she could be.

Now it was the first week of June, and the last week of classes. Jubilee had loved going to college: the professors, the other students. The studying until the wee hours of the morning, even the homework. Renee had thought she was crazy when she'd told her she was excited about writing her first essay.

But Renee couldn't understand what it had been like, to live so confined like Jubilee had. Now that she lived away from Fair Haven, she realized how stifled she'd felt. She was *free*: free to make her own decisions, to spread her wings, to make mistakes. Lisa still called her regularly, but she was making an effort not to be so involved. After Jubilee's brush with death, her family seemed to have realized that life was too short to keep her in that bubble she hated so much.

Her family had also expanded in recent months: Harrison and Sara had welcomed their baby boy, Bennett, on a cold, rainy day in February, while Megan had given birth to her and Caleb's daughter, Evie, just a week ago. With three grandchildren to spoil, both Lisa and Dave seemed to have fixed their interests on the new babies of the family instead of on their stubborn adult children.

It was afternoon by the time Jubilee had finished speaking with her favorite professor, a biology teacher who'd encouraged her to pursue her dream of veterinary school. He'd advised her on the classes she needed to take, and he'd told her he'd be more than happy to write her a recommendation letter.

Jubilee sighed happily as she walked through campus. The sun shone above without a cloud in the sky, people talking and laughing around her.

She'd missed Heath terribly, of course. They tried to see each other every weekend, but sometimes life got in the way. Video calls had become their go-tos, although Jubilee had to make sure Renee wasn't around whenever those calls got a little raunchy—which they inevitably did.

Heath had shown her how much he loved her, time and time again. He'd been the first person to support her move to Seattle to start college, and he'd listened to her frustrations and fears and only given encouragement and a shoulder to cry on. She'd done the same, especially when he'd had to testify against Johnny Porter at his trial. To everyone's relief, Johnny had received a twenty-five-year sentence for all his crimes, and Rich was looking at a similar amount of time behind bars.

"Jubilee," a voice called.

Jubilee squinted. The sun was so bright that she couldn't make out who had said her name.

Then she spotted him: Heath. He was here, in Seattle.

It had been over three weeks since they'd seen each other in person, and Jubilee almost pushed a few people to the ground in her haste to get to him. She threw her arms around him, and he laughed, squeezing her tight.

"You're here! Why are you here? Oh God, I missed you."

He took her head in his hands and kissed her, right in front of everyone. If Jubilee weren't so happy to see him, she'd be embarrassed by their PDA. Someone whistled while someone else hooted. Giggling, Jubilee ended the kiss.

Heath somehow had managed to look handsomer than ever: his hair was recently trimmed, the auburn strands glinting in the sunlight. He'd gotten a tan, despite working in a school all day, and he seemed healthy and happy. Jubilee wanted to kiss him until they couldn't breathe, and it was only because they were in public that she didn't yank off his shirt and kiss him everywhere else, too.

"I missed you, too," he said. He caressed her cheek.

"How did you know where I'd be?"

"Renee." He grinned. "I had to bribe her with a latte to get her to talk. Your roommate is a good negotiator."

"Good thing she wants to go to law school." Staring up at him, she shook her head. "I can't believe you're here. I feel like I haven't seen you in so long."

"I have news, but I wanted to tell you in person." He took a deep breath. "I'm not returning to Fair Haven Elementary—"

"What? Why? Did they make you leave? They can't, they promised—"

He shushed her. "It was my decision. I've loved working there, but it's time to move on. There's something that's more important to me now. Or more specifically, someone.

"I'm moving here. To Seattle." His gaze searched her own

for her reaction. "I was offered a teaching position at Smithton Academy, and I'm going to take it."

Jubilee couldn't speak, she was so elated. They could be together. Renee would be annoyed that she had to find another roommate, but Jubilee could buy her some Thai food —Renee's absolute favorite—to make it up to her.

"That's wonderful, Heath. I'm so happy for you."

"I want us to live together. I've looked at apartments and townhouses, and although we won't be able to afford anything amazing, we could swing it. I have the opportunity for a promotion at Smithton within two years, if I work hard. Oh, and I'm not arrested, of course."

"Don't even joke about that." She poked him in the chest. "But why drive two hours to tell me this? We have phones, you know. Texts, email…"

He pinched her ass for that, and she squealed. "Cheeky. I'm not just here to tell you about my job." He took a deep breath, and then to Jubilee's shock, he went down on one knee in front of her before pulling a telltale box from his jacket pocket.

"Jubilee Thornton, you're the love of my life, the woman who means everything to me," he intoned, opening the box to reveal a diamond ring that shimmered in the sunlight, "I can't imagine life without you. Will you make the happiest man on earth and marry me? Be my wife?"

The tears had started the moment he'd gone down on one knee, and now Jubilee was crying too hard to answer coherently. Someone nearby yelled, "Are you going to answer him?" prompting laughter from the crowd.

Jubilee smiled so hard her face hurt. "Yes, yes, yes," she sobbed. "Of course I'll marry you."

He stood up and kissed her, making the crowd cheer around them. Jubilee giggled. The crowd cheered even louder when he slipped the ring onto her finger.

"I'm so glad I wrote that list," she said as they walked back to her apartment. "Otherwise we might never have gotten together."

He hugged her close. "List or no list," he said, his voice laced with promise and heat, "I would've made you mine."

I'LL BE HOME FOR CHRISTMAS

A THORNTONS CHRISTMAS NOVELLA

It's Christmas time, and the entire Thornton clan is spending the holidays in a cabin deep in the Washington woods.

What could go wrong with twelve adults, four kids, and a dog all staying together in one big cabin?

Only the most chaotic—and memorable—Christmas ever!

Expect kisses under the mistletoe, lots of (spiked) eggnog, and even a surprise wedding as the Thornton clan celebrates the most romantic holiday of all.

Author's Note: *I'll Be Home for Christmas is set six months after the last book, Till There Was You, ends. It's recommended that you read the other books first, as this book is an epilogue to the entire series.*

CHAPTER ONE

HARRISON & SARA

The idea had been Harrison's, and once Caleb had gotten on board, the rest of the family had followed. Harrison wanted all of the Thornton siblings, their spouses and significant others, and their children to rent a cabin near the Cascades during Christmas.

As Sara Thornton, formerly Flannigan, watched her husband and the rest of the Thornton clan bustle inside the huge cabin, she wondered how great of an idea this really was. *Nothing like putting a bunch of people together in a cabin to create some chaos*, she thought wryly.

The cabin could house up to fifteen people, with seven bedrooms and four bathrooms, a huge living room and kitchen, and a hot tub out back. Constructed solely out of pine, it resembled a log cabin you'd imagine one of the pioneers living in centuries ago—if you didn't include the indoor plumbing and central heating. Although it hadn't gotten dark yet, someone had already turned on the outdoor Christmas lights, the colors twinkling merrily.

The selling point was that it had enough rooms for each couple and one more for the kids. James, Sara's son, hadn't been pleased that he had to sleep in the same room as the little ones, but when Sara had promised him he could help Harrison and the guys cut down a Christmas tree, he'd gotten over his disappointment with his rooming situation quickly. James also enjoyed looking after the babies, no matter how much he tried to act otherwise.

Sara couldn't help but smile as she inhaled the scent of evergreens. She'd never been in the woods like this. She'd grown up poor, her family having had to make do with cheap artificial Christmas trees strung with popcorn.

"Mom, Mom!" James scampered up to her, his cheeks rosy. At almost ten years old, James was growing so much that soon he would be taller than his mother. He shared her blue eyes, although Sara preferred to blame his sauciness on her ex-husband, James's father.

"Mom, there's a bird stuck in the chimney!" His eyes widened. "Uncle Caleb is trying to get it out."

"That's great. Where's your brother?" Sara and Harrison's son, Bennett, now ten months old, was just starting to become mobile, and Sara had asked James to watch him while the adults got their suitcases out of all of the cars.

"He's with—um. Aunt Lizzie? I think?"

Before Sara could grill James about Bennett's whereabouts, James scampered off again after Caleb shouted something unsavory from the nearby living room.

Along with Harrison, his five other siblings were also staying at the cabin: Caleb, with his wife, Megan, and their infant daughter, Evie; Mark, with his wife, Abby; Lizzie, with her husband, Trent, and their toddler, Bea; Seth, with his girlfriend, Rose; and Jubilee, with her fiancé, Heath.

Sara found Bennett in the living room and scooped him up, kissing him on his chubby cheeks. She couldn't believe her baby would be a year old in just two months. Where had the time gone? Bennett giggled when Sara kissed him again before wiggling to get down. He'd been lifting himself up lately and, with the help of his parents, had walked some. Sara definitely wasn't ready for her baby boy to be running all over the place yet.

"Where's the broom?" Caleb asked as he crouched under the chimney, Harrison and Mark close by. "We need to get this damn bird out. Otherwise it's going to get roasted for tonight's dinner."

"You could smoke it out," said Mark, his voice low and rumbling. "Not sure a broom would help."

"I think if you light a fire, it'll fly out," said Harrison as he peered up into the chimney. "Then again, it might just catch on fire."

"Please don't set the cabin on fire," said Sara. She caught Harrison's gaze and smiled. "I'm going up to our room. Bennett needs to take a nap."

Harrison smiled back, and Sara couldn't help the flutter in her chest at the sight. Even after two and a half years of marriage, Harrison still managed to make her giddy.

"I'll see you up there," said Harrison with a wink.

Caleb rolled his eyes. "Get a room, you two."

Mark snorted. "Didn't I just catch you and Megan kissing in the pantry?"

"I never kiss and tell."

Sara, with Bennett in her arms, left the men to figure out the logistics of getting a bird out of the chimney while they bickered and bantered. Upstairs, she found her younger sister Megan nursing Evie in one of the rooms.

It still felt strange sometimes to be around such a huge family, considering it had been just Sara and Megan, along with their mother Ruth, for years. Sara often needed a break from all of the commotion, and she had a feeling Megan felt the same way.

Sara set Bennett on the floor before collapsing onto an overstuffed armchair next to Megan. "I'm already exhausted and we just got here," she complained.

Megan laughed. "Tell me about it. But it'll be fun. If all else fails, you can get drunk on spiked eggnog." She patted Evie's bottom, then touched the infant's thatch of bright red hair. "Are you still nursing Bennett?"

"Not much anymore," Sara said with a sigh. "Is it terrible that I wished he wouldn't stop?"

"Not really. I'll be a wreck when Evie decides she's done. Then again, it'll be nice to drink again."

"Hard to believe my baby sister has a baby. The wild child has been tamed."

Megan grinned. "Don't tell Caleb that."

Sara heard James clomp up the stairs right before he found her and Megan. "Mom, they got the bird out!" He crouched down next to Bennett and began to help his brother race cars across the cabin rug. "Uncle Caleb totally said the f-word, too."

"Oh dear," said Megan, trying to bite back a smile, "I'll have to tell him to behave himself."

James shrugged. "Travis said the b-word last week in class, and he got detention. I told him it was his own fault."

Travis was James's best friend and their former neighbor, and although Sara sometimes wished Travis would get his mouth washed out with soap, she was glad that James had such a good friend to count on. She knew how tough it could be without any friends when you were young.

"Why did Travis call someone the b-word?" asked Megan.

Sara almost tossed a car at her sister's head. Instead, she sent her her most judgmental older sister glare.

"Oh, I can't remember. It wasn't a big deal." James shrugged and made a point not to look at either his mother or his aunt, which raised Sara's suspicions immediately. Although James was in fourth grade now, he rarely kept secrets from Sara.

"Really? Sounds like a big deal to me," said Sara. "Especially if Travis got detention for it. Did he call someone in your class that word? Because that's not nice of him to do, you know."

"I know it's not. *I* didn't say it." James was sulky now as he slowly pushed a car toward Bennett. "I don't know why it's a big deal, that's all," he said again.

Sara decided not to press James despite her intense curiosity. This wasn't the first instance of Travis getting into trouble for saying a bad word, but as far as Sara knew, he'd never called a fellow classmate one. So what had brought that on? Had the two boys gotten into some argument? But wouldn't their teacher have contacted her if that had been the case?

Sara had been working at James's school as one of two third grade teachers until she'd given birth to Bennett. She'd decided to stay home for the foreseeable future, although that didn't mean she didn't still talk with her former coworkers from time to time. If something had happened, Sara knew that Karen, James's teacher, would've told her as much.

Bennett squealed at his older brother's antics, effectively distracting Sara for the time being.

Later that evening, when the kids were asleep and the adults were sitting in the living room together in front of the fire, Sara nestled closer to Harrison and said quietly, "I think something's up with James."

With his good looks, charm, and his fancy medical degree, Harrison Thornton had seemed like the last man who would fall for a girl like Sara, a girl who'd grown up in trailer parks and had gotten a bad reputation in school simply because she'd turned down one of the asshole jocks.

Every time Sara looked at Harrison, she knew how lucky she was that he'd looked past the rumors and seen *her*. And he'd fallen in love with her, just as much as she'd fallen in love with him.

"Really? Like what?" Harrison rubbed her shoulder, keeping his voice as low as hers.

They sat on the couch furthest from the fire. At the moment, Jubilee and Rose were toasting marshmallows over the fire while Heath and Seth supervised. Abby and Mark were talking quietly nearby, while Megan, Caleb, Lizzie, and Trent were debating the merits of real Christmas trees versus artificial ones. Currently, Caleb was arguing for real Christmas trees with perhaps a little too much gusto, Megan looking on with an amused expression on her face.

"I don't know. He wouldn't tell me what happened at school. Travis called someone the b-word—"

"He called someone a bastard? Or a bitch?"

Sara snorted. "You would ask that. I don't know. I didn't ask him to clarify. *Anyway*." She huffed out a breath. "He told me it wasn't a big deal, but if he and Travis fought with some other students..."

"Hmm." Harrison frowned. "I'll ask him about it. Maybe it's not something he wants to talk about with his mom."

A prick of hurt bloomed in Sara's chest, although she'd thought the same thing. Was her little boy so old now that he couldn't talk to his mother? She didn't want to think about such a thing.

Seeing her sad face, Harrison squeezed her shoulder. "I'm sure it's nothing. Like he said, it's not a big deal. Maybe we should take him at his word."

"You're such a guy," was her complaint, which just made Harrison chuckle.

"And you love me for it." Whispering into her ear, he added, "Want to take this party upstairs to our room?"

"I thought you'd never ask."

HARRISON USED to hate the mornings. During medical school, he'd dread hearing his alarm go off in the morning. It wasn't that he didn't enjoy medical school, but he'd never enjoyed getting up early.

Now, though, he loved the mornings the most. This morning in particular made him appreciate them even more.

Next to him, Sara still slept, her shoulder rising and falling with each breath. Her brown hair was spread across her pillow, reminding him of how they'd enjoyed each other just last night. His body heated. Pushing her hair aside, he kissed the nape of her neck, inhaling her sweet scent.

Sara murmured something but only turned over to face him, still asleep. He began to kiss her forehead, then her cheeks and her nose. She finally yawned and opened her eyes with a low groan.

"What time is it? Bennett is probably awake. I should go get him—"

"It's early, and there are ten other adults in this cabin who can entertain him for a bit. Besides, James will let us know when he's awake."

He kissed her, the kiss deepening within moments, and then Harrison was pushing Sara into the soft mattress. It didn't take long for him to strip her out of her clothes and plunge inside her warm depths. Every time he made love to her, it was like coming home. Moving inside her, feeling her tighten around him. The way she said his name, how she moaned and arched. How her body had changed after she'd had Bennett, but it had only made him love her even more, this woman who'd flipped his world upside down and who'd given him not one but two sons to love.

Harrison's eyelids were heavy, and he was about to doze again when a knock sounded on their door. "Breakfast!" Jubilee called. "Get up or starve!"

Harrison groaned. "When did my little sister get so ruthless?"

"When you're the youngest in your family," Sara said wryly, "you have to be pretty ruthless to survive."

After breakfast, the men put on their outdoor gear to find a Christmas tree. The women had been invited—no one could ever say the Thornton men weren't men of the twenty-first century—but when a fiercely cold wind started blowing through, none of them wanted to traipse through the woods.

"Have a good time. And be sure to ask James what's wrong," said Sara, her expression serious.

Harrison had noticed that James seemed distracted lately. This morning, he'd only eaten five pancakes, when he'd been known to eat double that if given half a chance. Sometimes Harrison caught his stepson staring off into space, and then sighing deeply, like the world was resting upon his shoulders.

"Is this legal?" Mark asked as they began to trek through the nearby woods.

"Who's going to know?" countered Caleb with a grin. "Besides, it's just one tree."

"Do any of you even know how to cut down a tree?" asked Heath.

Trent snorted. "If the six of us can't figure out how to cut down one tree, there's no hope for humanity."

Seth grunted a laugh as he dragged a sled behind him with the saw and ropes while Caleb and Trent searched for the best tree. Heath was on duty to make sure Caleb and Trent didn't pick a tree that would be too big to get through the front door. Mark would wander off when he saw interesting wildlife; he had always preferred animals to human company.

Harrison stayed back with James, who scuffed his feet along the ground, his hands in his pockets. Normally, James chattered like a magpie, although as he'd gotten older, he'd begun to shed anything he'd deemed babyish. Showing too much enthusiasm for anything seemed to be the latest thing that only little kids did, not mature fourth graders like James.

"Hey, what about this one?" Caleb called out. The group

conferred, apparently decided it wasn't the best tree, and kept walking.

Harrison pulled his coat tighter as the wind blew harder. He hoped it wouldn't rain while they were out. He didn't really relish the thought of dragging a tree back to the cabin as he was soaked through.

"So, James," Harrison began, "your mother says that Travis got detention for saying a bad word. Want to tell me about it?"

James kicked at a rock. "No."

"Why not?"

"Because I don't want to."

Harrison wavered between annoyance and curiosity. James picked up a stick and began to drag it along the trees as they passed them, the clicking sound countering the sound of the other men arguing over various trees some yards ahead.

"Well, your mom is worried, so I told her I'd talk to you. Did you and Travis get into a fight with somebody?"

"Not really."

"Is that a yes or a no?"

James hunched into his coat, and Harrison could just make out the beginnings of a blush on his cheeks. "We didn't get into a fight," James finally said. "It's complicated."

Harrison had to bite back a chuckle at that pronounce-ment. The last thing he needed to do was make James self-conscious. Putting his hand on James's shoulder, he said, "You know you can talk to me, right? I'm not going to get mad or anything."

"Yeah, I know."

Right then, Trent motioned at Harrison to come over to

the group. Harrison jogged toward them, not the least bit concerned about the damn tree.

Finally, everyone decided this tree was *the* tree, and Harrison made James stand back as Seth began to saw at the trunk. When Seth got tired, Mark took over.

"Timber!" yelled Caleb as the tree listed sideways before falling. The tree itself was maybe seven feet tall, so when it hit the ground, it didn't make the loudest noise imaginable.

Harrison helped tie up the tree before the group made the trip back to the cabin. It was already getting dark despite the early hour. Harrison's breath fogged in front of him.

Worry poked at him as James trudged alongside him. What he'd thought was something innocuous made Harrison concerned something truly serious had happened.

It was time to bring out the big guns.

"If I promise not to tell your mom," Harrison said, "will you tell me what happened?"

James's eyes widened in surprise. "Really?"

Harrison knew that Sara would tan his hide for promising this, but he nodded. *Sometimes you have to play dirty.* "Really."

James narrowed his eyes, but then shrugged. If Harrison got himself into trouble, that was his own problem. Harrison knew that his stepson was a smart cookie no matter his age.

"Travis called Eric the b-word because Eric was making fun of me. He saw me give Sophie a flower the day before."

Who's Sophie? Harrison had to practically bite his tongue in half to keep from asking questions.

"Eric was saying that I was kissing girls under the slide, which is *not* true. I've never kissed any girls. Then Eric and his friends started singing that song. 'James and Sophie sitting in a tree, K-I-S-S-I-N-G."' James frowned, rather ferociously. "Travis told them to stop and then he called Eric a bitch."

Harrison choked. "James, don't say that word," he said, although it was difficult when he was trying not to laugh. He set his hand on James's shoulder. "I'm sorry Eric was making fun of you. That wasn't nice. But who's Sophie?"

A blush climbed up James's cheeks until his face was cherry-red. "A girl," was all he said.

"I figured that. Do you like her?"

James ducked his head. "Yeah. She's nice."

"Did she like it when you gave her a flower?"

"She just laughed and ran away. I don't know." James sighed. "I think I'm in love."

He said it so seriously that Harrison's initial bout of laughter faded. He could understand falling in love with a girl who seemed not to love you back.

Up ahead, Caleb and Mark argued as they crested the hill that led to the cabin. Heath said something that made the group laugh. By the time they got to the house, the argument was forgotten in the midst of jokes as they untied the tree to take it inside.

Harrison hung back with James. "If you like Sophie," he said, "then you should tell her how you feel. The worst that could happen is that she says she doesn't feel the same."

James frowned. "You think so?"

"I do. Being honest is really hard, especially with girls. It's scary. I was terrified to tell your mom how I felt about her."

"Really? Why?"

Harrison thought of how he'd fallen hard and fast for Sara while the world seemed intent on keeping them apart. When Sara had ended things, he'd been afraid he'd never get over his broken heart. Until he'd discovered that his own mother had interfered and had tried to keep them apart. Harrison hadn't wasted a moment in getting Sara back and convincing her that they were meant to be together—no matter what anyone else thought.

"Love is scary because you don't know how it's going to end." Harrison gazed off into the distance. "Maybe the person you love won't love you back. Maybe she'll break your heart. But maybe she feels the same, and it'll be worth it. Love is all about having the courage to act on it."

James stuffed his hands into his pockets. "I guess that makes sense."

Slinging an arm around James, Harrison hugged him close before ruffling his hair. James made a muffled protest.

"I know I'm not your real dad, but I love you just like if you were my own. You know that, right?"

James rolled his eyes. "You're my dad, Dad. Don't be dumb."

The guys were currently trying to figure out how to get the tree through the door without scraping off all of the needles. James ran ahead to watch, leaving Harrison to bite the inside of his cheek to keep the tears at bay.

What was it about kids that tore you up inside? Not just James, but Bennett, too. Sara had given him so much that sometimes it was overwhelming.

After everyone went up to bed that evening, Sara practically pounced on him the second he shut their bedroom door.

"Well?" she demanded, hands on her hips. "Did you talk to James?"

"I did." Harrison began to undress. "But I can't tell you what we talked about."

"What? Why? What happened? I'm his *mother*."

"Everything's fine, I promise. But I told him I wouldn't tell you." Sara looked hurt, and Harrison pulled her into his arms. "Don't be upset, baby. James is growing up, that's all. And I bet you everything he'll tell you on his own."

"I don't believe you, but thanks anyway." She sighed, laying her head on his chest.

He kissed the crown of her head, his hands moving downward until he cupped her ass. "How about I distract you really well tonight?"

That earned him a smile. "Sounds like you have your work cut out for you, Doctor Thornton."

Her throaty voice sent his body into overdrive, and before she could protest, he tossed her over his shoulder and took her to bed to show her just how well he could distract her.

CHAPTER TWO

CALEB & MEGAN

Megan dug around in the box of ornaments before dumping the entire box onto the floor, much to Bea and Evie's glee. Bea, Lizzie and Trent's toddler, squealed with delight and reached for a glass ornament.

"Oh no, don't take that one. Don't cry. Here's your stuffed dog."

Bea wasn't interested in being dissuaded. Lizzie, currently hanging ornaments on the tree the guys had finally gotten inside, laughed.

"What did you do? Bea-Bea, you don't need that ornament." Lizzie picked up her daughter and placed her on her hip, distracting Bea with some twinkly lights. Bea stopped crying within a few moments.

Megan blew out a breath. At the moment, she, Lizzie, and Trent helped decorate the tree. The rest of the crew was either helping with dinner or hiding in their rooms.

Evie sat on her boppy pillow, watching the proceedings

with her wide blue eyes. She giggled when Trent dropped an ornament that rolled next to her foot.

"What's happening in here?" Caleb scooped up Evie and gave her loud smacking kiss on the cheek. "Trent, that dog ornament is crooked."

"If you care so much, how about you help us?" Trent countered.

"Nah. I found the tree." He sat down next to Megan on the floor with Evie. "It's a good tree, isn't it?"

"Oh, it's amazing. The best tree in existence. Thank God you found it."

Caleb hooked an arm around her waist and gave her a kiss louder than the one he'd given Evie. Megan laughed, pushing him away halfheartedly.

"Your daddy is very silly," she said to Evie. "Don't listen to him."

Watching Caleb with Evie never failed to fill Megan with joy. The second Evie had been placed in his arms, Caleb had embraced fatherhood without reservation. He'd changed diapers, gotten up in the middle of the night to soothe Evie back to sleep, dressed her, bathed her. If he could've nursed her, he probably would have, Megan had thought wryly.

Megan loved motherhood, but one thing she didn't like? The fact that she and Caleb had made love a grand total of three times since Evie's birth.

At first, Megan hadn't wanted to have sex, and Caleb hadn't pushed her. Once she'd recovered, though, the demands of caring for an infant, plus their jobs, meant that sex was too often an afterthought. Either Megan was too tired or Caleb had to do a late-night shift at the police station, and by the time they were even in the same vicinity, both just wanted to sleep before Evie woke up and demanded the rest of their energy.

When Harrison had first come up with this Christmas-in-the-woods scheme, Megan knew it was her chance to get into her husband's pants. Last night, she'd put on her nicest lingerie and had stayed up in their bedroom waiting for him...only to fall asleep before he came to bed.

I need to come up with a plan, because I'm not leaving this place without getting at least one orgasm in the bargain.

"Let's get the star to put on top," said Lizzie. "Caleb, you're the tallest. Come on, be useful."

"I'm always useful." He handed Evie to Megan.

"No, it's not straight. Put it on that branch that's sticking up."

Lizzie instructed Caleb as he sent her exasperated looks. As a younger sister herself, Megan knew all too well how easy it was to annoy your older siblings. Trent, with Bea on his hip now, just looked amused and wisely kept his mouth shut.

Seeing Caleb now, Megan felt desire stirring inside her. It didn't help that his jeans outlined his firm ass, or that his hair was a bit longer than usual and curled near his collar. He laughed when Lizzie growled at him, and the sound made Megan bite the inside of her cheek to keep from shivering.

She'd put Evie to bed after dinner. After that? She'd corner Caleb by the woodpile if she had to.

When Caleb looked over his shoulder and winked at her, she knew he wanted to enjoy her as much as she wanted to enjoy him. She gave him a seductive smile, and he got so distracted that Lizzie had to pull on his arm to get him to pay attention again.

Megan first cornered him in the kitchen. After putting

Evie down for her afternoon nap, Megan heard Caleb's voice and followed it to the source, only to find him the only person in the kitchen.

Would she really get lucky the first time? Maybe she would get a Christmas miracle early.

"Who were you talking to?"

Caleb grinned before taking a large bite of his sandwich. "I always talk while making a sandwich."

"Why? Does it need moral support before you eat it? And where is everybody anyway?"

"Outside, I think. I think a few wanted to go for a hike."

"And you decided it was time to eat another lunch."

He grinned. "You know me so well."

Sidling closer, she fluttered her eyelashes, but to her consternation, he was too intent on finishing his sandwich. *This is not getting off to a great start,* she thought sourly.

She poked him in the chest. "Caleb."

"What?"

He swallowed and was about to take another bite when she snagged the sandwich from him and set it on the counter.

"Hey, I was eating that—"

She kissed him, only to jump away like she'd been scalded when she realized he'd been eating something with horse-radish. She *hated* horseradish.

He laughed. "Sorry, babe."

Megan wasn't about to give up yet. Taking him by the arm, she pulled him into the nearby pantry and shut the door. Caleb, not being stupid, didn't need her to explain what she was doing.

She trailed a hand down his torso until she reached his

belt buckle. "I've missed you, Caleb," she said, her voice husky. "Haven't you missed me?"

When she cupped his quickly hardening erection, he groaned. "Baby, I always miss you, but everybody and their dog has been around today—"

"Since when do you make excuses not to have sex?"

"Since you gave birth to our nine-pound, five-ounce daughter and needed time to recover."

She paused. Had he avoided her because he thought she was still healing? She'd told him she was recovered, but perhaps he hadn't believed her. Her heart flipping over in her chest, she gave him a sultry smile.

"I am totally, completely," she said as she began to unzip his jeans, "recovered, and if you don't make love to me in this pantry right now, I think I might die."

He leaned down to kiss her, but she laughed and pushed his face away. "No kissing. There's no time." She stroked his cock.

Caleb groaned, more loudly this time, and she shushed him with a giggle. Swiping her thumb over the tip, she watched him in the dim light, loving the way the tendons in his neck stood out as he tried to keep himself quiet.

"Do you want everyone to come running?" She squeezed him just to see his face contort.

"Someone's going to be *coming*." Turning her so she faced away from him, he kissed the side of her neck as he pushed her sweater up her back. "God, I've missed you. When you kept saying you were too tired—"

She tipped her head back to gaze into his eyes. "You said the same thing. We have both been pretty tired."

His lips twisted into a wry grin. "How did we end up becoming so boring? Remember when I arrested you?"

"I should've brought handcuffs."

That earned her a smack on the ass. When Caleb unbuttoned her jeans and pushed them down her hips, something clattered on the counter out in the kitchen. They both stilled, waiting.

And then Mark opened the pantry door, stared at them—with their pants undone and their faces flushed—and he just rolled his eyes.

"You better get out of here. The rest of the crew will be here in a minute," was all Mark said.

Megan was fairly certain he smiled as he shut the door, but with Mark, you could never be sure.

THE REST of the day was a series of near misses: Caleb pulled Megan into the bathroom, only to forget to lock the door and for James to open the door and catch them. That time, no clothes had come off, and for that, Megan had said a fervent prayer of thanks.

After dinner, she pounced on Caleb when he went out to get some firewood. He sat her on top of the woodpile—only for it to go tumbling to the ground, Megan with it.

"Maybe we should just wait until it's time to go to bed," said Caleb with a laugh as he helped brush the dirt off of Megan. "Like normal people."

"Tonight we're wrapping presents after the kids go to bed, and then Jubilee is going to make her spiked eggnog."

"Then we'll just not drink it, like we usually do."

She chewed on her lip. "We could sneak out early."

"That's the spirit." He patted her ass and grinned. "If we aren't banging like rabbits in a few hours, I'll be a monkey's uncle."

Despite Caleb's assurances otherwise, they did not, in fact, end up banging like rabbits. Evie wouldn't go to sleep, and Megan realized she had a tooth coming in that made her especially fussy. Caleb took over when Megan was at her wit's end, and by the time they were both in bed, they were too tired to do so much as kiss each other on the cheek.

The next few days—and nights—were taken up with activities and dealing with Evie. By Saturday, both Caleb and Megan were determined to get into each other's pants (as Caleb put it), even if everyone and their dog interrupted them.

"Meet me in the woods near the birdhouse at ten o'clock," Megan whispered in Caleb's ear that morning before having to go help with breakfast.

At ten, Megan was waiting for Caleb to show, praying someone hadn't asked him to do some chore or another. By ten after ten, she was afraid he wouldn't show when hands grabbed her from behind.

She yelped and whirled as Caleb burst out laughing. "You scared the crap out of me!" she complained, slapping him on the chest. "I thought you might not come."

He waggled his eyebrows. "And miss the chance to ravish my wife against a pine tree?"

The laughter died between them, and it was only a millisecond later that they were kissing like mad, hands coasting all over each other. Megan tangled her fingers in

Caleb's hair, rubbing against him like a cat in heat. God, she needed him. She'd waited way too damn long for this.

"Pants. Off. Now." Caleb unbuttoned his jeans while Megan did the same, although her hands were shaking so much it seemed to take forever.

He pushed her up against a nearby tree, the bark digging into her back. She couldn't even care at that point, she was so ravenous for him. With his dark hair falling across his forehead, his green eyes gleaming, he made her heart pound like mad every time she looked at him.

Caleb kneeled down and pulled her jeans down to her ankles along with her panties. The bite of the wind only heightened the sensations, although being surrounded by trees helped keep the worst of the wind at bay. It helped that Caleb's hands were hot on her skin, and when he kissed her sex and licked through her folds, all she could feel was him.

He licked her as she gripped him by his hair. She undulated against his tongue, gasping and moaning. Her release built at record speed until she came so hard the tree shook behind her. Caleb gave one last kiss to her core before he stood up and thrust inside her.

They both groaned. The sound echoed through the trees, and as Caleb thrust, the tree shook and rained down pine needles.

Megan couldn't help it: she started laughing, which then turned into a moan, but it was also still a bit of a laugh. Because she was *finally* making love with her husband who she adored, and God Almighty, why had they waited this long to get back into the groove?

"God, I love you," groaned Caleb as his rhythm got more jagged. "Even if you're laughing at me."

"I'm not laughing at you, I'm laughing at our circumstances—" Her last word trailed away as Caleb hit a spot inside her that sent her body into overdrive.

Panting, she clung to him. Her second orgasm burst upon her right as Caleb came. He kissed her wildly, and she shivered as she felt him fill her with his heat.

A long moment later, Megan groaned, but for an entirely different reason. Her back was sore, and when Caleb lifted up her shirt, he laughed and swore at the same time.

"Is it that bad?" she asked, trying to peer over her shoulder.

"No, the scratches are light, but if you go around wearing a tank top, everybody is going to know what we were doing." He kissed between her shoulder blades.

She sighed. "I guess that's the price I'll have to pay." Twining her arms around his neck, she kissed him, not caring in the least that her back was all scratched up.

When she heard someone tromping through the woods toward them, she said, "Well, they've found our hiding place. Where should we meet up next?"

Caleb's smile was slow and wide. "Hot tub. Midnight. Be there or be square."

"Oh, I'll be there. I need to make your back look like mine, so we're even."

CHAPTER THREE

Mark & Abby

Abby picked up a fast-moving Bea before she could get too close to the fireplace that had just been lit. Bea wiggled and pointed, saying something that sounded like "daddy" over and over again.

"Your daddy is upstairs," Abby said as she carried Bea away from the fire. It was the evening of the third day after everyone had arrived at the cabin, and Abby had been enjoying a brief quiet moment before Bea had run into the room.

The toddler babbled as Abby sat her on the floor and started playing with the stuffed animals scattered on the rug. She wondered where Lizzie and Trent were; it wasn't like them to take their eyes off Bea. Then again, Bea was so fast that they might not have noticed her absence yet.

"There you are!" Lizzie took a deep breath as she crouched next to her daughter. "One second she was there, and the next she'd run off. You're going to give me a heart attack."

Abby decided she wouldn't mention the bit about Bea getting close to the fireplace. No reason to upset Lizzie further.

As an ER nurse, Abby had worked with all kinds of children—and adults. You never knew who would show up in the emergency room on any given day or night. Abby had always enjoyed the babies, though, although she'd never love to see anyone in distress, especially infants and toddlers.

Bea giggled as Lizzie kissed her cheek. Abby's heart twisted in her chest as she watched them. She'd known coming on this trip would bring up feelings she thought she'd dealt with. She'd told herself to swallow the feelings of envy and sadness, but when you were surrounded by your nieces and nephews, it was next to impossible to keep those feelings in check.

Abby had known for some time that she couldn't have children. Or at the very least, it would be difficult to conceive. When she and Mark had first married, she'd told herself she was content that it was just the two of them. They had their horses and cats and all kinds of animals on Mark's ranch. And in the beginning, it had been more than enough.

Except lately, Abby had wanted a baby of her own more and more. It wasn't simply proximity to babies, although she knew that played a part in it. She'd dream of being pregnant, of holding a baby of her own—a baby equals parts her own and Mark's. Sometimes the need felt all-consuming. She'd always dismissed the idea of having a biological clock. Now, she felt it ticking louder and louder.

"Bea likes to run away from us lately," Lizzie was saying.

"I think she does it because she knows it'll freak us out. Do you think it would be super weird to get a baby leash?"

When Abby didn't respond, Lizzie touched her arm. "Abby, did you hear me?"

Abby forced herself to shake off her melancholy mood. *It's Christmas. I can't be moping around on Christmas.* "Sorry, I was thinking about dinner tonight. What were you saying?"

Eventually the living room filled with people, especially since the weather outside was currently rainy and windy. The babies were almost as loud as the adults.

Arms wrapped around Abby before a low voice said, "Having fun?"

She leaned back into Mark's embrace, closing her eyes. Out of anyone in the world, he was the one person who could shake her of this sadness. Or at the very least, distract her long enough for her to forget.

"Has your family always been this loud?" she mused.

Mark snorted. "It's worse now that everyone is paired up."

Jubilee stole a cookie from Heath's plate, which made Heath chase her about the room until he caught her and hauled her over his shoulder. Harrison said something that sounded like, "Don't drop her!" while Caleb yelled, "Shouldn't steal a man's cookies."

As an only child, Abby had had to get used to how boisterous the Thorntons were when she'd attended her first Thornton get-together. Add to that that Mark was easily the quietest of the siblings, and it had been quite enlightening to meet everyone at once.

She and Mark stood some feet away near one of the windows, out of earshot of the rest of the group. Mark turned so they faced each other, although Abby found herself gazing out into the woods, watching the rain patter against the glass.

"You've been quiet today. Did something happen?"

She forced herself to smile. "Besides the usual family shenanigans? No." At Mark's skeptical expression, she patted his chest. "I'm fine. I'm glad we came, although I can tell you're itching to get away already."

That made him smile. "How can you tell? I love my family, but God Almighty, they're *loud*."

Right then, Megan laughed and Rose shouted, and then everyone seemed to be yelling and laughing at the same time.

"I don't believe you, you know." Mark touched her nose. "But you can tell me later what's bothering you."

To Abby's immense gratitude, Lizzie chose that moment to interrupt them both to play charades. Mark balked, but Abby pulled him into the group. Sometimes her husband needed a push to get out of his comfort zone. He usually thanked her for it later—usually.

Mark grudgingly marched into the middle of the living room to play. Abby struggled to keep from laughing: he looked like he'd rather endure the rack than play charades.

Abby sat next to Sara, who had Bennett in her lap. Bennett, being curious and busy, soon climbed from his mother's lap into Abby's without batting an eyelash. When Sara tried to get Bennett to return to her, Abby just shook her head.

Mark held up two fingers before miming what looked like drinking as his team shouted guesses. On the other team, Abby found her attention wandering, especially as Bennett turned to face her and began to babble baby talk. He was a pretty child, with his dark hair and brown eyes. Pudgy and darling, he began to fiddle with Abby's necklace before trying to eat it.

"No, don't eat that. You wouldn't like it." Abby took off her necklace and set it on the table next to her. Bennett's lip trembled, but to her relief, he didn't start sobbing. It helped that there were plenty of other things for him to fiddle with: the buttons on Abby's blouse or strands of her hair. She winced when he pulled her hair hard, disentangling his fingers before he could do serious damage.

Her heart did that little squeeze it always did when she was close to a baby lately. Like with Bea, Abby tried to push the feelings away, but this time, she couldn't. Bennett seemed determined to make her really see what she wanted—and, in a way, accept that she wouldn't have it.

Oh, they could adopt, and Abby had been seriously considering it. But neither she nor Mark had a lot of extra money to put toward an adoption at this time. They couldn't ask his parents for money, even if they were willing to help. Having Lisa Thornton interfering with their finances sounded like the worst kind of hell.

Bennett babbled, plucking at her shirt, and Abby moved him so he faced away from her. She leaned down and inhaled his sweet baby scent, his hair silky soft. He was so warm that she was glad she wasn't sitting any closer to the fire.

"You and Mark will make great parents," Sara whispered.

Abby's eyes widened. "Oh no—"

"I can tell when people have that gleam in their eye. When they want to have children." She smiled before taking Bennett from Abby's arms. "And this one probably needs a diaper change. Mm, yep, I was right."

Sara hurried away before Abby could—what? Explain that

she couldn't have children? She didn't want Sara to feel guilty for saying anything, as it was hardly public knowledge that Abby's body wasn't made for having children. She swallowed against the lump in her throat.

Right then, Mark mimed something else, looking completely exasperated, when finally Caleb yelled out, "Vineyard!"

"Finally," Mark muttered. "Took you long enough."

Abby felt perilously close to tears, but she refused to break down in the middle of a family game of charades. Getting up, she got upstairs to her and Mark's bedroom and shut the door, tears leaking from her eyes. She slapped a hand over her mouth to contain the sob wanting to burst through.

She let herself shed a few tears before wiping her eyes. Glancing in the mirror to make sure she didn't look like a total mess, she returned to the games downstairs before anyone had noticed she was gone.

Christmas Eve meant stuffing stockings. Everyone agreed that instead of buying gifts for everyone else, they'd only buy gifts for their significant others. "Considering we're all covered on that," Megan had said, "I don't think anyone will be too upset."

That didn't mean everyone didn't contribute to the kids' stockings and gifts, though. Sitting in front of the tree with the rest of the adults after the kids had gone to bed, Abby couldn't imagine the chaos tomorrow morning when the kids woke up. Good thing only James was old enough to really care.

Mark had bought James a cowboy hat to wear when he

visited the ranch. He'd begged Sara to let him have horseback-riding lessons, and she'd finally agreed that he could start in the spring.

Abby had bought the gifts for the babies, although Mark had asked her at least three times if she was okay with that. Was it strange that she'd wanted to buy the toys, the clothes, the tiny items? She didn't even know anymore. Maybe for a moment she could imagine she was buying those things for their baby, not someone else's.

"Can you hand me the scissors?" Rose asked as she wrapped ribbon around a box.

Abby handed over the scissors. "Is that Seth's present?"

"Yep." She leaned closer so Seth wouldn't hear. "He's going to flip out."

Callie, who was sitting next to Rose, woofed quietly as if in agreement.

"What did you get Mark?"

Abby smiled wryly. "Socks."

"Wait, really?"

"That's what he insisted that he wanted." Abby rolled her eyes. "Why did I marry him again?"

"These Thornton men, you know." Rose winked. "Sometimes I wonder if we're all just crazy for putting up with them in the first place."

Abby caught Mark's gaze, and she saw his eyes heat with desire. Feeling her cheeks flush, she resumed wrapping gifts, although if her current wrapping job was any indication of her distracted state, she would never admit to it.

Later that evening, she went upstairs to take a bath. Jubilee stopped her in the hall to ask, "Sorry to bug you, but do you have any extra tampons? I didn't bring enough."

As Abby got out her bag of supplies, she realized she hadn't had her period last month and she had yet to get it this month. Since she had PCOS, a condition that messed with her hormones and often resulted in irregular periods, she hadn't thought anything about it. But she'd never gone *this* long without some kind of period. She'd gone off birth control within the last year, mostly because she knew she didn't need it to prevent a pregnancy anyway.

She handed Jubilee some tampons and promptly locked herself in the bathroom to calm her pounding heart.

It was too soon to know. More than likely, her period was just extra late. She shouldn't get her hopes up. And yet...

Oh God, where's a pregnancy test when you need one?

She couldn't help but go into nurse mode right then, asking herself about any other possible symptoms. She hadn't felt sick to her stomach, but were her breasts tender? They'd been a little sore lately, but she'd attributed that to Mark enjoying her assets a little more vigorously than usual. She hadn't been extra tired, per se, but then again, she'd taken a nap yesterday and the day before. She'd attributed both simply to being drained from being around so many people in the cabin.

When Abby climbed into bed beside Mark, she was so preoccupied that she jumped a little when he touched her arm.

"Whoa, I didn't mean to scare you." He peered more closely at her. "What is it?"

She hadn't intended to tell him like this. She didn't even technically have anything to tell him in the first place. But then the words tumbled out, and she found she didn't regret saying them aloud. "I think I might be pregnant."

Mark stared at her, his expression completely blank. She was about to repeat herself, thinking he hadn't heard her, when he finally said, "How?"

"I mean, I'm not sure. I haven't gotten my period for two months, and that's rare, even for me. Do you think any of the girls brought a pregnancy test? Why am I asking *you* that?" She laughed, a little hysterically, vacillating between excitement and dread.

"Abby," Mark said, "what are you talking about?"

She twisted the edge of the bedsheet. "I mean, I think I might be pregnant. I don't know for sure. I won't know until we get back. Unless you want to drive an hour to the general store we passed?"

Mark took a deep breath. He ran his fingers through his hair, and for the first time in a long time, she realized he was well and truly stunned.

"I know we haven't talked about kids beyond the fact that I thought I couldn't have any. If you're not happy about this—"

"Abby. Jesus, am I happy about this?" He shook his head. "Everything about you is a miracle."

She laughed, giddy, and he kissed her with a love that she felt equally. When he placed his hand on her belly, she prayed that she was right. She prayed that even if she weren't right, she could give this amazing, kind, loving man a child someday. Mark would be a wonderful father, just like he was a wonderful husband.

"I don't want to get our hopes up. I'll probably get my period in the morning and this will have been just a brief little blip." She felt tears prick her eyes. "But I want a baby, Mark. I do."

"I know you do. I've seen how you've looked at the babies. I hated the thought I couldn't give you that." He kissed her forehead and wrapped her in his arms. "No matter what happens, I love you. And we'll have a baby, somehow, someday."

~

THE NEXT MORNING, Abby awoke to find Mark already gone. Frowning, she touched his side of the bed. It was already cold, so he must've left hours ago. Considering it was all of eight o'clock right now, she wondered why he'd get up so early on Christmas Day.

When she couldn't find him anywhere after going downstairs, she began to worry. She sent him a quick text, which he replied to within moments. *Be there soon.*

By the time he arrived, the kids had already unwrapped all of their presents and the adults were starting on theirs. Mark came into the living room, looking harried but exultant.

"Abby, I need to talk to you."

Abby followed him upstairs, not even realizing she'd followed him into the bathroom until he shut the door behind her.

"Nothing was open. That's why it took me so long." He handed her a plastic bag. "But I found a place, finally. Pretty sure the owners don't celebrate Christmas."

Abby peered inside the bag. "You bought me a pregnancy test?"

"Go on. Let's find out if this is happening or not."

Opening the box, Abby still felt a bit like she was in some kind of surreal dream. But seeing her husband watching her, looking like he was about burst out of his skin with anticipation, brought her back to earth. "I love you, Mark," she said wryly, "but not enough to let you watch me pee on a pregnancy stick. Shoo."

Flushing slightly, he muttered under his breath as she pushed him out of the bathroom. Then she got down to business. She knew very well that you had to wait a few minutes for these tests to give you results, but waiting those three minutes was pure torture.

Needing moral support, she let Mark come back inside the bathroom. And then they waited.

When the two pink lines showed up, Abby almost thought it was a joke.

"Is that…?" breathed Mark.

She stared at those two lines—those two blessed, blessed lines—and started laughing. "Yes. Oh my God. I'm pregnant."

Mark whooped so loudly that Abby was sure the crowd downstairs heard him. Someone knocked on the bathroom door, and Mark opened it to yell in Seth's face, "We're having a baby!"

They didn't wait for Seth to react. When they got downstairs, Mark—normally staid, reserved Mark—yelled, "We're pregnant!"

The family stopped talking. Even the babies seemed surprised. Then, they erupted into congratulations.

Abby hugged and was hugged by everyone, no one the least bit annoyed at the interruption of their Christmas Day festivities.

CHAPTER FOUR

Lizzie & Trent

Lizzie, unlike her husband Trent, enjoyed being around lots of people. Considering she felt the most alive on stage, it stood to reason that she found the energy of a lot of people invigorating.

When Harrison had proposed this plan of the entire family staying in a cabin for Christmas, Lizzie had jumped at the chance. What could be more exciting than spending Christmas with her crazy family? Then again, after getting married and having her daughter, there was little that could ruffle Lizzie. An almost-two-year-old tended to reset your priorities and make you rethink what was really worth getting frazzled over.

Trent hadn't been as enthused by the idea of spending Christmas with her family. He'd made amends with them—especially Lizzie's twin brother, Seth—and Trent even considered her brothers friends.

"That doesn't mean I want to stay in a cabin with them," he'd said wryly. "Your family is—"

"Loud? Fun? Interesting?"

"A lot."

Lizzie found Trent outside on the porch with Bea on his lap. He'd wrapped a big blanket around them both, although today wasn't as cold as the previous days had been.

"There you are. Are you hiding again?" Lizzie sat down next to them. Bea babbled and reached for Lizzie, and Lizzie picked her up and snuggled her under her chin. When had her baby gotten so big? Soon she'd be talking in full sentences, going to school, leaving for college...

Trent handed her the blanket. "I'm not hiding. I'm taking a breather. Caleb wanted to hang Christmas lights all over the house, and then he and Harrison started arguing about how they should do it." Trent rolled his eyes. "Remind me never to get between those two."

"Like your family isn't as crazy."

Considering Trent had four siblings of his own, he didn't get to criticize Lizzie's.

Trent grinned. "True. Then again, we aren't deluded enough to all go to a cabin in the woods to spend Christmas together."

"Could you even get Phin or Lucy to come? I've seen them both three times total and we've been married for two years."

"Phin is busy. So is Lucy."

Lizzie brushed her fingers through Bea's curls. "Busy...or do they just not like me?"

She'd never voiced her fears that Trent's family still didn't like her. Considering their history, she couldn't blame them.

She'd hurt Trent when she'd ended things between them over a decade ago after she'd had a miscarriage.

"What are you talking about? They don't hate you." Trent shook his head and forced her look at him. "They were too young to know what was going on between us then. And Phin isn't good with people anyway."

"Isn't he a lawyer?"

"Exactly."

Lizzie laughed, which made Bea laugh, and she felt her fears calm somewhat. She knew how important it was to be close to your family, and the last thing she wanted was to create a wedge between Trent and his siblings. Especially since they'd already lost both of their parents, so sticking together was even more important.

Lizzie's phone rang, and when she glanced at the caller ID, she put her phone on silent without answering. Trent raised an eyebrow at her.

"Just a spam call," she lied. It had, in fact, been her producer, Terry. Lizzie had released her latest album in the fall, and since it had sold so well, Terry was pressuring her to go on tour. Except Lizzie couldn't bear to leave Bea or Trent behind. She'd considered taking Bea with her, but how could she separate her from Trent?

And Trent had his restaurants to oversee, so having him come too was out of the question. Lizzie had dodged Terry for two weeks now. She'd thought that since it was almost Christmas, he'd be too busy to bug her. She should've known better.

Why don't I just tell Terry no? She wasn't sure why she hadn't yet. Maybe it was because part of her really wanted to go on tour again. It had been so long since she'd performed for multiple audiences over the course of a month. Meeting fans, seeing new cities. She itched to get out of Fair Haven, which also scared her. Would she end up running away again like she had all those years ago? It seemed ridiculous, yet the fear remained each time she thought about Terry wanting her to tour.

Bea wiggled, wanting to get down. "No, it's too cold," Lizzie said. "You didn't put a coat on her?"

Trent shrugged. "She was sitting with me, and it's not that cold out. And you know she hates getting bundled up."

"Trent, she doesn't even have shoes or socks on."

"Well, she had socks on earlier. She must've taken them off." He narrowed his eyes at her. "What's gotten you so pissy?"

"I'm not pissy. And don't swear around Bea. I'm just worried about her getting cold."

"We can always go inside."

"No, not if you don't want to. I can go get her shoes. It's fine."

Lizzie didn't know why she sounded so irritable, but she pushed the thought aside as she went to get Bea's things. *I need a drink. Or five.*

Her stress level only increased when Terry called her a second time and left her a message that was only "Call me back" and nothing else. Lizzie was rather tempted to toss her phone into the nearest lake and tell Terry after the New Year that was why she hadn't gotten back to him.

That evening, things only got worse. Bea was cranky and fussy, probably because of too much activity, and by the time it was dinner, she was crying and refusing to eat. She tossed her food onto the floor, which Callie the dog enjoyed way too much. Her cries got louder and louder until they were ear-piercing. Her head aching, Lizzie picked up the screaming toddler and took her upstairs, her own dinner left to grow cold.

Bea screeched like a banshee, crying so hard that her face was red and her cheeks splotchy with tears. Lizzie should've insisted on Bea's nap this afternoon, but Bea hadn't wanted to nap and Lizzie hadn't wanted to fight her.

Lizzie made soothing noises, rubbing Bea's back, before turning on some quiet music. She walked the length of the room with Bea. Her cries quieted somewhat, but she still refused to fall asleep.

"Want me to take her?" Trent touched Lizzie's shoulder.

Lizzie handed Bea over, and to her consternation and relief, the toddler stopped crying completely. Trent bounced her like he would do when she was just a tiny baby. "There's nothing to cry about," he murmured. "You're just mad. Why is Bea-Bea so mad? You didn't eat any dinner, either."

It was stupid and petty, but Lizzie couldn't help but feel hurt that Trent could calm Bea and not her. And here she was, wanting to get out of Fair Haven and tour. Was she really so selfish? Her gut twisted, and she wasn't sure if she was madder at Trent or at herself.

"I can put her to bed. Do you want to go back down and finish eating?" he asked.

She wasn't hungry, but she nodded anyway. Kissing Bea on the cheek, she wandered downstairs, only to find everyone already in the living room and dinner over.

"I saved your plate," said Jubilee when Lizzie went into the kitchen. "It's in the microwave."

Lizzie almost wanted to tell her she shouldn't have bothered. Morose, she heated up her food and picked at it, only to throw out most of it when no one was looking.

When Trent came back down and sat next to her, putting his arm around her, she flinched. It was a tiny thing, but enough that he noticed.

"Hey, what is it? Bea went to sleep, if you're worried. I think she just had too much fun today."

She forced herself to smile. "I know. Thanks for putting her to bed. She wouldn't stop crying for me."

"And now you're beating yourself up about it." She looked away, because he was right. "Don't, Lizzie. God knows Bea has done the same to me. She's not even two. There's no logic to it."

Lizzie settled against him, inhaling his scent. She and Trent had fallen for each other in high school, but they'd been too afraid and messed up to get together until two and a half years ago. When Lizzie had accidentally gotten pregnant with Bea, it had become the fresh start they'd needed.

"Eggnog?" Abby handed Lizzie and Trent two mugs. "Be careful, though. I saw Caleb put in a decent amount of rum."

Just what I needed, thought Lizzie. She drank one mug and then a second one until her worries faded—at least for the moment.

TRENT KNEW when his wife was hiding something from him. He'd never tell her as much, but she was a terrible actress. She tended to get quiet when something was wrong (a big red flag), and then she'd avoid him (another red flag). The two combined were basically a sign screaming, SOMETHING IS WRONG!

Now he just had to figure out how to get her to tell him what it was.

After two years of marriage and having known Lizzie for over a dozen years, he knew well enough that pushing Lizzie to talk meant she'd shut him out. It was rather akin to sticking your hand in a bear trap: one second everything was fine, the next you had metaphorical teeth sunk into your wrist.

At breakfast that morning, the adults were preoccupied with eating when James burst into the room. "It's snowing!" he practically screeched. "It's snowing!"

Snow certainly wasn't unheard of in the Puget Sound, especially at higher elevations. Trent went to the nearest window to see fat wet flakes of snow slowly falling to the ground.

He doubted it would stick, but he wasn't about to tell James that.

Soon everyone was outside as the snow fell harder, covering the trees and ground with white. "I didn't think it was cold enough to stick," said Trent as Lizzie started making a snowman with Bea. "Did you know it would snow?"

"No. The weather app didn't say anything." Lizzie began scrounging for enough snow to pack into balls, Bea digging around in the snow until she reached the muddy ground, giggling the entire time.

James came to help them with the snowman while Caleb started a snowball fight. Suddenly it became a girls-versus-boys snowball fight, Jubilee grabbing at Lizzie to come play.

"James can watch Bea. Can't you, James? We'll be right here anyway."

Lizzie laughed, but to Trent's ears, it sounded hollow. Trying to get into the mood, Trent packed a snowball and, when her back was turned, hit Lizzie between her shoulders.

She whirled, glaring. Finally, a light came into her eyes. Game on.

He grinned as she threw a snowball at him but missed. Yelling, she chased after him, but not before he hit her almost square in the face with one. She sputtered and swore.

"It's okay," he jibed, "we all know you have terrible aim."

"Oh, really? You really want to be talking smack when I'm making the biggest snowball ever?"

"You'll never hit me with something that big."

"It's on, Younger. You better run."

Trent had longer legs, but he had to admit that when she wanted to win, his wife was fast. They ran into the woods, Lizzie gaining ground despite Trent's best efforts. He leaped over a log, only to catch the side of his arm on a branch. He swore. He stopped to make sure he wasn't bleeding, only to realize that he no longer heard Lizzie running after him.

He turned the second Lizzie sneaked up on him and threw the snowball straight onto this head. Snow enveloped him, and he sputtered when the stuff got into his eyes and nose and mouth. Lizzie guffawed. Until Trent tackled her to the ground and held her wrists down despite her best attempts to wiggle free.

"You have snow all over you," she giggled, her cheeks flushed. "You look like the abominable snowman."

"And you look like somebody who's going to get her come-uppance for that prank."

"Do your worst. I'm ready."

He kissed her, tasting both her and melted snow, and

before long they were kissing so deeply that Trent completely lost track of time. He'd missed this, this closeness. Hadn't they gone on this trip to take a break from the real world? Except that the real world had followed them here anyway.

Lizzie tried to wiggle free again. "You're going to have to let me up eventually," she complained.

"Not until you tell me what's wrong."

At that, her expression shuttered. She pushed at his chest, and he let her go reluctantly.

"We should get back."

"Lizzie—"

"Nothing's wrong. I don't know why you'd think there was."

"Bullshit." He stepped in front of her. "Why are you keeping something from me? Didn't we vow to tell each other the truth?"

"I'm not lying to you!" Her mouth twisted. "I just haven't told you some pertinent details."

"Are you going to tell me or am I going to have to force it out of you?"

She rolled her eyes. "The macho thing does not work for you, husband. Fine, you want to know?"

She blew out a breath. The light breeze played with the dark strands of her hair, her cheeks flushed and her lips a bright red from kissing. In that moment, Trent couldn't help but feel like she was the most beautiful woman in existence.

"Terry has been bugging me nonstop because he wants me to go on tour. And I want to go."

"I don't understand."

"I can't go, though. I can't leave Bea behind, or leave you behind. Or worse, take Bea and separate you two." It was as if she hadn't even heard him. "I'm a terrible mother, because sometimes I want to get out of Fair Haven and see the world again. I want to get on stage and sing in front of an audience, not just be a mother or a wife. So no, I didn't tell you, because it was my burden to bear. And I'm over it. I'm going to tell Terry it's not going to happen."

"Why can't it happen? If it's because of me and Bea, then we'll go with you." The idea sounded insane, but when he spoke it aloud, it didn't seem quite so crazy.

"You can't come with me. You have your restaurants. Your family."

"Lizzie." He embraced her, and it only took a moment for her to melt against him. "You're my family. You and Bea. Yes, I love my siblings, just like you love yours, but that doesn't mean I need to stay in Fair Haven to look after them." He grinned. "I think Ash would be offended if he thought I needed to look after him."

"But the restaurants. They're doing so well, leaving—"

"For one, I could work remotely. Secondly, I have three awesome managers to assist in the day-to-day."

"And Bea?"

"She's a baby. She doesn't care where she goes as long as it's with us."

Lizzie blinked and shook her head. "I don't see how this will work."

"Maybe it won't, but isn't it worth a shot?" He tipped her chin up. "Music makes you happy. I've seen that. Wanting to continue that part of your life doesn't make you a bad wife or mother. If anything, I'd be worried if you didn't care about music anymore."

Her chin wobbled. "I don't deserve you."

"Now you're just being stupid."

She laughed before moaning. "God, now I'm getting excited." Her eyes began to sparkle, and Trent could see her mind whirling with plans. "How do you feel about going to Europe? France, Germany, Spain, Italy—"

"I was thinking Spokane. Maybe Boise?"

"Shut up." But her smile belied her words, and by the time they got back to the cabin, Lizzie had returned to her old self again.

The snowball fight having concluded, a few adults had stayed outside to finish the snowman. Bea squealed *Mommy!* when she saw Lizzie.

She swung Bea into her arms and gave her a loud, smacking kiss. "What do you think about going to Italy?" she asked.

"You're going to Italy?" asked Seth, who was adding pebbles to the snowman's torso as buttons. "Since when?"

"Ask Bea. She's the one making the itinerary."

Seth sent Trent a confused look. Trent just shrugged and wrapped an arm around his wife and daughter, kissing both.

CHAPTER FIVE

Seth & Rose

Rose had never thought of herself as the marrying type. Considering everything she'd gone through, she'd always thought she'd prefer to live on her own. If she did fall in love, she wouldn't bind herself to any man who could take advantage of her later on.

Until she'd met Seth Thornton.

She didn't begin dreaming about wedding gowns and bouquets and terrible reception dancing, but she did begin to wonder if marriage might be in the cards for her. She saw how happy his siblings were with their spouses. She saw time and time again how Seth proved to her that there were good men in this world, good men who could love you unconditionally.

It had been over a year since she and Seth had gotten together, and a year since they'd moved in together. While he'd worked on his rediscovered love of woodworking, she'd returned to school to finish her degree in English.

She'd been content—or so she'd thought. Until the day Seth had mentioned the idea of them getting married, and then had never said a word about it again. Why bring it up at all? Had he changed his mind?

"Hey, did you hear what I said?" Heath, Rose's older brother, asked.

They were currently making hot cocoa in the kitchen for this evening. Normally they'd drink spiked eggnog, but it was early enough that James hadn't yet gone to bed. So, Rose had volunteered to make the hot cocoa, making sure to spike all of the drinks not meant for minors.

"No, sorry. What did you say?" She stirred the pot where she'd just poured boiling water over chocolate. None of this powdered hot cocoa nonsense, no way.

"I wanted to ask your advice. You know Jubilee and I were planning to get married in the spring. But I wanted to move up the date."

Rose raised an eyebrow. "Why aren't you asking your fiancée this? Spoiler alert: I'm your sister."

"I'm aware." He lowered his voice, although they were the only two people in the kitchen. "I got Jubilee to go get a marriage license with me a week ago, thinking we'd move the wedding up to early February."

"That's a terrible time of year to get married."

"Stop interrupting. I know. I want us to get married here. On Christmas Day."

Rose stopped stirring the pot of chocolate. "What, as a surprise wedding? Sounds like a good way to piss off your potential bride, Heath."

"Jubilee hates wedding stuff. You should have seen her

when her mom brought over a binder of different kinds of ribbons. Who has a ribbon binder?"

Rose snorted. "Lisa Thornton does. So, how are you going to pull this off?" She began pouring the heated chocolate drink into individual mugs. "Are you just going to drag her to the altar and hope she doesn't tell you no?"

"That's the thing: that's why I need your help. I need you to distract Jubilee enough so I can get everything together."

At that, Rose paused and looked her brother in the eye. "Me? Have you told anyone else?"

"Harrison knows. He offered to marry us himself."

Rose didn't want to ask how that conversation went. Considering Harrison had been against Heath and Jubilee's relationship in the beginning, it was hard to believe he was now willing to officiate their surprise wedding.

Heath, though, seemed so earnest that Rose didn't have the heart to say no to him. "Fine. But if Jubilee gets angry, it's on you. Tell her I had no choice."

"You're my favorite sister, you know that, right?"

"Pretty easy when I'm your only sister."

As she and Heath brought the mugs of hot chocolate out, Rose couldn't help but feel a twinge of envy at Heath's scheme. It wasn't as though she was desperate to get married. It was more that Seth had asked her, she had said she would like to, eventually, and then…nothing.

She sat next to Seth on the couch, handing him a mug. "Don't worry, I added a little something extra to it," she said.

"You're an angel."

Sitting in front of the fire, Seth had the look of a mythical creature, with the flames dancing across his sharply cut features. He tended to wear his hair short like he had in the

Marines, and it only emphasized his strong jaw and cheek-bones. Once Rose had joked that she could cut diamonds on his cheekbones, and to her immense amusement, he'd blushed redder than she'd ever seen on a man who'd once been in the military and had fought overseas.

Callie, Rose's black German shepherd, lay down on her feet, her tail wagging and brushing the backs of Rose's calves. Rose leaned down to stroke the dog's silky head.

"Why did we agree to this?" Seth grumbled as his family laughed and partied like they had every night since they'd arrived at the cabin.

"Because you love your family, and because it's Christmas. Don't be a Scrooge."

"Ho, ho, ho."

Rose sipped her hot cocoa, but when Callie got up to bark at something random, a bit of Rose's drink sloshed and got onto her chin. She laughed as she wiped it off.

"Did I get it all?"

Seth leaned toward her. "Almost." He brushed his thumb to the corner of her mouth before running it along her bottom lip.

Rose couldn't help herself: she let the tip of her tongue taste his thumb. He groaned, a low rumble, that made Rose shiver.

She knew that Seth wanted her; she knew that he loved her. But did he love her enough to marry her?

She wished she had the courage to ask him why he'd never brought up the subject again. She'd faced down so many things in her life already—what was one simple question?

Because if he tells you the answer you don't want to hear, it'll break your heart.

"Let's go upstairs," said Seth.

The door hadn't yet fully closed before Seth had Rose in his arms. He tasted like chocolate, his hands roving down her body. Desire instantly heated in her belly. He kissed her shoulder as he slid her sweater, then her camisole, off. Now that she was clad only in her bra and jeans, he was like something ravenous, all heat and lust, and Rose wanted to sink into that maelstrom without another glance back.

He kissed her belly, cupping her sex through her jeans. And yet, her brain wouldn't let go of her anxiety. It was like it had latched its fingers onto the edge and refused to set her free. Even as Seth began to pull her jeans down her legs, she couldn't get into the moment like she normally did.

And then for a moment, she was reminded of how she'd disassociated when Johnny had touched her, and it was like a splash of ice-cold water on her senses.

"Wait. Wait." Her voice was a whisper; she couldn't get the words out, make them loud enough.

Seth felt her freeze before he heard her. "Rose? What is it?" He reached for her, but she flinched. The hurt on his face made her feel even guiltier.

"I'm sorry. Can I take a rain check? I'm really tired."

When she got into bed beside him, she forced herself not to stiffen when he touched her back. Breathing deeply and pushing her anxiety away until she felt some measure of calm take over, Rose finally rolled over to face Seth.

"I'm sorry," she whispered.

"Did I do something? You know I'd never hurt you." His gaze roved over her face, anguished and confused.

"I know you wouldn't. It's just one of those things. I'm sorry."

"Stop apologizing."

"Sorry."

He laughed softly and Rose snuggled next to him, letting the beat of his heart lull her to sleep.

THE NEXT DAY brought enough activity to keep Rose's anxiety at bay. She helped bake cookies for Christmas Day, which really just meant she mixed ingredients and wasn't allowed to do anything else. Apparently her inability in the kitchen had preceded her.

"Did you set the timer?" asked Megan. "I don't want those to burn."

"Yep. Twelve minutes exactly."

"Why are the only people in the kitchen of the female persuasion?" mused Jubilee as she took a bite of a just-baked cookie.

"Because they're lazy bums and I told them if they got near my baked goods I'd beat them with a spatula." Megan handed Jubilee a bowl of dough and pointed her to a cookie sheet.

Considering Megan ran her own bakery, Rose couldn't blame her for being territorial in the baking department. To be fair to the men, Caleb and Heath had tried to help. But when Caleb had used baking powder instead of soda for one recipe, Megan had kicked them both out.

Rose began to mix up another batch of sugar cookies, only to forget if she'd put baking soda in it. She glanced over her shoulder at Megan, and then rethought that decision. *I'll just put in another teaspoon to make sure. It can't hurt.*

To her immense embarrassment, Rose watched as the cookies puffed up so much in the oven that they looked like cookie bubbles. Jubilee leaned down and bit her lip, probably to keep from laughing.

The timer went off, and Rose took the cookies out of the oven. They immediately deflated, rather like sad balloons losing helium. Megan had come by to look and had yet to say anything.

"Too much baking soda," she pronounced. She took a bite of one and grimaced. "Yeah, tastes terrible. Throw those out."

Rose felt stupidly like crying. *They're just cookies. Don't cry over cookies.* Dumping the baked goods into the trash, she said to Jubilee, "I'm going to go get some air," before she hurried outside.

It had snowed again this morning. Rose inhaled the cold air as she walked into the edge of the woods. She'd never known such stillness as she had found here. She let that stillness wash over her, calming her pounding heart. Sitting down on a log, she watched as her breath fogged in front of her.

After what Johnny had done to her, Rose knew she wouldn't get over that trauma anytime soon. Her therapist had assured her that she was doing as well as could be expected, but that she couldn't castigate herself if her anxiety and PTSD flared up. She'd hoped that being away from Fair Haven would've helped. It would seem that Johnny would haunt her no matter where she went.

"You'll freeze out here." Seth covered her with his coat and sat down next to her on the log.

"How did you know I was out here?"

"Jubilee said you looked upset. I put two and two together." His brow furrowed. "Is this about last night?"

She wanted to keep all these negative emotions to herself, but she knew that that never helped. Biting her lip, she tried to find a place to begin. How did she even explain her feelings when she didn't understand them fully?

"Promise me you won't interrupt me until I'm finished," she said. When Seth frowned, she poked him. "Promise."

"Fine, fine. I make no guarantees that I won't commit murder if someone hurt you."

"It's no one new."

He grunted. At least Johnny would remain in prison for a long time. There was some comfort in that.

Rose explained about her doubts, about how Seth had asked her about marriage but had never mentioned it again. She tried to explain that last night, it hadn't been anything Seth had done. She'd just gotten herself all tied up in knots.

"I think I was—I am—just afraid that you don't want to marry me after all. That I'm too messed up, too broken, to commit to. It's stupid, but there it is."

Seth didn't say anything for a long moment. The wind shook the tree branches, and snow fell in powdery flourishes to the ground. A bird sang nearby.

"You can talk now," said Rose with a weak smile.

"I'm trying to figure out what to say."

Her stomach twisted. Her anxiety started to pulse, and by the time Seth opened his mouth to speak again, she trembled with anticipation. *Is he trying to tell me he wants to end things? Oh God, please no.*

"The reason I didn't mention marriage again was because when I asked you, you seemed indifferent to it. I thought you needed time." He grimaced, anguish in his expression. "I know I can't fix you, or fix what happened. I wish I could. I wish I could beat the shit out of Johnny and make your ghosts disappear, but I can't. I try to give you time, and space, just like you give me the same when I have nightmares."

"So you do want to marry me?"

He laughed, incredulous. "Rose DiMarco, I wanted to marry you the day I met you and you told me to go to hell." He wrapped an arm around her waist and turned her to face him. "I bought a ring for you the day we moved in together. I just didn't know when would be the right time to ask you."

"You did?" Now she was crying.

"Of course I did, hummingbird. I love you. Even when you say stupid things like *if* I want to marry you."

She laughed as he kissed the tears from her cheeks. "I thought you didn't want me."

"Now that's just idiotic. You're mine and always will be."

"I love you. I'm sorry I'm a mess."

"What did I say? No apologizing." Clearing his throat, he reached inside his coat pocket and pulled out a small velvet box.

Rose's breath caught. He'd brought it with him?

"Rose, my love, my hummingbird, the woman who can't cook and who tried to shoot me more than once—"

"You deserved it."

"Shush. I'm proposing." He opened the box to reveal a sapphire ring surrounded by emeralds. "I saw this ring and it reminded me of you, so colorful and beautiful. Will you marry me, Rose? Be my wife?"

Her throat was clogged with tears and she felt a little silly, sitting on a log in the woods as Seth proposed, but she didn't care. Nodding, she whispered something that sounded like "yes." Seth smiled and then placed the ring on her finger. It sparkled in the light.

"Thank God," he muttered before kissing her. "I thought you were going to leave me."

"So we're both idiots?"

"Looks like it."

She kissed him until it was getting so dark that they couldn't see each other's faces anymore.

When they returned to the cabin, Rose waited for someone to notice the ring. She and Seth had placed bets on who it would be.

Rose was putting away her coat when she heard her brother's voice. "What is that?" he pointed to her hand, eyes narrowed.

"Oh, this?" She couldn't stop from grinning. Her face hurt from smiling. "It's an engagement ring."

Heath's eyes narrowed to slits as Jubilee and Sara gasped, grabbing Rose's hand. Heath turned to Seth. "You didn't buy her a diamond?"

"Diamonds are boring." Seth shrugged.

Before Heath could argue, Rose interjected, "I agree with Seth. I prefer colorful stones. And the ring he bought me is gorgeous."

"Oh, congratulations! I'm so happy for you two." Jubilee hugged her. Soon, the rest of the family was packed into the entrance hall and they were being inundated with congratulations.

"Maybe you should've waited until we'd gotten back," said Rose later on in their bedroom. "Because now your family will never leave us alone."

"There are worse fates." He kissed her temple. "As long as

you marry me, hummingbird, I don't give two shits what my family does."

That made her laugh, which made Seth kiss her, and then everything else was forgotten besides being in each other's arms.

CHAPTER SIX

JUBILEE & HEATH

"Rose DiMarco," said Jubilee the moment she got her sister-in-law alone, "what the hell is going on with your brother?"

"I've been asking myself just that for a long time."

Jubilee rolled her eyes. "Ha-ha. Something is going on, and I know that you know, because you keep looking over your shoulder—"

"I'm looking for *your* brother."

Jubilee pointed a finger in Rose's face, although she couldn't stop from smiling, regardless. "Tell me what's going on or I'll tell Megan that you ruined that last batch of cookies."

"You wouldn't."

"I would. Now, spill."

Currently, the two women stood in Jubilee and Heath's room in the cabin while the rest of the family were either downstairs or outside. It was Christmas Day, and they'd just

265

opened presents, which had mostly entailed watching James and the babies rip open packages with glee. Bea and Bennett had ripped open their gifts with a bloodlust that would've been frightening if it hadn't been so cute. Evie was too little to do much other than pull on the ribbons as her parents helped her unwrap her gifts.

As the festivities had gone on, Jubilee had felt Heath watching her. That wasn't strange. It was more that he was watching her, and then when she tried to catch his gaze, he'd look away. But a smile would play about his mouth.

Jubilee had realized Heath was hiding something from her when he'd disappeared during presents before returning with snow on his sweater. Which meant he'd gone outside for something. Which meant he'd brought something inside, but not into the living room.

Rose chewed her lip, clearly torn between Jubilee's threat of cookie blackmail and keeping her promise to her brother.

Finally, she said, "I can't tell you."

"Of course you can. You just say, 'Jubilee, Heath is concocting some crazy scheme. This is what it is.' Now, your turn."

"Nope. Not telling." Jubilee launched herself at Rose, but Rose just giggled and pushed her away. "I'm not telling you! Just be patient. It's a good surprise, I swear."

So it was a surprise. Now Jubilee was rather desperate to find out what it was. If it had been a gift, Heath would've given it to her this morning. So, not a gift. It wasn't as if he'd propose to her a second time (would he?). Seth had already proposed to Rose the day before, and Jubilee couldn't imagine Heath would want to have Seth rib him for copying him.

"Jubilee, will you come take a walk with me?" Abby

caught her in the hallway after Rose had scurried away. "I want to get some fresh air."

Jubilee wanted to decline, but at Abby's hopeful expression, she couldn't say no. After she got her coat, she and Abby began to ramble along the perimeter of the woods. Snow crunched under their boots, the sky a dreary gray. If Jubilee squinted, she could just make out a patch of blue sky that would peek out from the clouds every so often.

Jubilee was tempted to grill Abby about Heath's behavior, but she also doubted Abby would know. She blew out a frustrated breath. There were many things in life she hated, and having to be patient was one of them.

"Congratulations, again," said Jubilee. "You and Mark will be amazing parents."

"I hope so. I never thought I'd be able to have children, so this was a surprise." Abby's cheeks were flushed. "I mean, I shouldn't have been surprised, considering who I married. I was surprised he didn't get me pregnant the first time he so much as looked at me."

"Oh, no, ew. Please don't make me think about my brother that way."

Abby laughed as Jubilee gagged. Really, a girl could only take so much, let alone talking about her brother's virility.

"Do you think you and Heath will have kids?"

"We'll have to get to the wedding first. My mom is doing her best to interfere, to no one's surprise."

"I might have heard about that. Have you told her to back off?"

Jubilee stopped short, blinked, and then burst out laughing. "Have you *met* my mother?"

"Okay," said Abby, her lips twisting, "good point."

"I'm to the point that I'd rather just elope. I told Heath we could, but he acted like the idea was crazy. It's funny, as a kid I wanted the huge wedding: the dress, the cake, all of it. But now I just want to be married. The wedding would be a bonus."

"I felt the same. That's why Mark and I had a small ceremony."

"You guys were smart. But my mom also had a heart attack when Lizzie married Trent at the courthouse."

"It wasn't that she was six months pregnant?"

"Okay, it might've been part of it."

At that point, they'd walked almost a mile from the cabin. Jubilee caught Abby glancing at her watch, and she wondered if this had been a setup.

"I'm getting cold. Let's walk back," said Jubilee.

Abby hesitated, but when Jubilee kept walking, she caught up with her quickly. Abby then started walking more slowly than normal, something that amused and annoyed Jubilee in equal measures.

Just what the hell was going on?

Abby looked at her watch a second time, only to see Jubilee watching her. She blushed but said, "Let's sit outside for a bit."

"In the freezing cold? Why?"

"It's not that cold."

"A walk is one thing, but this isn't porch weather."

"Oh, good, you guys are back." Heath took Jubilee by the arm. "I wanted to show you something."

Jubilee found herself being taken to the back of the cabin, she was torn between curiosity and concern. What in the world was Heath up to?

"Heath—"

"Wait. Look."

Heath had taken her to a spot in the backyard facing the woods. All she could see were trees, snow, more trees.

"What am I looking at?"

"Shh. Just wait."

She waited, tempted to ask him what this was all about. But then she saw movement in the corner of her eye.

"Do you see it?" he whispered, pointing.

At first all she saw was snow. Squinting, she realized that amidst the brush and snow was a snowshoe hare, its fur already having turned white for winter. They were only a few feet from the hare. The hare stilled, its nose twitching, and Jubilee hardly dared to breathe. For a moment, all three of them stood still, watching each other.

The hare bolted into the woods.

"I saw it yesterday and this morning. I wanted to show you."

She squeezed his arm. She'd told him ages ago about how she'd always loved seeing snowshoe hares in the winter, but they were rare in Fair Haven. She couldn't believe he'd remembered.

"Was this your big surprise?" she teased as they went inside the cabin. "You sent me on a walk with Abby just so you could wait for the hare to show up again?"

Heath pushed open the back door, which led to a back staircase. "Not exactly. Come upstairs with me and I'll show you."

She was tempted to make a dirty joke, but she was too impatient to discover what plan Heath had concocted. He led her into their bedroom and shut the door.

Jubilee was about to ask what was going on when she saw it: a wedding dress lay on the bed. The same dress Jubilee had loved when she'd tried it on, but her mother had vetoed it because it wasn't a longer gown.

"Heath," she said, "what is going on?"

Jubilee didn't look excited. She looked...alarmed. Heath's speech about how he'd surprised her with a surprise wedding, how he knew how much she hated planning a wedding she didn't even want, all of it—it flew right out the window.

"Why do you have a wedding dress? Wait, maybe don't answer that."

He scrubbed a hand through his hair. "It's for a wedding. Our wedding."

"Our wedding."

"Yes."

"Our wedding that's happening next year?"

"I thought, with everything happening with your mom and how you were dragging your feet about planning the wedding, that I'd surprise you with a wedding. Here. Today. On Christmas Day."

Jubilee's mouth opened and closed in shock. Then: "Heath David DiMarco, are you serious?"

"Yes, but you don't have to do it. I should've asked you. This was a stupid idea—"

"No! Heath." She grabbed his arm, her cheeks flushed. "This is amazing. I'm just pissed I didn't think of it myself." She shook her head. "Did you really plan our wedding? What about the license? Who's marrying us?"

Heath pulled out the license that they'd already applied for. "It just so happens that Harrison can marry us."

"He *agreed* to marry us?"

"He did."

"Goodness, I don't want to know how much you bribed him to do that." She touched the envelope with the marriage license inside it. "This is really happening?"

"Only if you want it to."

"Oh no, you're not getting out of it that easily. I need to get ready. Did you bring everything? Shoes? A strapless bra?"

"I brought it all." At her incredulous look, he mumbled, "I Googled what you would've needed, okay?"

She snorted a laugh. "I would love to see *that* search history. Thank God, though. I was afraid I was going to have to wear this dress in my sports bra."

Her face fell then, and he touched her arm. "What is it?"

She grimaced. "My mom and dad. I can't get married without them here. I know my mom drives us both crazy and that's why you planned this, but she'd never forgive me—"

He pressed a finger to her mouth. "I got it covered. Don't worry."

"Heath DiMarco, you sneaky jerk!" But her smile belied her words, and she then pushed at his arm. "Get out of here. You can't see the bride before the wedding. And tell Rose and Megan I need them to help me."

Heath kissed her. "I love you. See you soon."

"I love you, and you're a nut. Get out of here."

After getting dressed in a suit and tie, Heath went downstairs to wait for Jubilee. The rest of the family hurried about with various tasks, although the cabin was already decorated for Christmas. He'd enlisted Megan's help with the cake, which Sara had taken over when Megan went upstairs to help Jubilee with her hair and makeup.

That was when he realized: he'd gotten Jubilee's underwear, but he'd completely forgotten to buy wedding rings.

"Shit." He turned to Harrison. "I forgot to buy us rings."

Harrison straightened his tie, frowning. "That's not good. Although I guess you could use Jubilee's engagement ring for her."

Seth slapped Heath on the shoulder and handed him a silver ring. "Use this. Just give it back to me when you have the real rings."

Heath knew this ring: Seth had gotten it to remember his friend who'd died in the war. "Are you sure?"

"Positive."

"Thank you. This means a lot."

Before either man could get too emotional, a knock sounded on the front door. Heath breathed a sigh of relief as he went to answer it.

"Lisa, Dave," he said as he ushered them inside. "I'm so glad you could make it."

"It wasn't exactly how we were expecting to spend Christmas," said Lisa as she handed Heath her coat. "But I am not missing my youngest daughter's wedding."

Despite Lisa's crisp words, Heath knew she would've been devastated had she not been invited to this impromptu ceremony. Dave would've been upset, too, even though his demeanor remained cool and collected. No matter how much she drove her daughter crazy, Lisa would always be Jubilee's mother.

When the ceremony finally began, Heath knew he would

remember this moment for the rest of his life: Jubilee walking down the stairs, wearing a wedding gown, her hair in some complicated braided updo. Her dress was ivory with lacy three-quarter-length sleeves, the skirt wide and bell-shaped. She'd placed a poinsettia in her hair. But what made Heath's heart pound was the love for him on her face as she walked toward him.

"Mom," said Jubilee as she spotted Lisa. Lisa rushed forward and they embraced, tears in each woman's eyes. Lisa murmured something in Jubilee's ear before Dave gave his daughter a hug, too.

As Jubilee hugged her parents, Megan and Rose followed her entrance, and then the entire family stood in the living room in front of the fireplace and waited for the wedding to begin.

Heath squeezed Jubilee's hand. "You look gorgeous."

"Thank you."

Harrison cleared his throat. "You two ready?"

"I think so," said Jubilee.

Heath elbowed her a little, and she laughed. "Yes, I'm ready."

"I'm ready," said Heath.

"Before the vows, I wanted to say a few words," said Harrison.

Heath heard someone groan; Jubilee laughed.

"I heard that, Caleb. You're the one who needed a box of tissues earlier."

Caleb snorted. "He's lying."

Bea took that remark to mean she should start talking to her parents, and Heath was fairly certain he heard something along the lines of "dog isn't here" from the toddler.

"Anyway," said Harrison, "I wanted to say that I didn't always agree with this relationship."

Heath's eyes crossed. "Here we go."

"I thought that you were too old for my baby sister. I told you both to stay away." Harrison chuckled. "I should've known that would never work. But I realized that it hadn't been about protecting Jubilee: it had been about protecting me."

When Heath had asked Harrison to marry them, he hadn't been sure of his friend's response. Although Harrison had come to accept their relationship, that didn't mean he'd want to assist in making it official and legal. But Harrison had agreed without hesitation.

Now Heath watched Jubilee as Harrison spoke, drinking in her beauty. He could see tears shining in her eyes already.

"You were my little sister, of course, but you were also the one who hung on to life so hard that there was no way you weren't going to thrive. I remember when you were only five years old, and you asked me to tell your cancer to go away. You were too busy to die." A few people chuckled, but the collective sound was definitely watery now. "I did my best: I tried to keep you safe. I wanted you to live that life that cancer tried to take away from you.

"But I realized that I wanted to keep you safe because that meant I wouldn't have to worry. I finally saw how much you loved Heath, and God Almighty, how much he loved you. And I'm not about to stand in the way of love, because I know how precious and rare it is."

Heath cleared his throat, mostly to get rid of the annoying lump in it. Jubilee was crying, trying to dab at her face so as not to mess up her makeup, and then everyone was crying and laughing at the same time. Abby handed Jubilee a tissue before handing one each to Heath and Harrison.

"So, let's get this party started." Harrison wiped his eyes before beginning the ceremony.

"Do you, Jubilee Christina Thornton, take Heath David DiMarco to be your lawfully wedded husband?"

Jubilee's gaze was fixed on him. "I do."

"And Heath David DiMarco, do you take Jubilee Christina Thornton to be your lawfully wedded wife?"

"I do," said Heath.

Jubilee smiled, and Heath couldn't stop smiling. They exchanged rings, Jubilee scrunching her nose at him when he placed her engagement ring back onto her finger.

"I'll get you a real wedding ring," he vowed. "I promise."

"Of course you will, and I'll pick them out."

"Hey, we're not done yet," said Harrison. "I now pronounce you husband and wife. You may kiss the bride—"

Heath wrapped his arms around his new wife and kissed her, bending her over his arm. The family hooted and hollered, the kiss only ending when Mark muttered nearby, "There are kids here."

Everyone converged on Heath and Jubilee at once. Congratulations flowed, hugs were abundant, and Heath shook each Thornton brother's hand like they hadn't known each other for years. Harrison made a point to murmur in his ear, "If you hurt her, I'll kill you."

"I hope you'll be very happy together," said Dave as he pumped Heath's hand. "Take care of my little girl."

"Oh, Jubi, congratulations." Lisa dabbed at her eyes before she kissed Jubilee's cheek. "I'm glad you invited us."

"I wouldn't have had you miss it for the world," she said.

A few hours later, Heath had managed to get a moment of privacy with Jubilee—his new wife, which he could hardly believe—and said, "I love you, Mrs. DiMarco."

"And I love you, Mr. DiMarco." This was the best surprise you've ever done for me." She tipped her head back, gesturing with her chin. "So you gonna kiss me under this mistletoe, or am I going to have to do it?"

He pulled her into his arms, right where she belonged. "Don't worry," he said, "I'll kiss you now and forever. Even without mistletoe."

And then he showed her exactly what he meant.

ABOUT THE AUTHOR

A coffee addict and cat lover, Iris Morland writes sexy and funny contemporary romances. If she's not reading or writing, she enjoys binging on Netflix shows and cooking something delicious.